Snakehead

*Also by Chad Merriman
in Large Print:*

The Avengers
Blood on the Sun
Hard Country

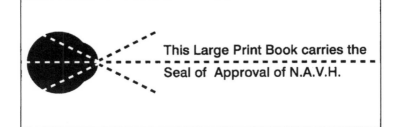

This Large Print Book carries the
Seal of Approval of N.A.V.H.

Snakehead

Chad Merriman

Thorndike Press • Waterville, Maine

Published in 2004 by arrangement with Golden West Literary Agency.

Thorndike Press® Large Print Western.

The tree indicium is a trademark of Thorndike Press.

The text of this Large Print edition is unabridged.
Other aspects of the book may vary from the original edition.

Set in 16 pt. Plantin by Liana M. Walker.

Printed in the United States on permanent paper.

Library of Congress Cataloging-in-Publication Data

Merriman, Chad.
    Snakehead / Chad Merriman.
       p. cm.
    Originally published under author's name
    Gifford P. Cheshire.
    ISBN 0-7862-7113-2 (lg. print : hc : alk. paper)
    1. Yakima River Valley (Wash.) — Fiction. 2. Cascade
Range — Fiction. 3. Large type books. I. Title.
PS3553.H38S63 2004
  813'.54—dc22   2004058807

Snakehead

As the Founder/CEO of NAVH, the only national health agency solely devoted to those who, although not totally blind, have an eye disease which could lead to serious visual impairment, I am pleased to recognize Thorndike Press★ as one of the leading publishers in the large print field.

Founded in 1954 in San Francisco to prepare large print textbooks for partially seeing children, NAVH became the pioneer and standard setting agency in the preparation of large type.

Today, those publishers who meet our standards carry the prestigious "Seal of Approval" indicating high quality large print. We are delighted that Thorndike Press is one of the publishers whose titles meet these standards. We are also pleased to recognize the significant contribution Thorndike Press is making in this important and growing field.

Lorraine H. Marchi, L.H.D.
Founder/CEO
NAVH

★ Thorndike Press encompasses the following imprints: Thorndike, Wheeler, Walker and Large Print Press.

Chapter 1

He had been in the saddle nearly four hours while he crossed Horse Heaven, coming from Umatilla Landing where his unending railroad chores had taken him, and the ride had been cold enough. Here on the river, which he had reached to find the ferryboat slowly loading wagons on the far shore, it was miserably colder, with a downstream wind whipping past him to boil into the rock palisades of Wallula Gap. Even his horse looked across the half-mile of water in brute exasperation and impatience. The stream was the Columbia, the River of the West, and the steam flattop over there was taking aboard what appeared to be settler outfits bound for the Yakima country. Above the slip, under leafless trees, Wallula Landing's hundred chimneys fed ragged smoke into the troubled air.

And then the horse lost interest in that side of the river and swung its head to the rear. Curious as to what its keener ears had picked out of the sounds of wind and water, Luke Preston glanced back toward the slant that came down to the water from the flat under the westshore cliffs. It seemed to him that the wind had suddenly swept up grits and flung them into his face, the sting of it driving the chilled slackness from his tall, heavy frame. In a country as empty as it was vast, it scarcely seemed possible for him to encounter at this lonely spot the man he saw riding down toward him from the Horse Heaven trail.

Recognition had caused the fellow to straighten out his own chilled slouch and to raise slightly the gloved hand that held the bridle reins. That was all the reaction Preston observed, and then Lawson Keel rode on down to him, his features resuming the amiable mien that Preston knew to be only a controlled, surface trick.

Keel only nodded when he reined in his horse; then he said, "What's holding that thing up over there?"

"Ferryman's taking his time. It's warmer there than out on the river." Then, having no taste for small talk with this man, Preston said, "How long've you been behind me, Keel?"

"Not long." Keel swung out of the saddle and began to stamp his feet and slap himself with his arms. "You were about a mile ahead when I came off the Yakima fork." He was nearly as tall as Luke Preston, but thinner and of about the same age, which was thirty now and closer to the age of discretion than they had been when they first met in Blackhawk, Colorado. Then Keel's eyes grew amused, and he added, "Apparently you don't like to have me behind you, Luke."

"You know damned well I don't."

"We've been here a long while, Luke. We've sidestepped one another, but I haven't made you any trouble."

"I wasn't expecting trouble in Blackhawk," Luke snapped. "Which is why I didn't watch my back there, too."

Keel shrugged, a chill showing through the look of amusement he managed to maintain. He could afford serenity, for his was the upper hand, the power to destroy while coming off no worse than nicked himself. His base now was Walla Walla City, where he owned a flour mill and a general mercantile establishment. He fell silent, while Luke looked up toward the distant town and the steamboat that lay tied to a wharfboat below it, bobbing on the water. Then Luke saw that the ferry-boat had finally left its slip and was cutting out into the choppy current. Keel pulled a cigar from his pocket and clamped it in his teeth but didn't try to light it in that wind.

They stood in continuing silence until the ferry had nosed against the near landing and made fast. The families with the wagons looked miserable but resigned, drags from the summer's influx, and the vehicles groaned with farm tools and household equipment. When the families were off the ferry, Luke and Keel led their horses aboard, still ignoring each other. The ferryman took their money, also without a word, and started back across the river.

Standing at the head of his horse, Luke watched Wallula enlarge in scale and felt the wind brisk up even more and grow colder still. The steamboat was the *Nez Percé Chief*, he saw as he came closer, and recognition told him he had a chore to attend to in Wallula, too, before he went on up the Walla Walla valley. The town above the packet had sprung to life in the Idaho stampedes during the '60s, which had sucked thousands of men and thousands of tons of freight through here. A disorganized array of buildings shaped a sandy street: stores, saloons, a fleabag hotel, a stage-express office, a livery barn and several wagon yards. Now, late in '74, there was something of recent vintage, the freight shed and loading platform of the uncompleted Walla Walla & Columbia River Railroad.

Luke's horse had been rented at the livery stable for the ride to Umatilla Landing. Keel turned wordlessly in the other direction, and Luke rode on to the big red barn. Elvek, the stablehand, stood in the yawning doorway with a manure fork in his hand. Luke swung down, tossed him the reins and handed him the rental.

A gaunt, whiskery man, Elvek had a tobacco-stained mouth and a hangdog air, but he had more than once done Luke a favor. Now he said sociably, "Talkin' for the railroad in this town can get a man's head knocked off, but I want you to know I got a little money saved to buy some of that stock issue Doc Baker's announced. A share or two, anyhow."

"That's fine, Elvie. We could use more people like you up the valley, as well as down here." The WW&CR owned thirty-two miles of right of way between Wallula and Walla Walla City, but with over two years gone since construction began, it still had only twenty-six miles of track. The six-mile gap, as Elvek and everyone else knew, crippled the line in its struggle against its many opponents. Unless the coming stock issue was fully subscribed and the track completed, the adversaries would win hands down.

Elvek shook his head sorrowfully. "Used to hear nothin' but railroad talk, except from these Wallula wagon freighters and the cowmen out on the ranges. Now Doc's tryin' to give 'em one, and they all act like he was bringin' in the plague."

"Not everybody, thank God," Luke said. "We've got a few more like you."

Elvek led off the horse, and Luke turned back to the doorway. He hadn't cared to show his own pessimism, but Elvek was right about the nearly solid front of hostility that had been generated in the valley by the still unfinished railroad. The last ten miles of track had had to be built out of revenue, and with the wheat haul over for the year, revenue wasn't even apt to meet the overhead. The stock that Dorsey Baker, the line's president, would soon offer to the public simply had to be bought, and that called for investors with a lot more money than the hostler had scraped together.

Leaving the barn, Luke angled across the street and entered a saloon designated only as: NAN'S. That was all the identity it needed, he reflected. Nan Alpert and her dark beauty had become known from Dalles City, far down the Columbia, to Lewiston in the deep interior, in the few years she had been here. But Luke reminded himself that the name was Nan Browder, now. She had been called that for quite some time.

Wallula Landing harbored a host of sojourners, with construction workers now laid off by the railroad but hanging around waiting for work to resume, and hands similarly idled by the shutdown of Baker's sawmill at Slabtown, a mile up the river, adding to the normal population. Nan's establishment was the hangout of the older residents, including the teamsters and cowmen who, after the gold boom died, had come to regard Wallula as theirs alone.

These had been the first to cry havoc when Baker began to promote the railroad and then, in spite of their antagonism, to build it. The teamsters had long fattened on the lucrative wagon hauls between the river port and the inland towns and communities. The cowmen feared that the railroad would bring in hordes of the settlers who already were beginning to chop up the cattle ranges. These people had become

13

the core around which had grown a massive antipathy on the part of the farmers, merchants and travelers who should have welcomed the new venture, and this aspect was hard to understand. Partly, Luke supposed, this sprang from fear or envy of Dorsey Syng Baker himself who, in addition to practicing medicine, running a big mercantile establishment and then a bank in Walla Walla City, had been and still was a leading figure in the cattle business. Luke had ridden for him a year or two, after coming from Colorado, before Baker asked his help with the railroad.

Even if he hadn't known he was off limits in Nan's place, Luke would have been made conscious of it the moment he stepped in. Even in late afternoon the room was filled, and he was aware of the tension injected by his arrival. He recognized a few cowmen off the desert and benchlands wheeling every way but west from the town, and men from the wagon yards and freight lines still running into the interior. He saw glances meet and mouths tighten.

His gaze flicked over this in indifference and came to rest on Nan. Prettier even now, he thought, than when he had known her in Blackhawk. She was at a table in a back corner with Kirk Browder, her husband, and Pete Lastrade who was purser on the *Chief*, now tied up below the town. The men were drinking, but Nan was not. Luke saw a questioning look on her face but received no welcoming nod of her dark head. Browder and Lastrade both scowled at him, Browder with a particular reason to hate him because Luke had once been a friend of Nan's. Luke put his flat stare on them, also, and walked over to the bar at the side.

The bartender knew better than to refuse service, although his expression conveyed a strong wish to do so. At Luke's order, he poured a shot of whiskey and set it up and then turned away. Luke tossed off the drink and didn't want another but ordered it. The bartender looked grumpier than ever. Luke let that one sit, watching the smoky room in the backbar mirror. For an instant his gaze settled on his own reflection, that of a powerful man with a rugged, weather-stained face and shaggy dark hair under a well-worn hat. Some picture, he thought, for the operations boss of the WW&CR. Then he saw another figure move up beside it, tall also, but slender, the figure of a well-built woman.

Nan's voice said in an undertone, "Luke,

you know I don't want you to come here."

"Got business here, Nan," Luke said. "I just didn't want you at that table."

"Luke, what are you — ?"

The voice fell silent, for Luke was walking down the room toward the table Nan had left. He saw Browder and Lastrade tense in their chairs, and tension rolled against him in waves from other parts of the watching room. Nan hadn't followed him. A greasy purser's cap was the only river uniform Lastrade wore, and he pushed it slowly to the back of his round head.

"I just come from Umatilla Landing, Lastrade," Luke said. "Seems a shipment of our strapiron got unloaded there by mistake off your boat. You know anything about that?"

Lastrade looked at him with flat eyes. "Hell, man, we unload tons of freight along this river. How'd I remember what went where?"

"All you need to remember," Luke said, "is that freight consigned to the WW&CR comes to Wallula, the way it's billed. We needed that iron. The delay cost us plenty."

A surly contempt showed on Lastrade's fleshy lips, for costing the railroad had been exactly what he was after. Browder leaned forward, his eyes akindle, for he ran a wagon freight line to Walla Walla City in addition to loathing a chapter in Nan's past she apparently had never explained. Neither of these two was a small man and neither was soft, and the room was filled with excited men of the same pattern. Lastrade grinned finally, knowing if the thing got out of hand, he could count on plenty of help.

He said, "Well, I'm sorry if there was a mistake, Preston, but they do happen."

Luke nodded his head. "Like a shipment of rail spikes that got unloaded at Castle Landing off the same boat. Yours. It took me a month to run that one down."

Lastrade shook his head in mock sympathy. "That must make it tough trying to build a railroad."

"It sure does," Luke agreed. "And it's why I intend to see it doesn't happen again."

His hand shot out so fast it had gripped Lastrade's shirt before the purser knew what was coming. Lastrade reared back in the chair and found himself being lifted upward and to his feet.

"No you don't, Luke." Something hard jammed into Luke's back, and Nan's cool voice resumed, "Sorry, but I'm not letting anybody wreck my place of business for any reason. Get out of here."

"Leave 'em be, Nan," Browder protested. "Pete can take this boy. Back off from it, you hear?"

"No," Nan snapped. "Pete, sit still. I think I'd enjoy shooting *you*."

Luke straightened, letting go of Lastrade, very conscious of the continuing pressure in his back. She would do it. He had seen this woman in action before and knew there was no bluffing in her. He turned to see her dark eyes flashing fire, telling him why Browder and Lastrade were suddenly quiet and obedient. Her expression didn't intimidate Luke, but he thought he had made his point. Lastrade might not sidestep a brawl in which he could expect help if things went wrong. Yet he didn't want his chronic, so-called mistakes on behalf of his friends here reported to the steamboat company.

"Beat it, Luke," Nan said. "And after this, stay away from here."

"Sorry, Nan." Luke shook his head. "As long as your place is a hangout for scum trying to wreck the railroad, it'll be my business to come here."

He threw a dollar on the bar for the

drinks on his way out.

Riding a fresh horse secured from the livery stable, he headed up the river road toward Slabtown to conclude his business in this vicinity before leaving for the upper valley on the next morning's train. The escarpment he saw beyond the river was the clipped-off end of the huge Horse Heaven country, and as he traveled, the 'scarp began to stand back to create the wide, fanning plain at the Yakima mouth. This secondary river, winding down from the snowpeaks of the Cascades, was the watercourse of the region's second vast group of fertile valleys now yielding rapidly to settlement. To his right the bare desert of the lower Snake and Walla Walla wheeled off into the distance, its hard light softened now that the day was nearly gone.

Some distance upriver he rounded a flat point and saw Slabtown on ahead, standing above an eddy in the river where a boom impounded a black island of sawlogs brought down the Yakima from the Cascades forests. The sawmill, which in the beginning had run from dawn to dusk cutting the ties, rail stringers and bridge timbers for the WW&CR, had little to do now with its storage yard full and track construction halted for lack of funds.

In the beginning, Slabtown had been the river terminus of the railroad, but after a year or so, Dorsey Baker had seen the wisdom of connecting with the established, though hostile, town. This had been done so that Slabtown was now on a spur, and coming nearer. Luke saw the closest thing to a railroad yard the new line possessed. Out on the main line there wasn't a siding or turntable between there and end of track. The trains going up the valley each morning had to travel backward all the way down.

Both the work train, once busily hauling materials to the end of track, but now idle, and the regular freight and passenger consist stood beside the millyard, steam down. Luke turned into the yard short of them and rode toward a huge, open-sided shed that sheltered the sawmill and its machinery. Off to the right were the commissary, blacksmith shop, bunkhouses and cookshack that, with the mill, were the sum total of Slabtown. Two saddle horses, wearing the Baker brand, stood with trailed reins in front of the slab-sided office on the near side of the mill. Luke dismounted and left the livery mount with them and then went in.

Chapter 2

The three men who sat by a sheet-iron stove were engaged in an earnest conversation that trailed off when the door opened and Luke Preston came through. Two of those indoors only nodded, for Luke saw them frequently. But Bill Green, Baker's cattle boss and Luke's boss not so long before, grinned and stood up to shake hands. A rangy, slack-muscled man who had brought the Baker herds through droughts and blizzards and driven them to markets a thousand miles distant, Green had helped to found what had been, before the railroad started eating it up, the Baker fortune. His easy grin came to his weathered face spontaneously, but Luke had a feeling that something worried him.

"Glad to see you, Bill," Luke said. "How's it going out on the bunchgrass?"

"Middling," Green said, resuming his seat.

The blocky, stubborn-looking man sitting on the other side of the stove was

Newall Truax, at present a construction boss with little but repair work on the finished track to engage his time. Glancing at Truax, Luke said, "I located your strapiron at Umatilla Landing, Newall. It'll be up on the next boat."

"The same old monkey business, eh?" Truax said, with a snort.

Originally a government surveyor, he had got interested in a line between Wallula and Walla Walla City when there was still hope that the Northern Pacific, building west from St. Paul, would make it part of its transcontinental system, make it a full-scale railroad, instead of the partly built narrow-gage with wooden rails and dinky, crawling trains that had finally come into being, and was already fighting for its life. Truax had made a survey for the NP, which had turned down the route as too expensive, but the comedown in scale hadn't dampened his enthusiasm for the line he was building. The NP had since bogged down in financial difficulties of its own and was stalled at the Missouri river. So the WW&CR, if and when completed, would be the first real railroad north of Nevada and California. Luke knew how much it meant to Truax to finish it and then see it pay off.

"The same old thing," Luke agreed, "but maybe I've put a stop to it. Nearly all the stuff that's gone astray came off the *Chief*. The purser's a friend of Kirk Browder and that bunch. I had a talk with him before I left Wallula." He turned to the third man, who was Frank Baker. "I don't suppose you've seen your father since I was through the other day."

A slight, clean-cut man of about twenty-three, Frank strongly resembled the doctor in build and facial features, but his was a gentler, less driving disposition. Originally he had been trained to run his father's farming operations in the upper valley, but when the sawmill was built to cut materials for the railroad, he had been put in charge.

Frank said with a shake of his head, "I suppose he's still in the back country doing spade work on the stock issue."

Bill Green said mildly, "Which maybe he shouldn't be doing."

"Why not?" Frank asked, surprised. "Somebody's got to talk sense into the people if the stock's to be sold. I don't think you've forgotten what a fizzle the bond issue was two years ago."

"I sure haven't," Green said. "But maybe Doc's trouble is his dogged notion that what makes sense to him will to other people if he just explains it to them. It's never come to Doc he's an uncommon smart man, and that makes him testy with anybody he can't educate right off. Now, that don't matter much with a cowman or farmer or maybe even a doctor. But when you deal with the public, it matters plenty. It was John Boyer who made a go of the store and is making a go of the bank. I've come to think that Doc'd have done better if he'd put John in charge of the public end of the railroad, too, at least the money raising. That nice way John's got with people would have made a big difference, I bet."

Frank nodded, too worried about the railroad's future to resent Green's criticism of his father. "You're probably right, Bill, but you know him. No matter how many horses he drives, he's got to have the reins all in his own hands."

"He's a born loner," Green agreed. "But don't get me wrong. That's not the only reason I think the stock issue'll flop like the bond sale did and the first stock Doc tried to sell when we organized the company."

"What's the other reason, Bill?" Luke asked. Green was as good a friend as Dorsey Baker would ever have, and he wouldn't be disclosing his private opinions this way if he wasn't worried deeply. Of the twenty-four men who had incorporated as the WW&CR, he and a handful of others were the only ones still backing it with all they had. Baker had been forced to buy the stock of the rest which, added to what he already owned, made it ninety per cent his company. But the flaws in his personality were legitimate worries to the others, and Luke wanted to hear Green out. "You mean the doctor's refusal to sell enough stock to surrender control of the railroad?"

"That don't help him," Green said. "They use it to claim he wants 'em to help pay for a railroad he'll run for his own profit. But that's not what I mean. Lately I've been wondering if there could be a snake in the grass." He glanced at Luke and added, "To put it your way, a snakehead the whole line's been hung up on, not just a train."

"A secret enemy?" Truax said, surprised. "Have you somebody in mind?"

Green shook his head. "No, but it'd have to be somebody with money to buy up the controlling interest if Doc'd let go of it. And enough influence to keep the opposition steamed up. It's not natural to have so plagued much trouble without it being organized somewhere along the line."

"That makes sense, Bill," Luke said, keenly interested. "It would explain a lot that never did seem natural. Nobody's going to take Doc's railroad away from him after the way they've made him go it alone, unless he's forced to it. And that's the position he could be in if the stock issue fails."

"It's the position he's damned apt to be in," Green amended. "He's got a lot of resources, but they're not ready cash, and he refuses to borrow money on 'em."

"Shun debt as you would the devil," Frank said. "I've heard him say that a thousand times."

Truax glanced at Luke with grimly amused eyes. "I'm just the construction boss, Luke. You're the trouble shooter. Why don't you find this snakehead of Bill's and get it fixed?"

"I'll try," Luke said. "And if there is one, I'll sure try to get it fixed. Glad I run into you, Newall. I intended to leave word about the strapiron with Frank."

He nodded and left them and went out to his horse, lost in thoughts stirred up by Bill Green's speculations. The WW&CR had so many open enemies, it had never occurred to him that some secret and powerful manipulator could be behind it all. If such a one existed, he would be at his most active now with the stock issue only weeks away. That might not make him any easier to detect, but it made the importance of doing so all the greater.

Luke awakened at daybreak in a cold upstairs room at the Wallula Hotel and for a moment postponed the start of another working day. The wind had risen in the night to split shrilly on the corners of the creaking old building, toss trees and sift sand through cracks until he could smell it in the room. That meant there would be drifts on the track, that morning, to stall the train until they had been shoveled off.

He hated to leave a warm bed for that kind of prospect but did so, hurrying into his trousers and boots and then washing and shaving in the chilly air. He felt better when finally he could settle his wool shirt down over his head and start to warm up again. Then, carrying his hat and coat, he left the room and descended the stairs. He came off the treads in a cramped, shabby lobby to see that the dining room was open, already filled with wayfarers eating at the long table. He hung up his hat and coat and went in.

Half an hour later he crossed a sand-filled porch and stepped down to a blown street. The train he had seen in Slabtown was now standing at the rough, diminutive depot, taking on an all too scant load of freight and express from the steamboat that was still tied up below the town. The mixed consist included two boxcars and two flats, for the sake of appearances more than necessity at this dull season, with a passenger coach tacked onto the rear end. At the front wheezed and trembled the *Walla Walla*, a Porter-Bell pony locomotive. This had been shipped around the Horn from the East, but the narrow-gage cars had been built by millwrights at Slabtown.

Waiting for the loading to be finished, Luke smoked a cigarette. A few passengers, two of them women, came over from the hotel and boarded the little coach. When he saw the boxcar doors being closed, he also went aboard the hind car, which was barely six feet wide, with two rows of benches down the sides on which the passengers would sit facing each other during the six-hour ride to railhead. The women had gone to the front end, and they sat with downcast eyes. Some of the men showed symptoms of a hard night in the town's pleasure spots. The stage that had already left had taken out almost as many passengers, Luke knew — in too big a hurry, they would have told each other mirthfully, to wait for the steam cars.

The locomotive emitted a piercing whistle completely out of proportion to its size, the women winced and shut their eyes, the cars shuddered, jerked and began to move. The women glanced at each other uneasily, and Luke noticed how they braced themselves with their hands. He settled back on the hard seat in the rear of the car and watched the town and trees slip past. Sam Dunbow, the conductor, swung up at the last moment, a habit in which he took pride. He grinned at Luke and began to collect the fare to the end of track.

The country south and east of town was also rolling desert, dotted with sagebrush, rabbit bush and huge dunes of sand. The train came to the first trestle over the loops of the Walla Walla River and stopped with the engine over the water, while the engineer hauled up water in a bucket to fill his tank. A mile farther on they passed the juncture of the spur to Slabtown, rolling by them at the maximum speed of six miles an hour imposed by the wooden, iron-surfaced rails. But within half an hour the train came to a stop at the first sand deposit left by the night's high wind.

Dunbow swung down with a sigh, and Luke followed him to help clear the track. The engineer was already down and plying a shovel. To that point the freight and stage road had paralleled the track, but there the road crossed to the far side of the Walla Walla, which it and the tracks both followed to the upper end of the valley. Luke saw Kirk Browder's wagon string pulling along over there. The skinners, aware of the stalled train, were making derisive gestures. Luke helped the two-man train crew clear the track, and the train went on.

At Five Mile Station, where no passengers or shippers flagged the train to a stop, the desert fell behind. On either side of the river rose gullied sagehills, crisscrossed with rabbit trails, and this wasp-waist was the natural division between the desert and the great, rich valley. Beyond the stricture and within the valley was Divide Station, where again no flag was up.

Listening to the whacking of the car wheels on the uneven track, Luke fell to thinking of what an enormous achievement this short, initial section of the line had been. The work had begun on the desert in spring, and all summer the hot winds had blown, with extraordinary persistence, the floating sand and alkali dust, inflaming the eyes of the workmen. To make matters worse, the rigid economies forced on Dorsey Baker by the lack of financial support kept wages low and camp fare plain and sometimes skimpy. The finished line was only halfway over the desert when the whole bunch went out on strike.

Higher wages and better food had run up costs. So had the drift fences installed at the worst trouble spots to stop some, but not all, of the vagrant sand. And all but ruinous had been the discovery that the wooden rails on which Baker had relied would not by themselves stand up under the beating of the car wheels. So a strapiron surface had been applied on the wearing edges of the rails, and now it, too, was wearing out.

It was unthinkable that the man who had got that far and even farther against equally discouraging obstacles should yet fail or be made to fail. Dorsey Baker was not only a man of great ability and courage; he was a sick man driven to realize great ambitions in what he believed to be a limited time. At fifty his hair and beard were a snowy white. His spare body was stooped, gaunt, pain-wracked and partly paralyzed on the left side. He had lost two wives, leaving him with a brood of children of nearly every age from Frank's down. Busy as his many undertakings kept him, he had been both father and mother to the children until he married yet again and started yet another baby crop.

When Idaho gold withdrew its transient support, it had been Baker who saved the Walla Walla country from being returned to the Indians who gave it its name. Or at least from being turned over to the stockmen who even yet were jealous of its bunchgrass ranges. For Baker had shown the dirt farmers, who previously had grown produce for the inland mining population, that the arid benchlands would produce wheat as abundantly as it grew in the bottoms.

The Walla Walla had grasped *that* idea, Luke reflected, for an export crop would turn the impending disaster into a permanent prosperity. The idea took root, and wheat was planted not only in the creek valleys but on the high ground as well. Fine harvests were reaped to be sent down the river to Portland and thence by clipper to the hungry markets of the Orient. But there was a hitch, and a ruinous one. For a decade the wagon outfits, and the river packets connecting Wallula with Portland, had fattened on the mining trade. Their rates were so steep that a sack of wheat shipped to Portland cost as much in freight as it would bring on the market. The wheat boom threatened to be even shorter-lived than the mining boom.

That was when Baker began talking about a railroad, and he had made every effort to swing the Northern Pacific, still a long way from being completed, down the valley. The only tangible result had been Truax's survey and estimate that the valley section alone would cost $673,000. The NP lost interest, and Baker's response had been to declare that the valley must build its own railroad. At his insistence the county held an election on a special bond issue for that purpose, but the cost estimate had so completely dampened enthusiasm that the issue was resoundingly voted down.

So Baker had made either the most magnanimous or the most foolhardy move of his busy life. Cornered, but far from beaten, he had announced that with strict economy he could build the road, himself, for half the original estimate. This the valley proved willing for him to do, provided he did it with his own money and

$50,000 put up by the other twenty-three stockholders who shared his faith. He wouldn't consider using the bank's assets at the risk of its depositors and stockholders. Borrowing was precluded by the personal rule Frank had quoted at Slabtown, "Shun debt as you would the devil." So he had gone ahead, committing himself to raise nearly $300,000, assuming he could build the railroad as cheaply as he claimed. He would have to have the public's help, but he believed, in the early stages, that through performance he could win it. The performance had been magnificent but, instead, he had reaped a harvest of bitter enemies, detractors and jokesters at his and the line's expense.

Luke came out of his thoughts to realize that the train was stopping, not yet come to Touchet Station. When he heard the whistle and bell cut loose together, he realized what was wrong. The train slowed to only a snailing pace, and pretty soon cattle appeared in numbers on either side of the train. There had been no money with which to fence the right of way, and this end of the valley was still cow country. Soon the cattle beside the tracks thinned out, the bell and whistle grew silent, and the train picked up speed.

Luke knew this could have happened by chance, or the cattle could have been drifted there purposely to harry the train crew and disgruntle the passengers. The local cowmen had an even more humorous trick. Whenever a dead steer or horse was found on the range anywhere near the tracks, the stinking, unwieldy carcass was dragged in and deposited between the rails for the swearing trainmen to get out of their way somehow.

Chapter 3

The real trouble came between Touchet and Dry Creek Stations, a jarring, noisy stop so abrupt the passengers were hurled against each other and, some of them, into the aisle between the benches. Luke landed on an elbow in the vacant space next to him but was on his feet and moving before the car stopped pitching. He dropped to the ground with Dunbow on his heels, and he heard the conductor mutter disbelievingly, "Snakehead here? The iron on this end's still in good shape!"

A snakehead it was, a length of strapiron that had worked loose and curled upward under the pounding of the car wheels. This had driven its end through the floor of a boxcar, prevented from doing far more serious damage only by the low speed and the practiced engineer's quick shutting off of the steam. Even so, momentum had twisted the length of iron into a hairpin that turned back on itself without pulling out of the car it had impaled. The engineer dropped down from the cab, red-faced and swearing but resigned. He carried a hacksaw and crowbar. The only thing to do was to cut off the impediment, hammer back the protruding end so it wouldn't catch on something, replace the iron from the lengths carried on the train, and go on, the passengers frightened and the schedule once more ruined.

Dunbow said grimly, "One of these days a piece of that stuff's going to come ramming up through the floor of the passenger car. And there goes the last of that kind of business."

Luke was aware of that danger and its discouraging effect on potential passengers, even if no one was hurt, and he knew that luck alone had kept it from happening so far. He crawled under the car with the other two and watched while the engineer made the time-consuming cut and Dunbow finally flattened back the protruding end of the iron still caught in the car floor. Then Luke took a good look at the wooden rail that had been stripped so violently of its metal surfacing.

He said presently, "That's one that never worked loose. Somebody pried it." He pointed to marks in the wood where the spikes had been that had secured the strapiron. They proved what he said.

"The mangy coyotes," Dunbow said bitterly. "They knew we'd pick up speed on this end, where the track's newer. A little faster, and we'd have piled up certain."

"We won't gain time on this end anymore," the engineer agreed. "We wouldn't dare."

"And that's what they were after," Luke said.

Time was a vital element in the struggle for freight and especially for passenger business. The trains could beat the wagons, barring trouble, but the fast stages could still outdistance the trains with passengers. The men crawled out from under the car, and the train was moved forward. Then new strap had to be put on the rail so the train could pass over it on its return trip. Even though they worked at top speed, an hour was lost before they could go on.

It was two-thirty in the afternoon when the train came to the end of the track close to the point where Mill Creek came into the Walla Walla. Since the old Whitman Indian mission stood in the forks of the streams, this point on the line had been named Whitman Station. The stage and wagon road had long since crossed back to the near bank of the river and again paralleled the track. A short way off stood a stage station and road ranch, eloquent in apposition of the unyielding old and of the new struggling for survival. By the tracks was a storage shed that served to protect from weather and thieves freight brought from, or inbound to Walla Walla City, still six trackless miles to the east. Running the connecting wagons and stagecoaches was another of Luke's headaches.

The train pulled in by the shed and stopped, and Luke stepped down to the ground. For a moment he stood looking on beyond the station to where, in the distance beside the grade, he could see Truax's construction camp. This was a clutter of torn and dirty tents that now housed only a custodial crew, for the construction workers had of necessity been laid off. In his line of vision and just beyond the freight house were the two mudwagons over from Walla Walla City to bring and pick up passengers and express. They had brought a fair load of travelers to take the downbound train, but the passengers just arrived on the train wouldn't fill both coaches.

He watched the train crew unload freight

and express while he waited for the exchange of passengers to be made, then walked on past the rustic depot to the lead stage. Pasco Pasquel, who had just helped the last of the two women into his ungainly vehicle with a flourish, turned to look at him with a grin.

"*Como 'sta,* Luke? You ride on box with Pasco?"

"You've got company, *amigo.*"

"*Bueno,*" Pasco lowered his voice. "I theenk we also got trouble."

"What's that?"

"I tell you."

Pasco's was a fast turn-around schedule, while the freight wagons that made the connection needed all day. He was in charge of the passengers and carefully supervised the loading of the overflow vehicle. When he was finally satisfied, Luke followed him up to the box. The tandem stages rolled out then, incongruously substituted for the steam cars.

"Well, Pasco," Luke said. "What's worrying you?"

"Cleent Morgan."

Luke pricked up his ears. Clint Morgan was the kind of spearhead for the disaffected cowmen that Kirk Browder was for the embittered teamsters, both equally

40

hostile to the railroad. "What about him?"

"Last night I see Morgan in Danny Traxler's saloon, Luke. He is talkeeng with these two *hombres*. They are — what you call? — the hard cases. They are making the beeg medicine." Pasco hesitated. "It look to me."

Luke turned that over in his mind. Viewed independently, Browder and Morgan were hardly more than gadflies, pestering the railroad but so far doing no harm. Yet if there was a guiding hand behind both, uniting them and the other natural opponents of the railroad, they had to be taken seriously, particularly with the stock offer coming up.

"What made you think they were making medicine?" he asked.

"I see these *hombres* before," Pasco said. "In Virginia City where I drive stage before I come here. These hard cases, they nearly get strung up, Luke. Somebody pay them to blow up a water flume and shut down somebody's mine."

Morgan never kept very fragrant company, but would he go so far as to import dynamiters? Men who went in for that kind of sabotage would also pry loose strapiron, not caring that they endangered lives. Could Morgan be the guiding hand?

41

Luke couldn't credit it. Clint Morgan had plenty of low cunning but not the brains to mastermind a concerted plan of action against Dorsey Baker and his new enterprise.

"You theenk we got trouble there?" Pasco asked.

"I think we've got trouble all over the landscape. Thanks for telling me that." On the next breath Luke found his eyes narrowing while his thoughts chained on. Morgan could well be the tough, unprincipled field man, the go-between, allowing the person or persons working secretly against the railroad to remain safe in their respectable roles. If Morgan was really such a link, he and his Nevada imports were men to watch even more closely than the Kirk Browder crowd at Wallula. "Maybe you and I'll take a look for those dynamiters this evening," he added to the driver.

"If they are steel here," Pasco agreed.

The stage clipped along, with the two men on the box turned back upon their own thoughts. This was the broadest part of the valley, and any way a man looked, he saw the far, enfolding hills, highlands and mountains. They were all beautiful views, toward the Umatilla highlands or the Blue

Mountains or the Snake River benchlands, even in the chilly late fall. In spring and summer they were superlative, from the Blue Mountain forests in their richest hues to the high wheatlands and bunch-grass ranges and down to the homesteads on all the basin's many streams.

The afternoon was nearly over when Pasco brought his stages and passengers into Walla Walla City. Little remained in the valley metropolis, Luke reflected, to remind him of the old Steptoeville that had changed its name so ambitiously at the start of the mining rush. Fort Walla Walla still stood on the edge of town. The old bridge still lay across Mill Creek. But the trail to the mines had become Main Street, and now many of the frame false-fronts had been replaced by masonry buildings, substantial and dignified.

Pasco stopped at the Stine House to unload, and Luke followed him down to the sidewalk. "Meet me at Traxler's bar for a drink after supper," Luke told the driver. "About eight."

"Weel do," Pasco agreed.

Luke walked down the busy sidewalk until across from him he saw a narrow brick building whose lower floor was labeled along its front: PAINE BROTHERS & MOORE. Originally this had been the general mercantile store Dorsey Baker and John Boyer had run through the days of the mining trade. His gaze lifted to the floor above, which also was identified by a sign, and one of monumental simplicity: THE BANK PLACE. This was the present home of what officially was Baker & Boyer, Bankers, but the doctor had never thought it necessary to change the original identification, although there were now two other banks in Walla Walla City. Luke crossed the street and climbed the stairway ascending to that floor.

When he stepped through a door at the head of the stairs, he came into a lobby separated by a counter and wickets from the bank's clerks and the desks of the partners. He saw at a glance that Dorsey Baker wasn't there, and Boyer was talking to a homesteader in cowhide boots.

Waiting, Luke rolled a cigarette and looked at this man who had followed Baker west by only a few years, then his brother-in-law through a wife of the doctor's who had died. They had run their store together, and while everyone had respected Baker's strict honesty and fair dealing, it had been Boyer's personality that had drawn much of the trade, as Bill Green had said. A portly man of inexhaustible affability, Boyer was never too busy to stop and visit, nor was his head too full of his own affairs for him not to remember details of the affairs of others. Even more important, a native tact spared him the unfortunate fruits of Baker's tart, if honest, tongue. Not sharing in Baker's other enterprises, Boyer was not nearly as wealthy now, but he had put all he could raise into the WW&CR. While he had been made treasurer of the company, he had been given little voice in its management. Green had been right again in counting it one of Baker's worst mistakes not to have put Boyer in charge of public relations.

Luke noticed that Boyer and the settler were shaking hands, then the latter turned off toward the door. Boyer's gaze shifted to Luke, his eyes warming, ready to give him his time no matter how many bank duties pressed for his attention. Luke went over to him. He didn't get up here often, and they shook hands.

Boyer had the warm voice that went with his amiable countenance, and he said, "I hope you're not after money, Luke. The bottom's been scraped clear out of the barrel."

"No, I hoped I might find the doctor here."

"You see him, you hold onto him," Boyer said. "I'd like to see him, myself. He's still out trying to shed light into dark corners, I suppose."

Luke nodded. "I saw Bill Green in Slabtown. He's not very hopeful of the stock issue going over."

"I know. Bill was in the other day."

"What do you think, John?"

"That Bill's a good weather prophet." Boyer sighed. "They're not getting behind it like Dorsey was sure they would, now that he's got the track to within six miles of town. He still refuses to believe that, but I sense it and so does Bill."

"Too bad."

Knowing Boyer wouldn't betray the fact that he was very busy, Luke offered his hand again and then walked down the stairs shaking his head. All Baker asked was $75,000 from the public with which to finish the track, replace the strapiron rails with T-iron and, if possible, to buy heavier, faster locomotives. That would eliminate many of the present troubles and double or even triple the running time. This was modest enough, reasonable enough and clear enough common sense to gain acceptance and a favorable response.

The farther Luke got down the stairs, the higher his anger mounted. Even those who criticized, or derided, or made a bogey of it, had been benefited by the narrow-gage railroad with the wooden rails. Once railhead was deep enough in the valley for the line to solicit patronage, Baker had announced a freight rate one-half that charged by the wagoners, forcing them to come down to the same level. Public clamor had compelled the steamboat company to follow suit, cutting their charge in half. When the river people realized the profit in hauling downbound wheat, Baker had induced them to cut their rate on that item even more and to put more boats on the run.

Thus the hoped-for export crop had been saved for the Walla Walla country, and the growing of wheat increased until it became the principal industry. What had been Baker's reward? By the time construction reached Mile 16, the halfway point, all the money he and his few loyal supporters could put into the company had been exhausted. Baker needed nearly as much again, and to avoid weakening his control of the company through a stock issue of that size, he had offered bonds to pay a handsome twelve per cent. There were so few buyers that construction beyond that point had all had to come out of revenue, with not one shipper out of two even willing for him to earn it. It was incredible, unless someone unsuspected had all the while injected a subtle poison into the entire public mind. The idea that had begun as a conjecture on Bill Green's part had become a strong probability in Luke's mind.

Reaching the sidewalk, he halted and glanced along the street, thinking over the town's citizens of enough influence to sway public opinion without mounting a soap box, and with enough money to take over a controlling interest. One of Baker's rival bankers? None was of that caliber. One of his former competitors in the store business? The merchants were benefiting from the lowest freight rates in history, and none was a man of exceptional wealth. A coterie of these, pooling their resources? Possibly.

Luke went to the room he kept at the Stine House, which he sometimes never saw for days on end. The supper hour was far enough away to give him time for a hot bath in the tin tub at the end of the hallway, and he used it, afterward putting on clean clothes and feeling much better physically. Yet he had hardly buttoned his shirt when a rap on the door took him over to open it. He found the desk clerk standing there with a letter in his hand, which he held out.

"Man from the post office brought this over," the clerk said. "It was marked rush. He said it come up on the stage from Wallula."

Luke took the letter, grunting his thanks, but didn't really look at it until the man had gone and he shut the door. There was no return on the envelope, and his name and address were printed. He tore open the cover and pulled out the contents, finding that the note enclosed was not printed but written in an obviously feminine hand.

His brow wrinkled while he read the terse message: "He's trying to do it to you again, Luke. Don't let him."

There was no signature, but from those few words there could be no mistaking who had written them. He had never seen Nan Browder's handwriting, but only she would say just that to him and know he would understand. He had still been in Wallula when the stage left, so why hadn't she seen him, instead of sending this? He answered that before he had completely asked it of himself. After what happened at her place, she hadn't wanted to risk seeking him. Why at just this time, with himself hunting a clue to the identity of the man secretly fighting not only him but the railroad? That was easy, too. The same urgency that affected him had worked on Nan. She knew that things were heating up because of the coming stock issue.

Yet there were other questions not so easy to answer. Why this act of friendship now, if it was really that? She could have cleared him there in Blackhawk if she had been willing to testify before the grand jury that had indicted him. Why help him now when she had still loved Lawson Keel enough to follow him to this country, even though Keel had thrown her over? Luke hadn't believed her love had died, even when she married Browder, whom a woman of her nature could hardly have loved and could have married only out of despair and loneliness.

He wadded the paper angrily and threw it into a corner, then went over, picked it up and burned it, letting the char and ash fall into the room's cuspidor. He did know why she hadn't testified on his behalf back there. A woman didn't testify against her husband. To her that was what Lawson

Keel had been, even though Keel had an entirely different idea of their relationship.

He knew these questions were dodges, anyway, to save him from facing the warning itself. The only way Keel could do it to Luke Preston again was through the railroad, which Luke owned only to the extent of the few stock shares he could afford, but to which he was dedicated mind and heart. The stock would be nowhere near as profitable as what Keel had taken away from him — and from others, getting him blamed for it — in Blackhawk, but control of the railroad would be. If Keel ever achieved that, this country would be in for a rate-gouging monopoly that would make the greedy wagon freighters look like pikers.

He hadn't got around to Keel in the short time he had been speculating on the identity of Bill Green's snakehead because Keel wasn't too obvious a suspect. Profitable as the Blackhawk coup had been, Keel hadn't brought enough money out of it to acquire a controlling interest in the WW&CR by either foul means or fair. He hadn't bought stock, yet hadn't been an open enemy of the project. On the other hand, he had every instinct to be the man. He ran a store that dealt with the farmers and a mill that bought wheat from them, and he stood high in their opinion. His position and personality were impressive with the town's other business men. If he was working in secret, backed by a group that could raise the money, Keel was indeed the snakehead.

By the time he had reached this conclusion, Luke found that he had started to sweat. What could he do about Keel when his own past, if exposed, could be enough to bring down Baker and the railroad?

Chapter 4

The Walla Walla City terminal of the railroad was related to the rest of the line only in that it sat beside the right of way where eventually passenger and freight depots would rise. Lined along the yet-to-be-built track, at present, was a freight shed temporarily serving to receive and store such freight as came in on the wagons from railhead, or came from some shipper to leave by company wagons for the end of track. Between the shed and a barn and blacksmith shop was a churned-up yard where spare wagons were backed to a fence with their tongues sticking up in the air. Extra wheels were strung along the fence, a couple of spare tongues lying by them on the ground. The mudwagons, which would not need to leave for a couple of hours to meet the day's train, were on the other side of the yard.

Luke looked out on this scene from a window of the office in one end of the drafty freight building. Tripp Yale, who took care of the horses and vehicles and did the physical work at the station, was busy at the forge over there. Luke had some tedious but unavoidable paper work to catch up on but was unable to settle to it, disturbed not only by the unexpected warning from Nan. The night before he and Pasco had paid a visit to every saloon in town without finding the men Pasco had seen talking with Clint Morgan. Nor was Morgan in evidence, and they had finally heard that he had gone down the river early that day. Luke didn't like the idea of Morgan and maybe his mysterious hoodlums being down there with himself up here, whether or not they were working for Lawson Keel.

A voice, young and pleasant, said behind him, "You're fidgety, Luke. What's the matter?"

Luke turned, both frowning and smiling at the young woman who sat at the desk near the office's front door. She was Sherry Yale, Tripp's daughter, who acted as freight clerk, passenger agent and whatever else was required of her on this end of the line. Her pretty young face and the loose way she wore her brown hair concealed what he knew to be a very confident woman, a man's woman engrossed in the predominantly masculine life around her. Once when Pasco was sick and Luke was out of town, Sherry had taken the mudwagons to the end of track. Dainty, frail and timid as she looked, he knew her to be plenty capable of turning down the wick of the occasional sport who made a mistake with her.

Since he had never been able to explain why he couldn't encourage what easily could be a nice friendship, he had always taken a jocular attitude toward her and did again, saying, "I'm just not cut out for this kind of life, Sherry. I should have taken on something easy, like running a lunatic asylum."

Sherry kept on posting freight bills, but she had heard and wrinkled her nose. "You saw Nan Browder and started mooning about her again." She looked up accusingly. "Well? You saw her, didn't you?"

She knew that the past had somehow related him with Nan, that he sometimes saw her. In view of his silence, she had, like a woman, assumed it to have been romantic.

"Only for a minute," he said.

"I bet."

He would have given her some light answer, but at that moment something outside the window drew his attention. A buggy had pulled up out there, and he saw Dorsey Baker swinging down, being careful to hide his crippledness, even without witnesses. Luke went to the back door and stepped out just as Baker came to the ground. He called a greeting that wasn't answered immediately. A broken-tipped whip stood in the buggy's socket. It had been there for months, the doctor, in his enforced frugality, refusing to replace it.

"Good morning, Luke," Baker said then, turning and leveling his cool eyes on Luke. "John told me you were in the bank yesterday. So I hurried out before you went down the line again." He gave Luke his spare smile instead of his hand.

A man forgot until he looked at the drooped left eye, the sagging side of the bearded face and mouth and the way the left arm was carried and the left leg dragged that he was partially paralyzed on that side. And a man who looked at his worn, shabby clothes and battered black hat would be apt to forget that he was probably the richest man in eastern Washington in terms of fixed assets and holdings not readily convertible to the cash he now needed so desperately.

Baker said nothing more until they had

gone indoors. There he gave Sherry Yale a slightly warmer smile than he had given his operating superintendent and trouble-shooter. He moved to the stove to warm himself and, looking at Luke again, said, "Locate the strap?" That was a relatively minor matter, but he concerned himself with details even smaller.

Luke told him about the straying shipment, another incident in a chronic experience. He described the hangup on the snakehead west of Dry Creek and went on to the more routine details of these periodical reports. Even though his worry about Morgan, the men he had imported and the man who might be behind him, was uppermost in his mind, he refrained from mentioning them. Baker already looked unwontedly tired and discouraged. Certainly he had enough to trouble him without adding more than could be offered only as speculation.

Since Baker seemed disinclined to mention it, Luke said, "Did you do any good in the backcountry?"

The doctor pondered a moment in gloomy silence, then shook his head. Luke knew from an earlier announcement that he had gone in to Dixie, Waitsburgh and Dayton, old waystations on the Idaho stage road that had become farm towns and were growing rapidly. That, too, was wheat country, and it should have stood solidly behind Baker's idea of running his line on to Lewiston eventually.

"Worse than none," Baker said finally. It was the first time Luke had heard his voice sound so flat and depressed. "The shippers up there are not only disinterested in the railroad, Luke. They're talking of starting a new river port of their own on the Snake. At the Tucannon."

Luke could only emit an exasperated sigh. Coming out of Idaho, Snake River curved along the north edge of the Walla Walla basin before it emptied into the Columbia. Except at low water it was navigable by steamboat. A port at the Tucannon would have several things to recommend it to the Waitsburgh-Dayton people, he realized. It would be only a fraction of the distance to Wallula, although the water haul would be considerably longer and more influenced by the seasons. Moreover, wheat shipped by that route would bypass both the monopoly-minded wagon freighters and the monopoly-suspect railroad on the route to Wallula.

"So the devil with them," Baker added on a gust of impatience. "When we're ready to extend the line beyond Walla Walla City, we'll go south through Weston and Centerville to the Umatilla."

The region to the south was also becoming wheat country, but the proper solution was to tap both it and the country Baker had just visited and now renounced for its stupid stubbornness. He probably hadn't bothered, Luke reflected, to conceal his contempt for their scheme and the ears they had kept closed to his reasoning.

He looked at the brooding doctor and felt the weight of the responsibility that had settled on his own shoulders. In his unvoiced opinion, the inland people didn't want their own river port as much as they wanted to sidestep the fight that had gone on concurrently with the construction of the railroad. He said, "Maybe those people up there won't help in the stock issue, the way things stand, but I wouldn't write off an eastern extension yet. Once the antagonism's put down, and the suspicion that the railroad'll only turn into another freight monopoly, I think they'll get behind you." Out of the corner of his eye, he saw Sherry nod her head. She was still posting the books, but her ears weren't required in her work.

"I didn't start the antagonism and suspicion," Baker snapped. "How can I stop it except by winning the fight?"

That was one way to stop it. Another that Luke couldn't mention was to root out the person or persons who had cultivated those ruinous emotions in the deciding majority in the valley that otherwise might not have succumbed to it. That was the terrible duty devolving on Luke Preston, who could do it only at the cost of his own doom.

Then, having garnered the latest report on the line's operations, Baker was ready to leave again. He said, "Tell Frank I'll get down to see him in a few days. I'm going to Weston, and maybe on a ways." As abruptly as he had arrived, he went on about his business.

"It's terrible," Sherry said somberly, when they found themselves alone again. "Having to beat the bushes for supporters, when this country ought to tip its hat to him. Someday I bet it does."

"I sure hope you're right," Luke said.

He forced himself to settle to work and caught up with his office duties that forenoon, checking and initialing a stack of invoices and time sheets for Boyer to pay, and tonnage and other figures Sherry had been stacking on his desk during his absence. She would take care of the stuff from there on, and she was welcome to it. All the while his worry had increased as to why Clint Morgan had gone down the valley and what had happened to his Nevada imports.

He had his noon meal at the hotel, struggling against a dictate of conscience rising from his talk with Dorsey Baker. By the time he left the hotel, he knew he had to have a confrontation with Lawson Keel and settle his mind about the man's part in the fight against the railroad, no matter what it cost him personally.

The merchandising concern he reached and entered was off Main. A gilt sign running across its front said: L. KEEL & COMPANY, and Luke speculated on the identity of the "& Company," for Keel had no apparent partners. The store stood across from Keel's flour mill so that farmers who sold him wheat could go over and spend the proceeds in his store. Their vehicles jammed the space in front of both buildings, and the store's interior was crowded and babbling with farm talk. A balcony ran across the deep end of the place, a stairs leading up to it. A boot and shoe department used most of the balcony, but at one end was a railed-off space that provided an office for Keel's bookkeeper and himself.

Glancing up, Luke saw Keel there at a desk, only his head and shoulders showing above the balcony railing. For a moment Luke's body was charged with reluctance, then he climbed the stairs, walked over to the gate in the low fence and went through. A dour man wearing an eye shade and black cuffs glanced at him in melancholy disinterest and went back to his figures. Keel was writing a letter and had a cigar in the fingers of the hand that steadied the paper. The only thing that betrayed a reaction, when he glanced up at Luke, was the accumulated ash that dropped off the cigar.

Instead of speaking to Luke, Keel turned to look at the bookkeeper and say quietly, "Herb, go and get yourself some fresh air." Apparently the bookkeeper was used to being sent away when Keel wanted privacy. He stood up and left. The babble on the lower floor would keep anything said up here from carrying. Keel drew on the cigar until Herb was out of earshot; then he said dryly, "Well, Luke, this is a surprise. Don't tell me our meeting at the ferry landing, the other day, inspired a desire to renew old acquaintances."

"You know it didn't," Luke said.

"So what do I owe this honor to?"

"I think it's time we laid down our cards."

Keel looked surprised, and a little wary. "Oh? How come?"

"I think you're trying to gratify your instinct," Luke said coolly, "for moving in on what better men have put together. Wiliness is all you ever were good at, Lawson. Cheating and double-crossing and, of course, deceiving. You're real good at those."

Keel's quick suck of breath convinced Luke that he was on the right track.

He added softly, "I could destroy your influence with the people you're manipulating to serve your own ends here, Lawson, if I told what I know about you."

There was a mock amiability now in the face he looked into. It reddened, and he saw Keel clench a fist. "It wasn't me who was indicted," Keel said angrily. "It was Wade Foster. And that indictment hasn't come under the statute of limitations yet, even though you did a pretty good job of burying Wade Foster. Good enough that I've got to thinking of you as Luke Preston, myself."

Luke brushed that aside, saying,

"Lawson Keel would have been indicted and Wade Foster given a clean bill of health if Nan Alpert had testified before the grand jury."

"She didn't," Keel snapped.

"Don't I know it? And I know why she hasn't exposed me here — she feels she's done enough to me already. But why haven't you tipped off the law? Nothing would finish Baker's railroad quicker than to have it come out that one of his key men is on the dodge from a swindling charge in Colorado."

Keel swallowed and sucked his cigar through a long moment. Then he stubbed it out, shooting a glance at his visitor. "What makes you think I want the railroad finished?"

"The parallel between the chance you had in Blackhawk and the one shaping up here makes me think so. But you don't have to tell me why you've kept your mouth shut. It's a trump card, but you know I could hurt you bad enough to jeopardize your scheme if you played it. So you won't unless you have to."

Keel smiled coldly. "A shotgun standoff?"

"Exactly."

"Don't forget," Keel pointed out, "that it

64

was you who brought the charges against me back there, trying to make your own defense. It would be the same thing here if I exposed you. Don't forget that I was cleared, while you disappeared before they could arrest you after the indictment."

"I only disappeared," Luke said, "because I'd have made out no better in a trial without Nan Alpert's testimony. You know that."

"It was supposed to be a secret indictment," Keel mused. "I never knew who tipped you off."

He was wondering if it had been Nan, perhaps if it had been Nan who informed him of the scheme here, now that her lips were no longer sealed by the foolish love she had borne this fellow. It must have occurred to Keel, also, that Nan could still clear Wade Foster if she ever became willing to take the consequences to herself.

Luke knew that he dared not endanger her, and he said indifferently, "All my friends weren't false ones, you know."

"So it's a shotgun standoff. At present." Keel shrugged. "Don't overlook, though, that yours is single shot, while mine's double-barreled."

"I'm not overlooking it. And I'm not apt to let you grab control of the railroad, at your own price and for your own purposes, if I can help it."

Keel's smile would have proved he was Bill Green's snakehead, even if Luke hadn't already been convinced of it. Luke only looked at him a moment, then turned and went out through the gate.

He had descended the stairs and gone out to the street before he realized why Keel had called his weapon double-barreled, for he wasn't the only one he would endanger if he revealed what he knew about Keel's past. Nan hadn't perjured herself, but she had withheld vital evidence, and Keel had relied on that to lock her tongue after he broke off their affair. He was much less sure of her now and uneasily aware that she could still reverse the situation, clearing the man who had been condemned and condemning the man who had been cleared. Now Keel must resort to intimidation in case of necessity, and if frightened badly enough, he might silence her permanently. He had enough at stake to impel a man of his cut to do that.

Luke returned to the freight yard to find Sherry, who had brought her lunch, back at work. He interrupted it to say, "Sherry, how does a woman who's loved and gone a long ways for a man feel after he's booted her out?"

Sherry's mouth dropped open. For a moment she only looked up at him with disturbingly pretty eyes. "Why, if she was any kind of a woman, she'd be madder than a wet hen. Who're you talking about?"

"Nobody," Luke said. "I just wondered."

Sherry looked skeptical but returned to work. After a moment she glanced across the room to where he had returned to his own desk. "Luke, was it *you* broke off your affair with Nan Browder?"

"I never had an affair with Nan Browder."

"Well, whoever she was before she married that teamster. Alpert, wasn't it? I forget." She hadn't forgotten for a moment.

"Her neither," Luke said.

"Hah."

Luke stayed at his desk only long enough to realize that he wasn't going to wait for the next day's train to go down the valley. He told Sherry to look for him when she saw him coming and went out through the back door and on to the barn. He kept a saddle horse there for local use, and it could have him in Wallula that evening.

Chapter 5

Wallula had settled down to its evening diversions when it heard the whistle. Elvie Elvek, standing in the doorway of the livery barn, looked at his fellow stablehand and said, "Steamboat comin' in? At night?" But both men soon knew it wasn't a river boat. The whistling kept up, heavy and urgent, and it was soon apparent that this came down the river on the wind. A man stuck his head out of an upstairs window of the hotel and pointed in that direction. "Fire up there, it looks like," he bawled to those below him. "I see a glow. Must be the Slabtown mill!"

Elvek felt his heart jiggle in his chest, and understanding seemed to make the screaming of the far-off whistle louder and more alarming. He heard voices rise excitedly on the street, which was soon full of men, some truly concerned about the fire and already storming off along the road up the river. Others came pounding toward the livery barn to demand horses, too many for Elvek and his helper to take care of, so Elvek slipped into the shadows and, half-paralyzed by his consternation, let them take care of themselves or strike out afoot.

As the last of these bolted off toward the cause of the alarm, some to help and some to enjoy the spectacle of what could be happening to old Doc Baker up there, Elvek came out of his shock. He owned a little piece of the railroad, and if the mill and the materials stored in the yard went up in smoke, there went the stock issue kerplunk. He glanced around to see that the boss hadn't put in an appearance, then ran down a row of stalls to where a horse was still tied, a nag nobody had wanted. Elvek threw a saddle on it and swung up. A moment later he was on his own way up the river.

The mill whistle had stopped blowing by the time he rounded the point, and he could hear men shouting all around him. The fire on ahead grew larger, redder by the minute, and a stream of foot and mounted traffic poured along the road, even behind him now that more people had been drawn into the night by the excitement. Elvek got within a hundred yards of the millyard, which as yet was unaffected by the fire, before the congestion forced him to stop and leave the nag.

Running on afoot he saw that the fire so far was confined to the shacks and bunkhouses to the north of the sawmill. Several of these burned savagely, the smoke piling down over the mill, huge embers shooting with it like comets. Elvek's lips pinched, for this was no accident. Somebody pretty smart had started it, for a fire in a bunkhouse wouldn't look too much like the work of a firebug. And it would do the job, for the bunkhouses were upwind from the more vital part, the mill and the stored railroad materials. He saw that a bucket line had formed between the river and the conflagration. For every man who worked there, though, one or two stood grinning, wanting the whole works to go. Elvek wanted to curse the onlookers, to tie into them with his bony fists, but there was a fire to fight and he aimed to help.

He stood figuring where to start, but a man nearly ran over him, so he climbed onto a lumber pile where he could see better. Men were swarming over the mill roof, he saw from there, using wet sacking to beat out the carried brands. Others worked in the yard, trying to save the piles of timbers — enough to finish the track if

Doc had the strapiron and could afford to hire the men. The shacks nearest the mill were being demolished, he also saw from that elevation, to form a firebreak, and he saw one of those burning on the upper edge cave in. And then in a patch of firelight, he saw Luke Preston. He didn't know why, but he felt better then and galloped off to join a bucket line he saw forming.

The fringe of shacks, sheds and bunkhouses north of the sawmill burned with the intensity of matchwood, with embers like popping corn flying up into the wind to be scattered dangerously. Luke worked with a crew trying to contain the fire in the section where it had started, his lungs tortured, face and hands stinging, body drenched with scalding sweat under cinder-burned clothing. A cable from the loghaul, which usually dragged sawlogs from the pond to the headrig, had been lengthened and run out. Now it was pulling down whole shacks between the fire and millyard, flattening them so that when they burned, as they would, they would create less of an inferno.

By then he, Frank Baker, and the mill and yard bosses had got five bucket lines organized to move up water from the pond, some of it to soak the sacks used to beat out embers, the rest to wet down the firebreak they were building. The trains that had been left on the track by the millyard for the night had no steam, and there was a question whether the men trying to fire the boilers could move that most vital of all equipment out of danger in time. He cursed the wind and the start the fire had got in one of the empty bunkhouses before it was discovered, and the fact that with the mill shut down there had been only a skeleton crew on hand. He knew that Wallula had turned out in force, some to help, but most to stand as spectators and root for the fire to put an end to Dorsey Baker and his abominable railroad.

The last of the shacks in the swath came down with a crash, and at that moment Frank Baker appeared from the smoke. He stopped beside Luke, panting, hatless and with the hair nearly burned off his head.

"I don't think we can hold it, Luke!" he said urgently. "It'll jump the break sure as hell!"

Luke had already succumbed to that conviction in view of the high wind and intense heat. "Unless we go a step farther," he said. "I think we better backfire, Frank, right now."

Frank groaned, for he understood more than Luke had said. The extreme measure suggested might only seal the doom of the whole property, yet there was a chance that it would help limit the damage to the area already surrendered. The mill was Frank's responsibility, so Luke left it to him to decide, and in that moment Frank displayed a streak of the cool courage that characterized his father.

"All right. Let's start one."

With brands snatched from the burning fires, they set new fires on the leeward edge of the narrow, flattened belt. This brought a yell from the spectators observing it that died away when they saw that the gamble might not pay off in their favor. The gigantic suction of the heat of the main fire pulled in air from all sides, creating a draft toward itself. In a moment it was apparent that the draft was equal to if not stronger than the wind against which it moved. As the deliberate fires gained strength, dampered by the compacted, water-soused fuel they fed on, the smoke faltered and gradually bent toward the main holocaust. When the spectators realized the fire itself would not sweep beyond the break, they pinned their hopes on the wind above, that still caught soaring embers and sowed them broadcast.

The next cheer rose from the firefighters when somebody shouted that the trains were pulling out of danger. But it was long moments more before the backfire was blazing with the same force as the main fire and moving toward it. When this was certain, the two bucket lines tied up there were freed to help protect the standing property. Even then it was touch and go for a long while, for here and there an outcry welled up where somewhere in dead grass, sawdust, dry lumber, or the underpinning and roof of the mill building, a spot fire exploded into life. Time and again men stormed these spots with water pails or wet flails to beat, stamp or drown the new threat.

It seemed hours to Luke, after the backfire was set, before the tide had turned beyond question. The firebreak held, and the mill and lumber piles still stood intact. The last of the burning shacks had caved in to create a final firestorm over the threatened sections and a new frenzy of action. After that the air was fairly free of brands, and the disappointed among the spectators began to drift off down the river toward Wallula. A good try on somebody's part. It had nearly worked, and if it had, there would have gone the railroad. As it was, the old Doc would be out of pocket plenty replacing what had been destroyed.

The office still stood, and Luke and Frank leaned against its blistered wall, silently regarding what, for all their luck, was a depressing sight. Luke felt for his tobacco and then grimaced, wondering if he would ever again enjoy a smoke. He had arrived at Slabtown hardly an hour before the alarm sounded, and he and Frank had been sitting in the office talking over the worries Luke had kept from the older Baker. They were discussing the advisability of putting armed guards around the mill and on the trestles when the outcry informed them that it was too late.

In the turmoil that followed they hadn't had a chance to speak of the fire's origin. Now, his voice hoarse from smoke, Luke said, "It had to be those two fellows Pasco told me about. Clint Morgan's imports from Nevada. Dynamiters there. Arsonists here. It's all one pattern."

"I wish we could prove that," Frank said bitterly. "But the two men are long gone by now, probably, and Morgan's kept his own hands clean."

"Maybe they're gone, and maybe not," Luke reflected. "They're professionals, and they didn't bring this job off. It's my guess they'll hang around and try again."

Frank started to say something but broke off when a man came out of the shadows toward them, and Luke recognized Elvek, from the Wallula livery stable. The hostler wore his usual hangdog look, yet it was changed somehow by a look of stubborn anger. His burned and blackened clothes showed he had put in some work on the fire.

Luke said, "Thanks, Elvie."

"I never come over to be thanked," Elvek said in sudden bitterness. "I heard you mention Clint Morgan, and there's something I better tell you. He's been in Wallula most of the day, left his horse at the barn. I went over to Nan's for a drink before supper, and him and Browder was there drinking and acting like they felt real good. Maybe it was the booze, but, more, maybe they knew what was going to happen up here."

"Thanks again," Luke said. "I wonder if he's still there."

"Likely. Usually makes a night of it when he hits town." Elvek turned and vanished again into the night.

"Going to see them, Luke?" Frank asked.

"I've got to."

"Then I'll go along."

Luke shook his head. "Those firebugs aren't happy with their night's work, and that cuts out your work till they're nailed."

Frank wanted in on the accounting, but he realized that the physical property of the railroad was menaced as it never had been before. He left to organize a fire watch and guard. Luke got his horse from the corral across the road from the sawmill and rode down to Wallula Landing.

He wasn't surprised to find Nan's place still open and doing a land-office business with the excited townsmen, most of whom had been at Slabtown either to fight or to savor the fire. Nor did he deem it peculiar that when he walked through the door, a quick awareness of his arrival swept across the room. He paid no attention to the men who turned toward him with their appetites for crisis restored. At the deep end of the room, at Browder's usual table, the teamster still sat drinking with Clint Morgan.

Striding toward them through an aisle that cleared spontaneously, Luke spotted Nan. She was at the far end of the bar, and he saw her hand lift and press to her breast, while a soundless protest shaped on her lips. He saw Browder flatten his hands on the table, while Morgan pushed his spine against the circular back of his chair. Not a word had been spoken in the room when Luke reached the table and stopped. Every ear was attuned to what was to be said and every eye waited to witness what was to happen next.

Luke looked flatly at Morgan, seeing a burly man at least his physical equal whose head was canted so that amused yet wary eyes stared back. "If you haven't paid off your Nevada boys, Morgan," Luke said, "you better dock them. They didn't earn their money. You must have heard that by now."

Taken aback by the specific reference, Morgan came forward in the chair. "Mebbe you know what you're getting at, there," he returned. "But I don't, Preston."

"If you didn't see the fire yourself, these people must have told you we saved the mill and yard."

"Oh, the fire," Morgan said. "What makes you think I had anything to do with that? I been here since afternoon, and you can ask Nan." He decided to drag her into it himself and called to her, causing her to lift her head and frown. "Where were me and Kirk, Nan, when that fire broke out?"

Nan's frown deepened, but she said dully, "Here."

"I'm not talking about you and Browder, Morgan," Luke snapped. "I'm talking about the two Nevada men you huddled with in Danny Traxler's saloon in Walla Walla City night before last."

That was too precise even for Morgan's tough brazenness. He blinked his eyes, his ruddy cheeks darkening, his eyes turning thoughtful and worried. "Hey, now," he breathed. "What's this?"

He glanced about uneasily. Browder was staring with a sprung-jawed blankness of expression, his gaze moving over the faces in the room which all were turned that way. Nan's face was one of these, hers a tangle of surprise, concern and something hard to figure out. Luke knew what had jolted them, the fear that the arsonists had been caught and forced to confess.

He let them keep thinking that for a moment, then repeated Morgan's startled question. "What's this? It's the one chance you'll get, Morgan, to walk out of here on your own legs. And then climb aboard your horse and head for the far side of yonder with the intention of never again showing yourself around here."

Behind Luke, somebody breathed, "Holy Moses."

Morgan's eyes bugged at the effrontery of being told in front of all those people to leave the country, which Luke knew there was no chance of his doing.

"If I don't?" Morgan intoned.

"If you don't walk out of here, I'm going to pack you out and pile you onto the first manure heap I come to."

Nan cried, "Luke, — no — !"

"No gun in the back this time, Nan," Luke warned. "I'm tired of having to come into your place after scum."

He was leaving Morgan no choice, even if Morgan wanted one, and the man boiled to his feet, a driving rage flooding his face. Browder, excited but apprehensive, slid out of his chair and stepped clear. Morgan stumped around the table, his arrogance forcing him to stick his thumbs under his belt. He hadn't minded taking tacit credit for the attack on the sawmill a while ago, alone here with men who hated Baker as much as he did. But Luke's startling knowledge of details had scared him. He knew if he showed even a trace of this after the insults, he would be turned from hero to laughing stock.

A practiced brawler, he abruptly shook

off his slackness, his body twisting, and surged forward, his shoulder working and driving a scaling, heavy fist at Luke's jaw. The drive carried him with the blow, but the jaw somehow slipped out of range, and Morgan gushed air from a fist that made a thunking sound low on his ribs. He took it flat-footedly, only emitting a grunt, then followed with his other fist. That one landed, and he hammered Luke backward until again his fist slid over a shoulder and Luke's fist smashed him full in the belly. Morgan pulled up then to stare at the hatless, hair-singed, fire-blackened figure so slippery and unstable in front of him.

"Been in a few yourself, huh?" he breathed. "Good. That'll make it more fun for me."

His eyes shuttled over the silent, waiting crowd, seeking partisanship and seeing a prudent neutrality now that none of them was sure of the outcome. Then he was the one bracing himself for, out of the corner of his eyes, he saw Luke come storming at him.

Luke saw nothing but the stung, furious but now cautious man at whom he charged. He had learned from Morgan's first rush that the man relied on the power in those huge shoulders, that his arsenal was limited to a fury of smashing punches meant to settle things fast. Moving in too close for Morgan to swing heavily, Luke belted him in the belly and again on the breast bone and watched pain flicker in those sweaty eyes. He drove Morgan back until he crashed against the table he had got up from, sending the table screeching backward, spilling a bottle and glasses to the floor. Morgan's heavy arms pushed at him, but Luke sent a punch whistling between them that hit Morgan under the jaw and snapped back his head.

Morgan used the table to brace himself. His haunches caught on its edge, he leaned quickly back on his arms, lifted his feet and drove them forward into Luke's face. It was unmerciful, and the hard soles and heels cut and smashed. Luke heard Nan's second cry of protest then. He saw lights explode in his head, felt the head jerk backward and tear at the roots of his neck. And then the floor whacked the back of the head, and he could only fight to hold onto his wits.

Morgan took a grinning moment to catch his breath, walking around his fallen adversary, staring down with gleaming eyes. He listened for a second to the ragged, choking sound of Luke's breath in a bloody mouth, then permitted himself to glance again at the watching faces. They were with him again, eager to see how he would wind it up. He was happy to show them and turned quickly, viciously, and kicked Luke hard in the ribs.

He didn't even see movement in the hand that somehow jabbed out and caught hold of his foot. He only felt himself yanked off balance, and while he danced on one leg and kicked savagely with the caught one, Luke came up on his knees. Morgan broke free, steadied himself and swung a leg to kick a face again exposed for a second. But Luke sprang onto his feet.

His face was scraped and bleeding, his head hung forward and breath still whistled through his ruined lips. Morgan boiled in to finish it and didn't even see the punch that came up between his arms, only felt its skull-popping impact on his jaw. He heard Luke breathe, "If that's how you want it," then felt a knee drive into his crotch. Sickened, he jerked back, pain racking through him and draining off the strength he needed to save himself. He felt fists dent him, he heard air tear over his own teeth, but he saw only shimmering images that all seemed to be Luke Preston.

His head rocked from blows to the mouth, the chin, then his knees gave way completely, and he let out a long sigh as he fell.

Luke looked around with sweat-stung eyes while he waited for his rushing breath to slow down. He thought there was a hint of satisfaction in Nan's eyes, but he wasn't sure. Browder, who had finally watched the fight he had wanted to see happen with Lastrade, stared in disbelief at his unstirring ally. Feeling vulnerable, maybe, having had a hand in the deed for which Morgan had made payment on account. The others, all those inclined to throw their support behind the best man, were at least impressed, disabused of the idea that the WW&CR could be kicked around with impunity.

Luke picked Morgan up like he would carry a dead man, slung across his shoulders. At the door he turned to glance back. Not even Browder cared to object to his carrying his threat to its conclusion. Luke staggered out into the night with his load.

Chapter 6

A mile short of Walla Walla City Luke turned off the stage road and headed through the dawn toward Tripp Yale's quarter-section on Mill Creek. The lane he followed ran flat and straight to a grove of bare locusts by the stream. He was not surprised to see smoke rising above the Yale house in the grove, for day came late with the year so near its end. Yet he noticed this with only a vague attention. Somewhere between there and Wallula Landing he had subsided into a stoic indifference, not only to weariness and the cold of the night. He had no great awareness even of the pain and soreness of his ribs and battered face and mouth.

He had hoped to catch Tripp outdoors doing his morning chores, but when he reached the dooryard, he saw no one around the outbuildings. In the next moment the door beyond the roofed back porch of the house swung open, and he knew there was no chance of keeping

Sherry from seeing him. She stepped onto the porch from her kitchen, and the consternation on her face told him he looked even worse than he felt.

"You're hurt!" she cried, running out to him. "What happened?"

"Just a little singed and a little beat," Luke said, swinging down. The dismay he saw in her eyes would have been rewarding had he had a right to evoke it. "Tripp up? I got a little job for him."

He trailed reins and turned to see Tripp framed in the doorway, his face reflecting Sherry's concern. A husky man who had run a blacksmith shop before Luke hired him to handle the Walla Walla yard, Tripp said dryly, "You look like you tied into a red-hot buzz saw and come out second best."

"You're not far from the mark," Luke agreed. "Somebody set fire to the sawmill last night."

Tripp's eyes narrowed. "It gone?"

"No, but it was a close call."

"Who'd you tangle with?"

"Clint Morgan."

"Save your questions," Sherry said, looking at her father impatiently. "Can't you see he's beat? Luke, you come in and let me tend to you."

"I'm all right, and —"

"She's right, Luke," Tripp cut in. "You need a little repair work, and some grub wouldn't hurt."

Luke followed him into the kitchen, Sherry coming behind him. Their breakfast was on the table, half-eaten. His knees were rubbery, and he needed Tripp's help to get out of his sheepskin coat. Sherry was already filling a washpan from the hot water tank on the side of the range, her face pale but set determinedly. He sank into the chair Tripp moved out from the table for him and told them what had happened in Wallula. Tripp went back to his breakfast, his face growing blacker while he listened.

"I want you to find Doc," Luke told him. "He'll be in Weston or someplace on south. There isn't much he can do, but he ought to know about it. Tell him. Tell him we've put guards on the mill, trestles, and way stations, and set some good men to riding the track."

"That sure won't help the budget," Tripp reflected.

"It sure won't. But it wouldn't help the stock issue to let them really pull something off, the next time."

"That's what they're shootin' at," Tripp

agreed, getting to his feet. "Well, I'll get going. Weston's a long ride."

"And now," Sherry told Luke, "maybe you'll let me clean up that face."

Luke started to protest that he could do it himself but was too beat, so he leaned back his head and closed his eyes. The hot, soapy cloth she used felt good, and her hands were swift and gentle. It pleased and yet disturbed him that, at the moment, she was less concerned about the railroad than the condition in which he had arrived at her house.

"I don't think I'm going to make it look much better," she decided. "But maybe it'll feel more like a face."

It was beginning to, but by the time she had washed off the soot, sweat and dried blood he was nearly too sleepy to sit up in the chair. Yet Sherry wasn't through with him, for, having cleaned him up, she went on to apply cold cloths to reduce the swelling around his mouth and eyes. When she was satisfied, he felt a great deal better and aroused to learn that Tripp had saddled a horse and left.

"And some breakfast for you," Sherry said.

"With these lips?" he asked.

"Try it."

She didn't wait for his agreement but went to the stove. She had put back some of their breakfast to keep warm, and he watched her fill a plate with biscuits, ham and fried eggs, the kind of hearty fare Tripp would require. She brought him coffee, and he was surprised to discover that he could drink it. She sat down across from him.

"Did Nan see the fight?" she asked, and glanced down at the coffee she had poured for herself.

Luke frowned at her but knew that as long as he failed to explain his relationship with Nan, it would obsess Sherry. "She was there. I don't know who watched. Clint Morgan kept me busy."

"She watched, and she didn't root for Morgan."

"Likely not," Luke agreed. "Nan's a poor judge of men, and she has her weaknesses with them. But she's a few cuts above the crowd Browder hangs out with."

"Is that why you can't forget her?"

She was crowding him harder than she ever had before, and he knew it was because the last hour had created a closeness between them impossible at the freight office. She had enough honest courage to ask for a confirmation or a denial, at last, of his interest in another woman. Since he dared not tell her the truth about himself, he had to confirm it.

"I guess it is," he said.

He watched a flatness come into her eyes, and then she shrugged. "Well, I've got to get to town and open the office. But why don't you sleep here and save yourself more riding? There won't be anybody else around all day."

"Thanks, but I've got another man to see before I hit the hay."

"Then go on. I'm not quite ready yet."

He knew she didn't want to ride in with him, and he said softly, "Sherry?"

"Yes."

"I'd have it different."

She smiled and turned away.

By the time he came back to the stage road, he had forced from his mind everything except the task to which he had committed himself when he took his job with Dorsey Baker. Only by the narrowest margin had the railroad escaped grave damage from the fire at the Slabtown sawmill. He was under no illusion that Morgan would let it go at that, especially after his humiliation in Nan's saloon, or that Morgan's hirelings had done more than take cover.

They had already proved the vulnerability of the line sufficiently to discourage many investors who might otherwise have bought stock in the coming offer. A more successful blow could be ruinous, and the attempt would probably be made to strike it before the public meeting to be held at the turn of the year. In spite of the precautions being taken, the railroad was still exposed in more ways than Luke liked to remember.

It would be useless to seek the protection of the law, especially to lodge a criminal complaint against men who had taken pains to cover their tracks. It was something that had to be met by himself and the handful of stalwarts trying to build a railroad for a country that didn't appreciate it. Essentially the job was his own, and he was convinced that the responsibility for the outright mischief was Lawson Keel's. The only thing he could see in his favor was the fact that Keel had to protect himself carefully in every move he made or ordered. With luck, this sensitivity of Keel's could be used to hold him in check and induce him to check-rein Morgan, Browder and their rash crowd until after the meeting.

A half-hour later Luke was closeted with Pasco Pasquel in Pasco's room in a fleabag hotel on the edge of town and Luke had told him of the previous night's events. It was the first word of it to reach the town and, while he listened, Pasco's brown, Latin eyes simmered.

"The sons of beetches," he said vehemently. "I should have shot that pair when I see them with Cleent Morgan in the saloon."

"Well, hardly," Luke said. "But what you can do is come down with a lame back and lay off driving stage a while."

"Me? The back she feels fine."

"Sure. But I want you loafing around where you can keep an eye on Lawson Keel for a day or so."

"Heem? Why?"

"I think he's the man behind Morgan, like Morgan was behind your old Nevada acquaintances. I want to make sure."

"*Bueno*. I keep the eye on heem."

Luke clapped him on the shoulder. "Fine. He'll hear today that the fire didn't do much real damage and that I licked Morgan for it and made some pretty sound charges in front of that whole crowd. He'll be worried about how I come to know so much, if Morgan was only carrying out orders. He'll have to see the man and chew him out for being careless and see that he don't go off half-cocked to get even with me."

"Ah, *si*," Pasco murmured. "Morgan, he has the orders not to come to Keel. So Keel must go to heem. At Morgan's cowspread. If he does thees, Keel is the ramrod."

Luke nodded. "But that's only part of it, Pasco. It was pure chance that you'd seen those Nevada hooligans before, but Keel and Morgan don't know it. Keel, at least, is smart enough to worry over how I got onto it and tied them to Morgan. We've got to get him so jittery about being linked to Morgan, himself, that he'll lay low till after the stock meeting."

"And how we do that?"

"You keep an eye on him, and if he leaves town on the sly, you follow without him knowing it. If he goes to Morgan's ranch, you let him know you followed."

"That's what I thought," Pasco reflected, "and it could get a *hombre* more than the bad back. But I do it. We gotta feex their wagon."

"That might not do it," Luke warned. "I put so big a dent in Morgan's pride Keel might not be able to hold him back. If those firebugs aren't holed up at his spread, Morgan knows where they are, and they'll be itching to finish the job, themselves."

"Where you be?" Pasco asked.

"In the hay for the next few hours," Luke told him. "You can tell Sherry what you're up to and have her get a relief driver. If you have luck with Keel and I'm not around, she'll know where you can find me."

Pasco nodded. "I let you know *pronto.*"

Luke left him and came out to a street grown busy with the day. The glances he drew as he walked to his own hotel reminded him that his appearance was something other than normal. Yet nobody tried to stop and question him, for the news of how narrowly the railroad had escaped a disastrous blow had not yet been circulated in Walla Walla City. The hotel clerk eyed him speculatively but made no comment, and Luke went up to his room. He was too tired to undress beyond pulling off his boots, and he lay down on the bed and pulled a blanket over him and was sound asleep at once.

He would have liked to stay there much longer, for he had driven himself long and hard and his punished body demanded repair. But it was only late afternoon when his uneasy mind roused him to a state of complete wakefulness and a very sore body and face. Getting up, he pulled on his boots and then rolled his first cigarette since before the fire. Only then did he notice the note somebody had slid under his door. Moving to it stiffly, he picked it up and unfolded it.

"Didn't want to disturb your rest," he read, "but I'd like to see you when you get up. I'll be at the Elkhorn. Bill."

That would be Green, the cow boss, who must have heard of the vicious attack on the WW&CR. Luke donned his coat and hat and went down to the street to see that the stages had brought in a full and probably inflated account of the violence in Wallula. With the day's pace slowing, farmers in for trading stood by their rigs talking with acquaintances, and townspeople were knotted here and there along the walks. Voices trailed off and eyes alerted with new interest as Luke came along. Some of them seemed on the point of halting him, and some wore expressions of poorly hidden satisfaction. Luke strode by, aware that the marks he bore symbolized for them the fact that the man he worked for could be hit hard enough to hurt.

The saloon Green had mentioned was in

the next block up, and there Luke found the same atmosphere. Green was sitting in a mild poker game with some cowmen friends, all of whom lost interest in the cards and looked up when Luke appeared at the table. But before anybody could say anything, Green threw in his hand and rose to his feet. He looked grim enough to discourage comment from the men he left at the table. He shook hands with Luke but said nothing until they were out on the street.

"It don't take much of a nose for weather," Green said then, "to predict frost the day the new stock goes on sale."

"It sure don't," Luke agreed.

"How much damage did that fire really do?"

"Probably not as much as rumor has it by now. The bunk and cook houses went. We saved the mill and yard. Nothing was lost we can't finish the railroad without — not even public support, because we didn't have that, anyway."

"But it could've cost Doc his chance to win enough support to wind up the project," Green said moodily. "The way this town's taking the news doesn't make me cheerful about it."

"We won't know till the public meeting,"

Luke agreed. "That's nearly four weeks off yet, and if we don't let anything more happen, we're not much worse off than before."

Luke had assumed that the cow boss wanted to see him only to get the straight facts. But Green had more than that on his mind and seemed undecided about offering it. The man pondered a moment, then said hesitantly, "This might sound looney, but I don't think you need to worry about another strike like that. It's had the effect that was wanted. The next'll be different, and it won't come till the meeting."

Luke stared at him. "What makes you think that?" He had a lot of respect for Green's opinions. It had been his nudge that had led the way to Keel's key role in the railroad resistance, a thing he didn't dare mention to Green now. As a plain working cowman, Green rubbed elbows with people Dorsey Baker and John Boyer never saw except in a business way, and he was sensitive to moods and undercurrents and was keen of mind.

"This street's all ears today," Green said. "If you just got up, you're hungry, and I could do with a bite. Let's get some supper someplace where we can talk."

Chapter 7

They ate in the Stine House dining room at a corner table where Green began to explain what troubled him. "There's already been a sort of stock meeting," he said, "with enough money pledged to raise two to three times what Doc's asking for. Enough to buy control of the company."

Luke looked at him in disbelief. "You mean that?"

"Well, there wasn't any meeting," Green admitted. "But somebody's been working up a deal they figure they can force on Doc. A lot of people've come to want the railroad finished, now it's so close to here, but they don't want to help Doc finish it because they don't trust him to run it for their benefit. You know that. But what you don't know is that quite a bunch of 'em are ready to put up not only enough to finish the job but to convert to standard iron track. With a mighty big if. They'd do this only if they could put their own man in Doc's place."

Luke sat dumbfounded. He didn't have to be told who that man would be, for a caper in which somebody else put up the money had Lawson Keel's name written all over it. "You didn't know this yourself," he said, "when I talked to you the other day at the mill."

"No, I just heard it yesterday."

Green went on to explain. It was hearsay, chained through several links by the time it got to him, which had made him discount it until the attempt on the sawmill lent it considerable force.

"The fire must've had two purposes," he reflected. "To discourage investors who don't hate or distrust Doc enough to come in on the undercover scheme and who might back him. And to show him, even if he wasn't hurt much, that he could be hurt enough to lose everything he's put into the line. Sort of softening him up, since he'd be a hard man to persuade to relinquish control of the company."

Green's sketchy knowledge of the scheme had come through Ridge Murdock, a cowman on the Touchet who had a brother growing wheat somewhere around Dixie. A committee had been to see the brother and talked him into making a pledge. The brother, in turn, had put the bite on Ridge, who wasn't having any part of anybody's railroad because he didn't want to see more stock range ruined by the plow.

"Ridge has got money, though," Green explained, "and I been after him to come to the meeting and subscribe to some of Baker's stock. I run into him yesterday and brought it up again. He laughed and said Baker could raise plenty of money for his railroad if he'd prove his good faith by stepping out of the management. So I dug what he knew out of him."

"Did he know who they want to put in Baker's place?" Luke asked.

Green shook his head. "The way I understood it, he's to be voted on after a deal's been made. Which there won't be. Doc'd sooner lose a leg than control of the line he's brought to this point in spite of every obstacle they put in front of him."

"And his refusal," Luke reflected, "will seem to prove his intention of turning it to his own benefit. If they could maneuver him into such a bad light, he'd be lucky to raise a thin dime himself."

Their food arrived, and having conveyed the gist of his new information, Green began to eat. Luke followed suit with much less appetite. He had no doubt who had started the secret promotion. Or who would be elected to take over the running of the WW&CR if Baker — who was stubborn but not stupid — was cornered so hopelessly that he would have to surrender control if there was to be a railroad at all. Nor did he doubt how mercilessly Keel would bilk his backers and squeeze the shippers if he managed to gather control into his own greedy hands.

All Luke Preston had to do to stop it was stand up in the meeting and tell one and all what a crook Keel really was. And then go to prison, himself. He had a feeling he would do it if there was no other way to save Baker, and the meeting was almost at hand.

He realized that Green had stopped eating and was looking toward the double-doorway opening of the dining room. "There went Pasco heading for the stairs," the cowman said. "He lookin' for you?"

"I expect," Luke said quickly. "I gave him an errand and he was to report back. Excuse me, Bill."

"Go ahead. I got to hit for the ranch, anyhow, soon as I eat."

Luke caught up with Pasco in the upstairs hallway, and Pasco's nod told him that he had met with success. But they went on to Luke's room to talk.

"Thees bum back you weesh on me," Pasco said then, placing his hands in feigned pain on his own, "it geeve me a lot of trouble."

"Keel made contact with Morgan?" Luke asked.

"*Si.* I know the livery where he keeps his *caballo* and I set on the bench with the bum back to the sun. No time at all, Keel comes for the *caballo.*"

"Before the news of the fire came in?" Luke asked, surprised.

Pasco nodded his dark head. "He knows the fire was to happen, and he has the eetch to know how it come off. I see he is heading for the *campo,* and it is easy. I get my *caballo* I have already saddled. I peek Keel up south of town and stay on hees tail all the way to Morgan's shack."

"He know you followed him?"

Pasco shook his head. "I change my mind about letting him know. Because, *amigo,* I sneak up behind the shack and hear there ees beeg squabble inside. Morgan, he ees not happy to come to on the manure pile in Wallula. I do not theenk he is listening to what Keel say about the fire being enough and to lay off. I wait till after Keel go away, and *poco tiempo*

Morgan is on a *caballo* and eet ees heem I am following." Pasco grinned. "The *hombres* from Nevada, they are holed up in Badger Canyon, over the hump from Morgan's *casa*. I do not get close enough to hear, but they make the medicine again, just like in Danny Traxler's saloon."

"Good work, Pasco." Luke dropped a hand on his shoulder. "I already heard something to make me think Keel won't start any more trouble till after the stock meeting. But those three are another kettle of fish."

"And I theenk we better dump thees keetle of feesh."

"Good. Get yourself some grub and a gun and have us a couple of fresh horses saddled. I was talking to Bill Green in the dining room, but I'll meet you at the livery as soon as I can."

Luke accompanied Pasco down the stairs and then went on to the dining room. Green had finished his meal but was still at the table, smoking a cigar. Luke wasn't ready yet to point a finger at Keel, even to a man he trusted as he did Green. So he said nothing about Pasco's discovery and their intentions while he hurriedly finished his own supper. And then Green offered his hand and left.

Night had fallen by the time Luke and Pasco rode out along a side street and struck the stage road leading to Whitman Station. A two-hour ride lay between them and Badger Canyon, but Luke felt no need to rush it. Even if Morgan and his men struck that night, in their hunger for a quick reprisal, they would hardly dare to approach the well-guarded railroad until the small hours of the night. So he and Pasco rode at a comfortable but mile-eating gait, seldom speaking and feeling the night's deepening cold.

They reached the railhead in little over half an hour to be challenged spunkily by the armed guards Newall Truax had posted. There were two of them, laborers idled by the shutdown of the construction work, and Luke told them he had reason to expect something to happen that night or soon. The guards assured him that the Dry Creek trestle was also manned, and the station and trestle at the Touchet. These were the closest points to Morgan's ranch and the easiest targets for a quick strike.

"Not that they'll pick the nearest," Luke told Pasco while they rode on, bending to cross the Walla Walla and head on to the southwest.

By then the overcast of the early night

had thinned away, letting stars break through. The wind came over the open bottom in sometimes gusty force, its nip reminding that the winter's really frigid period would soon arrive. Yet there was a serenity in the night, and watching the stars reminded Luke with something of a start that Christmas was nearly at hand. Having no family, that was something he rarely remembered until the valley towns began to decorate themselves for the season.

In another hour they had reached Pine Creek and raised a light that pinpointed Morgan's trashy headquarters. He wasn't much of a cattle operator, for he was a restless man and liked to deal in horses. Of recent years he had assembled cattle to drive to the overland railroad in Nevada and only for this special work did he hire a crew. In winter he usually lived here by himself. But he might not be alone tonight for, if he planned a move, he could have brought his henchmen down from Badger Canyon, which was in the highlands on the west of his shack.

Morgan had built in a wooded cove at the foot of the rising ground, and the natural cover had let Pasco slip in on the shack on his former visit. They needed another close look before they would know if they had to go on up to the canyon. When they had forded the creek, Luke pulled down, Pasco stopping beside him.

"So?" Pasco said.

"Let's get a line on 'em, then wait and see what happens. My feeling's that something will, after the way Morgan rushed out to see his pardners after Keel was here."

"*Si,* and soon." It was quite a ride from there to the railroad even at its nearest point. "You wait. It is *por nada* if we teep them off, and I know how to go in for the look."

Luke agreed to that, for if Pasco had got in close enough to the shack to listen without being caught, he could get near enough to check on the number of horses in the corral, perhaps to look through a window to see who all, if anybody, was inside the house. He waited in the creek brush while Pasco rode downstream, keeping to the shadows of the streamside cover. He lost track of him, presently, and kept his eyes on the shack off across the flat. He judged the time at around ten o'clock, and his feeling grew that something special was up for Morgan's light to be burning so late. Men who lived alone usually turned in soon after dark.

Pasco hadn't even had time to reach the shack and its clutter of outbuildings when Luke stiffened in the saddle, his nerve ends alerted and keen. Two ridden horses had appeared on the flat, off left of Morgan's setup and against the far landrise. They were probably carrying the pair from Badger Canyon, coming down to join Morgan, and Luke feared that Pasco would be seen before he had seen them.

Luke was considering what to do when the light in the shack window went out. Apparently they had set an hour to meet, and their moving this early in the night meant they were setting out on a longer ride than to the nearest point on the railroad. That could be down the valley toward Wallula or up the valley toward Walla Walla City. He waited impotently, afraid of Pasco's blundering into red-hot trouble but unable to reach him in time, without riding straight across the open ground.

Then a lone rider rode out from the dark buildings and joined the pair, and the three were coming at a trot toward the creek ford and Luke. All he could do then was move down along the creek the way Pasco had gone, far enough to keep the horses from sensing each other's presence. When he stopped, he dismounted and stood with a palm pressed to his own mount's nostrils to keep it from whickering, and waited. Through the thin screen at the edge of the growth he saw the nightriding trio cut in toward the ford and vanish. They couldn't lose themselves in the open country on the other side of the creek for some distance. He settled himself to wait for Pasco to rejoin him.

In only a few minutes he saw Pasco coming across the open, his boldness indicating that he had seen what had gone on. A few minutes later Luke had met him and they rode toward the ford themselves. Morgan and his companions were small figures off to the northeast when they came out on the far side.

"That means Walla Walla," Luke decided. "And they're staying off the roads."

"The depot and wagon yard? You theenk they have the nerve for that?"

"Morgan's vain enough. He'd figure something flashy like that was just the ticket."

It made sense. A blow struck in the heart of the valley would receive the utmost publicity, and while Morgan would take pains to see he didn't get caught, everyone would know who had struck it. He probably knew that after the Slabtown attack, no important part of the railroad would be left unguarded. But with a bold foray into territory where they were least expected, the three of them might be able to handle a couple of guards.

"If we catch them red-handed," Pasco reflected, "eet could be very bad for *Senor* Keel. If they catch the guards napping, eet could be very bad for *Senor* Baker."

"You'd better cut around and beat 'em in," Luke told him, sure enough of his guess to act on it. "I'll tag behind 'em in case we're wrong and they head somewhere else."

Pasco nodded and was gone.

Pasco rode due north until the night had swallowed him, and by then the other figures had vanished in the northeast. Luke rode swiftly until he had picked up the nightriders again, and they still rode on a straight line toward Walla Walla City. Afterward he matched his speed to theirs at a distance where he could barely keep them in sight. And then when buttes and gullies and more wooded streams began to break up the foreground, he would lose them for long moments. Each time he had to narrow the gap until finally he was forced to cling dangerously close in their rear.

By then their only possible objectives were Whitman Station or the town, and near midnight the trio he stalked eliminated the railhead by crossing the Walla Walla above the old Indian mission. Shortly after that, Luke nearly landed himself in trouble by overrunning them, for he came out of a draw that had swallowed them, and almost too late saw them halted on the other side of the buttes that had cut them from sight. If they had been leery of their backtrail and watching it, they would have seen him before he cut back into the shadows.

He saw from winking glows in the darkness that they were smoking, and their stopping to do it meant that they were killing time. It was hardly half an hour's ride from there to town. With no doubt of where they were going left, he was tempted to pass around them and join the reception party. Only moments later he was glad he hadn't yielded to that impulse, for all three threw away their cigarettes and dismounted. It was impossible to tell who was who, but a couple of them began to take something out of their saddlebags. Then the same two were kneeling on the ground, with the third man standing and watching them.

All at once Luke was sure that the two busy ones were preparing to live up to the reputation they had won in Nevada. Each of them was capping and fusing dynamite, making up a bundle of the explosive sticks, which they hadn't cared to do until near the end of their ride. This was only another shrewd guess, for the thin starlight showed him nothing beyond what he could read from their movements, but apprehension grew in him. A hurled bomb could deal with a number of guards and do its destructive work at the same time. Two bombs could wreak bloody ruin.

A pistol shot would knock the whole thing in the head then and there, and Luke drew his gun from its holster. A few bullets thudding near the touchy stuff would scatter them like scared pigeons. But the closer they were to railroad property when they abandoned it or found themselves captured with it in their possession, the more incriminating it would be. His throat was tightening like drying rawhide, but he didn't fire the gun.

Then, to his surprise, the one who had to be Morgan swung into the saddle and rode on, the powder monkeys continuing with their job. True to form, Morgan seemed to be dealing himself out of the more risky business of making the attack. Luke gave no thought to following him, for at the moment the pair with the home-made bombs were the real danger.

Chapter 8

The two men Luke continued to watch from the shadowy mouth of the draw seemed in no hurry. Before long they appeared satisfied with their accomplishment, but they only sat on their heels by their horses. The fact that they didn't kill time by smoking again weighted Luke's conviction that the objects near them on the ground were bundles of dynamite now primed with caps and fuses. He wondered what they were waiting on.

And then, adding to his mystification, Morgan came back. He was leading a nag of a farm horse he must have roped out of some nearby settler's pasture. The others sprang up, and when they began to transfer a saddle and its attached pouches to the new horse, Luke saw into their plan. It was clever enough to inspire his respect and deadly enough to appall him. Morgan's problem was the flat, open ground around the freight yard and buildings, which the guards he had to allow for could watch closely and cover with ease. But only a short distance down the right of way was a stand of stunted, dry-country evergreens, out of bullet range but easy to approach from the blind side. Given a whacking start from there, the docile farm horse would head speedily for the yard and barn, its only burden the dynamite.

Even Pasco, who was probably there by now, would hold fire if he saw a saddled but riderless horse coming in, and so would the other guards. By the time the carefully cut fuses had burned down to the detonating caps, the plug would be in the midst of them and the crowded buildings. If enough of its brand was left afterward to be read, it wouldn't be a brand Morgan needed to worry about. A plan of such vicious cunning would appeal to a man like him, and Luke wondered how far he dared let it proceed before he took a hand. It could be quite a ways, if he reached the yard before they did.

He waited, however, until the reunited threesome moved out again on its beeline, cross-country ride to Walla Walla City, the nag trailing behind at the end of a catch rope and one of the Nevadans riding bareback. Luke let the night swallow them and then cut off to their left where low hills would cover him. He knew they wouldn't rush with their hair-trigger load, and when he was out of earshot, he lifted his own horse to a lope. The animal had covered a lot of ground but had been lightly worked, and the recent hours of slow picking made it eager to deliver. It was hardly any time before Luke found himself passing by the last homesteads before the town.

He forded Mill Creek where the right of way crossed and eventually a trestle was to be built, and then followed the survey stakes due north. Soon he saw ahead of him the stand of trees he expected Morgan to put to use. He passed it by and, while he rode on toward the freight yard, waved his hat above his head to declare his friendliness. Even so, Pasco and Tripp Yale, guns in hand, were waiting warily at the edge of the yard when he came in. Tripp's presence told him the man had located Dorsey Baker, but there wasn't time to ask about that. Luke told them tersely what to expect and how they would have to meet it.

"Son of a gun," Pasco murmured. "I have heard of the dynamite floated down a flume into a stamp meel. And rolled down a heel on a wagon. But theese is the new wreenkle."

"With good chances of raising messy

hell," Tripp added, "if you and Luke hadn't caught onto it. Now all we got to do is shut the yard gate and let the nag go off outside, where it won't hurt anything but sagebrush."

"It's not that simple," Luke told him. "We want them, the nag, *and* the dynamite. So we've got to nail 'em when they come into the trees over there."

Tripp nodded. "Then let 'em claim they weren't up to mischief and had nothin' to do with the Slabtown fire."

There were, besides Tripp and Pasco, two men assigned there for guard duty by Newall Truax. Luke told Tripp to trade his shotgun for one of the construction hand's rifles and then wait on this side of the yard. If something went wrong and he saw the lethal horse coming toward him anyway, Tripp was to drop it in its tracks. Then Luke and Pasco left on foot for the trees. These were not dense and the stand was not large, but it would hide the Morgan party if it came in from the west side. Concealed within the trees on that side, Luke and Pasco waited tensely. It was their hope to take the nightriders when they first came out of the starshine and couldn't see too well, but too many things could go awry for them to feel easy.

Nothing was in evidence in the far night, and after long moments nothing had appeared. It was Pasco who got the first warning. "Something she is coming," he hissed, his eyes moving alertly over the sooty distance, *"Si, por seguro."*

It was several breaths more before Luke began to make out black dots moving in the distant darkness, a little south of where he had been looking for them. In a moment the objects seemed to have stopped dead still, but Luke was sure they were riders who had changed direction and were now coming straight toward the trees. He and Pasco separated then, stationing themselves where the larger trees hid them and spaced to divide the attention of the arriving horsemen. The night's silence seemed to grow heavier, and Luke felt a runnel of sweat slide down across his ribs. They were coming the last, dangerous distance with extreme caution. It seemed an unbearable time before they had enlarged enough to become, beyond mistaking, three riders and four horses.

He heard the click of Pasco's gun hammer being eared back, and his fist tightened on the grips of his own pistol. And then came the first evidence that Morgan's instinct for self-protection was still working. Instead of coming in among the trees together, the three halted about a hundred yards off. They did a little low-voiced talking, and then Morgan, some animal instinct seeming to warn him out of the trees, rode half around them to the north and halted for a long look at the freight yard.

Then he signaled with a hand and the other two men rode around on the south side of the trees. Luke saw, to his disappointment, that they meant to start the nag in from there. Morgan was either keeping himself clear for a quick getaway if trouble started or was afraid to be too near when the explosive charges were lighted.

Luke didn't know Pasco had slipped back to him until he heard a soft whisper at his elbow. "The luck she's run out. Morgan is one cagey *hombre*."

Luke grunted. Luck had had little to do with it beyond his guessing their intentions, and no one could have done that right down the line. Unless they captured Morgan and the farm horse, they had nothing of consequence, and taking them all at the same time had become impossible. He had no doubt that Morgan would be off at the first warning. So he had to let it go further than he wanted, allowing them to send the horse in and relying on Tripp to stop it in time with his rifle. He and Pasco would jump the trio while their eyes were magnetized by the nag's progress.

He conveyed this briefly to Pasco, ending, "We'll double up on Morgan. The others are small change."

Only one of the two strangers had swung down, and the other was holding his horse for him while he led the farm nag forward. A match flared, and on its heels a sputtering of sparks erupted, then the man whipped the mare's rump with his hat and yelled. The startled nag bolted and, while the man had headed it toward the distant barn, it went pounding off toward the town, a small, sizzling fire jetting from its side. The mounted rider went streaking after it to head it toward the freight yard, then lost his nerve and swung back.

"*Madre de Dios*," Pasco breathed. "The *caballo*, she have the mind of her own."

Luke stood frozen for only a breath, for Morgan's panicked shout jarred him out of it, "Come on, boys — let's get out of here!"

A rifle cracked, but Luke realized this was Tripp trying to drop the bolting farm horse before it reached the built-up streets of the town. Luke rushed to the edge of the trees, shouting, "Hold it, Morgan, or you're dead!" Morgan whirled his horse and shot in one blurred motion, and Luke's gun chopped down and fired. Pasco's gun opened up, but was aimed at the other two men, who came cutting around the thicket to join Morgan.

Then something shook the ground itself, and a tremendous, ear-flattening boom rolled over them.

By then the three targets to the west were streaking away. Both men in the thicket concentrated on Morgan, trying now to drop his horse, but the whole bunch had pulled out of effective pistol range.

"No use," Luke said, breaking it off. "I wonder how far that poor plough nag got."

They came out of the trees and walked back to where they could see the space on the east side. Luke grew aware of a powder smell much heavier than the shooting would have caused, and while darkness hid it, he could also smell settling dust. And then his gaze drifted to something that riveted it. Off to the right of the railroad property the first straggling buildings of the town made pale outlines in the deep night. Short of them there had been an old storage building, long vacant, that was there no longer. Some old fruit trees that had shaded it lay torn and tumbled on the ground.

"It's a mercy those bastards knew what length to cut the fuses," he told Pasco grimly. "Another hundred yards, and occupied houses would have received the full force of the blast."

"I theenk *Senor* Morgan weel keep riding," Pasco answered, "until he has put *mucho* country between heem and thees town."

They walked in to find Tripp, still holding the rifle with which he had tried to stop the escaping horse, waiting at the yard gate. Luke wasn't surprised that every window pane was shattered in the barn and freight shed, and he knew that this percussion effect had rolled over the houses on beyond the site of the actual explosion. That showed the devastation that would have resulted had the horse headed for the railroad barn as intended and equally the kind of insane risk he had taken with the lives of the Walla Walla citizenry. Instead of secret admiration and support, the man would reap outrage for having so recklessly endangered the very people he had expected to applaud him.

In another ten minutes the rudely awakened town was congregating in numbers where the old warehouse had been and at the railroad yard itself. Within half an hour Luke, Pasco and Tripp were closeted in the windowless freight office with Bike Cahill, the town marshal, Johnny Belknap, the deputy territorial marshal stationed at Walla Walla City, and Dorsey Baker. The doctor had heard the explosion even at his house on Mill Creek, guessed its meaning and hurried over.

"Lucky for me," Cahill was saying to the federal marshal, "that they got away. I'd sooner you had the job of chasin' 'em down than me havin' to stand off a lynch mob. And there'd have been one. There ain't a window left on the street over there, and if the plug had got a block farther, the coroner would have had his work cut out for him, too."

Belknap nodded agreement, but Luke noticed a sour amusement in Dorsey Baker's eyes. The town's sympathies depended on whose ox was being gored, and there would have been no such public spirit of vengeance if the railroad buildings had been flattened and some of its employees killed. Even these lawmen would have been harder to impress with Luke and Pasco's account of who had stolen and charged the lethal nag and brought it in. As it was, they had accepted it readily, and Luke had agreed to swear out warrants. They would have to wait for daylight to find hide or hair of the pitiful horse and to appraise the damage fully. If some bum or drunk had been sleeping in the destroyed building, the charge could be homicide.

Baker took little part in the talk until the lawmen had left, Tripp and Pasco going out with them. The doctor looked very tired and, alone with Luke, he said, "Good work, Luke. I can't tell you how grateful I am. If they'd pulled it off, the stock meeting would have been a circus. As it is, this might have helped us."

"They're mad at Morgan," Luke said. "But only because he nearly got some of them blown to smithereens."

"There's always sympathy for the underdog, though," Baker said. "I haven't had much luck arousing it so far, but this has shocked everybody. Most of them aren't really our enemies. They're just misinformed, misguided and misbegotten. At least some of them —" Baker allowed himself his thin grin — "qualify for that last."

Luke nodded. He had seen nothing of Lawson Keel, although the excitement had probably brought him out, but Keel's shock would have surpassed that of the ordinary townspeople. Already given reason to distrust the stability of his henchman, Keel must by now be sweating blood over the prospect of Morgan's being caught and betraying their covert dealings. The law had listened to Pasco that night. If Keel knew that Pasco had also trailed him to Morgan's ranch the day before the dynamiting, he would see himself being charged with having engineered it.

But Luke didn't consider informing Keel of that. It would be too dangerous to Pasco for the good it would do in keeping Keel off balance. As to the danger Keel posed to himself, Luke had only to look at the slight, frail man before him, tormented by infirmities, plagued by adversities and betrayed by the very people he had so often helped, to know with a clear, hard conviction that the die was cast. He would fight Keel every way he could, without revealing the secret of their past lives. But if Baker's survival depended on it, and no other way could be found, he would without hesitation speak out and pay the price.

"Where'd Tripp find you, Doc?" he asked.

"Weston. I think I did a little good up

that way, and I'm going back." Baker smiled his fleet smile again. "Not that they're enthusiastic about me building it, but they want a railroad. They haven't any river where they can start their own port, like the people around Dayton and Waitsburgh are talking about. Some of them have promised to come to the meeting, and I intend to see more."

"I sure wish you luck. I guess Tripp told you all about the Slabtown fire. I hated to hang the extra expense on you by ordering everything put under heavy guard. But I figured it's what you'd want."

"After tonight's little business," Baker drawled, "how could I question it?"

"Frank says he's got enough cull lumber around to replace the essential buildings. A couple of bunkhouses and a cook-shack will do from here out."

"So I figured," Baker said with a nod. "Tell him to go ahead at once. We've got to guarantee our ability to finish the line promptly if the people will be so good as to help out with the cost." He got tiredly to his feet. "If you'll excuse me, I'm going to try to sleep a while longer; then I'm going back down south."

"Doc, you need a week in bed."

"I could use it. But there's so much to

do and so little time." Baker offered his hand and left.

Luke looked around the empty office, his mind remaining on Baker. When the doctor spoke of the fleetness of time, he hadn't meant between then and the stock meeting now almost at hand. He had already suffered two strokes, and another might well be the end. The way he drove himself, that one could come even sooner than he feared.

Luke had slept through much of the previous day and was too wound up to sleep again immediately. He watched the last of the sensation seekers return to the town and their homes, and then sent Tripp and Pasco off to bed, saying he would stay to reinforce Truax's guards. Not that more trouble was likely then or for quite a while, but they had to play safe. When daylight came, he went down to the wrecked warehouse, which had been blown far and wide. There wasn't a thing left of the farm horse that he could find, and men poking among the ruins had found nobody caught in them by mischance.

That was for the law to handle, now, and Luke went on into town and got some breakfast at a place that opened early to cater to the traveling public. People who knew him, he observed, eyed him with a new respect that he hoped wouldn't wear off for a while.

As soon as the courthouse was open, he met the deputy marshal and lodged an official complaint against Clint Morgan and two John Does. He had little expectation that the trio would be caught very soon after their long head start, but that didn't make much difference. Keel was the real enemy of the railroad, and he would be as heartily glad to be rid of the three as Luke was.

Pasco was up in time to take his stages out that day, and Luke went down to Whitman Station with him and rode the train on down to Wallula Landing. All along the line he was reassured to see track riders and station and trestle guards going earnestly about their business. It was a heavy drain on the treasury, yet if it inspired confidence in him, it would inspire it in the public. At Wallula he found that Frank Baker, anticipating the doctor's wishes, had already put men to work cleaning up after the fire. He was also getting ready to put up new buildings for the crew that at present he could only hope to rehire.

And at Wallula Luke realized also that a

new interest had come to compete with the railroad question. Christmas decorations were going up on the business fronts, reminding that there was a softer side to life. He found the fir boughs and tinsel and season's offerings in the store windows very pleasant and was glad to have such a diversion. For immediately afterward, at the district schoolhouse in Walla Walla City, the fate of the railroad would be decided.

Chapter 9

Long before dark on the day of the public meeting, it was apparent that the attendance, in spite of bitter weather, would exceed Dorsey Baker's most hopeful estimates. Since before Christmas an off-and-on snowfall had piled up a frozen, six-inch blanket on country and town, fouling the roads and discouraging all but the most hardy from coming in even to trade for necessities. Yet, for reasons Luke understood well, the afternoon had seen men arrive, singly and in delegations, from as far away as the upper Pine and Dry and Touchet and from just about all the country from there in. Strong emotions were at work in them, and in the townspeople who meant to attend, of which Clint Morgan's backfired caper was only a part.

Making a rare change into a sack suit in his hotel room, that evening after he had eaten his supper, Luke felt no optimism because of this huge turnout. Clint Morgan and his cronies had not been caught, and few cared any longer if he ever was. Right after the holidays, Dorsey Baker had made the chilly, two-day boat trip down to Portland and come back with a bombshell more shaking than Morgan's homemade contrivance. He had announced it first at a directors' meeting he called hastily, and then it had been made public.

While in Portland he had dropped in for a casual chat with his old friend Ainsworth of the Oregon Steam Navigation Company, only to be told with equal casualness that the OSN was seriously considering the idea of building its own and full-fledged line from Portland to Walla Walla City. This left no doubt in thoughtful minds that the struggling little WW&CR had to be completed at full speed. It was that or it would find itself put out of business by outsiders far more notorious for self-interest than Baker would ever be.

Even the unthinking were stirred by the news, although they scoffed. "It's a put-up job," Luke heard a man say on the street. "John Ainsworth's cut from the same bolt as Baker and just helpin' him scare us into subscribin' for his stock."

"Maybe so," a listener argued. "But if it's the pure quill, and the steamboat company gives us a choice between their boats and their trains, we'll wish we had Doc back. He's got, and he's always had, a stake in this country. We never been anything but a milk cow to that steamboat crowd."

"That's how I see it," another man piped up. "We got to have our own railroad. Doc's the only one who ever tried to get one off paper. So what if he makes money out of it? We will, too."

"You wait till he gets one goin' and the wagons put out of business," the first hooted, "and see how much you make."

Luke knew the OSN threat was no strategem, that Baker was worried as never before. And while he prepared to go to the meeting, his own worry revolved around what the coming hours might require of him personally. The new threat had, if anything, helped Keel and his faction in their undercover efforts to wrest control from the doctor. Baker was a solitary, inflexible man, yet he might well yield to that bunch rather than let the project be killed in one-sided competition with the downriver Goliath.

The meeting had been posted for eight o'clock, but the town schoolhouse was bulging at the corners by a quarter to. Its lower floor had two large rooms that could be made into one by folding back doors, which had been done. Even so, the chairs and benches brought in and the aisles and spaces along the walls were so nearly filled by the time Luke got there that he was lucky to find a standing space in back. He didn't mind, for his tallness let him get a good view of things.

Hanging lanterns lighted the room, and an immense stove heated it to a point where the three hundred people he estimated in the audience were already busy with handkerchiefs mopping their brows. The few women who had braved the crowd were fanning themselves, and he saw Sherry sitting beside Tripp. He recognized a group, seated together, from the upper Walla Walla where Baker had done his most recent soliciting, and a group from up Dixie way. Mainly they were locals, merchants, lawyers, hotelmen, and farmers from out in the valley.

Baker hadn't yet put in an appearance, but there was a small platform and rostrum at the front of the room. Chairs flanked it facing the audience and seated there already were the town dignitaries. There were to be no ceremonies, but the occasion required the dignitaries' presence, and because of their political bents they were trying to show no partisanship. On the other side were the directors of the railroad. John Boyer was smiling genially, waving greetings now and then to various people he saw in the audience. Bill Green looked uncomfortable in his store clothes and was stony-featured. Frank Baker seemed nervous. Newall Truax was calm and impassive.

And then Luke spotted Lawson Keel in a front-row seat, sleekly dressed as usual and looking more bored than excited. Luke had a hunch that this was a pose, considering his purpose at the meeting. The ring-leaders in the faction supporting him might or might not be those sitting near him. Luke knew some of these, and others were strangers.

As punctually as a clock striking the hour, a side door opened at eight o'clock, hushing the buzzing of the audience and riveting all eyes, and Dorsey Baker came in quietly. He carried a folder in his good hand and didn't seem to have dressed up for the occasion, although he wore a coat, vest and pants that matched. He paused a moment looking over the audience, and his droopy eyelid made him seem to glare.

Maybe he did feel a little antagonism, Luke reflected. These were people who had voted down his attempt to get the county to sell bonds to build a railroad. They had spurned his offer of stock when he organized the WW&CR on his own hook and then had spurned the bonds he had tried to sell when finally he had built the line to the halfway point. It must gravel him to have to come to them now with a plea for their help.

If so, he gave no sign of it beyond the somewhat baleful cast of his eyes in the smoky, mealy lantern light as he mounted the platform and at once got down to business. A lifted hand stopped the applause, by no means unanimous, and he put his papers in front of him, glanced at them and then looked up.

"No sense wasting time," he announced, "explaining why we asked you to meet with us tonight. You know why. I've talked to most of you individually, and I hope you've come to agree that the completion of the railroad is vital to the best interests of us all. I have here —" a finger tapped the papers in front of him — "a detailed estimate of the cost that any of you is welcome to look over after the meeting. And so to business. I've been authorized by the directors of the company to offer stock to the people of the Walla Walla basin only, in the amount of $75,000. That includes all of you but excludes outside interests. I ask you to accept this offer in full and without delay for reasons you have all heard by now. Stock in the Walla Walla & Columbia River Railroad is hereby offered in that amount. In return, I promise you that, as expeditiously as can be done, the railroad will be finished, fully equipped and operating in time to benefit you in your next harvest. Our treasurer, Mr. Boyer, will be happy to take your subscriptions." Baker nodded his head and was done.

A stunned silence hung in the air at the pared-to-the-bone brevity of his appeal. Luke stood openmouthed and saw a stricken look on the faces of Boyer, Green and Frank. It was a situation that called for oratory, an impassioned pointing out of the dangers attending the entry of the OSN into the railroad picture, a rousing description of the future of the country if only its people would rise to the occasion, even a fatherly lecturing for their having failed him so miserably to that point.

Yet what Baker had said was the essence of the man. His belief in the reasonableness of all men had led him once again to assume that his listeners were as astute, as ruled by logic, as perceptive of opportunity as he. John Boyer stirred in his seat, about to rise to his feet and pitch in. He could have delivered what he knew to be required to win these people, but he changed his mind and sat still.

And then a man in the audience stood up and called for attention. He was not Keel, as Luke would have expected, but Sigmund Schwabacher, one of the town's leading merchants.

"Doctor Baker," he called. "Most of us have heard you go over the costs of building the line a number of times. Twenty per cent of it remains to be finished. According to your previous figures, this should cost half again the seventy-five thousand you're asking us to put up. May I ask where the rest of the money is to come from?"

The question irritated Baker. "The same place the money's come from since Mile 26," he said coldly. "From current revenue."

"But that'll take time, Doctor Baker," Schwabacher retorted. "With the OSN talking railroad, how can we afford to take that long?"

"If we resume construction, Mr. Schwabacher, I think the OSN will be discouraged from its proposed undertaking."

His questioner thanked him and sat down, but he had started a buzz of private conversations. Luke doubted that Schwabacher had anything to do with Lawson Keel. But he was a man who would be sympathetic toward Keel's idea of forcing Baker to show good faith by surrendering control of the company. Keel was looking around the room, seeming to wait to see if anybody else wanted the floor. When nobody moved, he got to his feet.

"Doctor Baker," he said, putting warmth and courtesy into his voice, "I know I speak for many of us here in voicing the deepest appreciation for what you've done. Yet it's a natural question to ask why, when a powerful monopoly like the OSN is thinking about a railroad of its own, you aren't asking for the full amount needed. Not only to finish the line but to convert it to standard gauge, which will be necessary as soon as possible. In short, three or four times what you're asking for." Baker bristled, but Keel said smoothly, "Bear with me, sir. I'm in a position to assure you that, if you will sell stock in an amount to deliver a standard, fully equipped railroad speedily, it will be subscribed."

"We want no outside financing, Mr.

Keel," Baker said with a wave of the hand. "I thought I had made that amply clear."

"It will be local money, Doctor Baker."

"Yours, Mr. Keel?"

"Some of it. The rest will be put up by a group that's asked me to represent it."

"Why haven't you been to see me, Mr. Keel? Why choose this occasion?"

Keel smiled then. He was weaving a web that Baker sensed. Luke saw a sardonic look on Bill Green's face, for Keel was verifying the truth of what Green had heard from a fellow cowman. Keel's eyes slid over the audience, and Luke could tell from the faces that showed surprise and the ones that looked gratified who was in on the maneuver and who was hearing of it for the first time.

Keel's attention shifted back to Baker. "The fear of monopoly is deep-seated in this country, Doctor, and with good reason. I'm sure you know you've aroused it yourself. Almost equal to the bogey you've raised in the OSN."

"Bogey?" Baker said angrily. "Mr. Keel —"

"Bear with me, sir," Keel cut in. "The fact remains that your refusal to reassure the country as to your ultimate intentions has handicapped you grievously. All we ask is your assurance that the railroad, if completed, will be run for the benefit of all the basin and not one individual or select group."

Wary now, Baker said, "And in what form do you ask this assurance, Mr. Keel, since my reputation doesn't seem sufficient?"

"The opportunity to buy stock in the amount I suggested."

"Which would also buy," Baker said, with his thin smile, "control of the company."

"Placing it in the hands of the people whose interests are vitally affected. Why do you refuse to let go of it, Doctor Baker?"

Two out of three in the room were with Keel by then, whether or not this was new to them. Baker had been worked into a corner where his refusal to listen to the suggestion seemed to prove an ulterior motive on his part. The doctor was aware of it, and he was also aware that any subscribers he might otherwise have won around had moved over to Keel and would stay there if he refused to prove his good faith in the way Keel demanded. Luke's neck muscles had tightened. Baker surely would relinquish control, hoping to retain his presidency and managership, rather than convict himself by his own obstinacy.

If that happened, Luke knew he himself would have to demand the floor and make plain to everyone why Lawson Keel was the last man on earth they should trust and follow.

There was a stir, and he saw that Sherry Yale had risen to her feet. She looked angry and frightened and grimly determined.

"I'll tell you why, Mr. Keel!" she said furiously. "And all of you blind people! How many times have you passed up a chance to buy all the stock or all the bonds you wanted? You could have had your controlling interest then, whoever you are that Mr. Keel is representing. Doctor Baker offered it. Why didn't you buy it? Why did you sit on your pocketbooks and let him and a mere handful of men that believed in him and in this country risk all they had and suffer every kind of hardship and ridicule and mean, dirty attack? It hadn't ought to be news to you that Dorsey Baker has gambled an enormous amount of his own money to build us that railroad because you wouldn't help. Only a fool would surrender control of it now, and even you people ought to have the sense to see it."

"She's answered him, Doc!" somebody yelled happily.

140

"I believe she has." Baker permitted himself his wispy smile, then turned and went out through the door that had admitted him.

Sherry had said what he ought to have said in his brief address but could not. Even Keel was taken aback and looked around with a baffled expression, and Luke was surprised at how many men were grinning.

One of these tried to shake Sherry's hand, but she only turned and began to work her way out of the room, Tripp rising to follow her. Keel followed, but in pursuit of her, and then the whole audience was on its feet, the astonishingly short meeting to which many of them had given a day's time to attend over already. Then Luke realized that some of them were not moving toward the exit but were either standing where they were or threading their way to the front of the room where John Boyer stood waiting to take subscriptions. Thanks to Sherry, or the threat of the OSN or to Clint Morgan's irresponsible endangering of the town, some of them were ready to help Baker finish his railroad.

Still not hopeful but nonetheless gratified, Luke began to move toward the outside door. He had reached the packed hallway when a man ahead of him said to a companion, "That man Keel's all right. He sure smoked Baker out, and that takes doin'." The jam at the exit had halted them, so the man kept talking. "I come here ready to put a little money into stock. The wagons can't handle the wheat we could grow if we had a real through line. But I'm damned if I'll risk my hard-earned dollars to give a few bigwigs a new way to milk us."

"Me, neither," the man beside him agreed. "Baker *or* the OSN."

Luke spoke up then, saying mildly, "How much were you fellows paying the teamsters to haul your wheat? Twelve dollars a ton, wasn't it? And what does it cost you now? Six dollars, I believe. So where have you been milked?"

They both turned to look at him, as did others packed around them. They recognized him, and while the marks of the fight with Morgan had healed, they remembered that and had a grudging respect for him.

"Oh, we're gettin' better rates," the first man said, turned hangdog by the challenge. "Right now, while Baker's raisin' the money and finishin' the line so the horse freighters can be run clear outta the field. It's then we've got to worry about, when we got no choice but to ship by rail or haul for ourselves."

"I've heard that wild story for three years," Luke retorted, "and I'm plenty tired of it. The man who planted it and keeps it going is the one who made out to champion you people tonight. What do you think would have happened if Baker had knuckled down to him? There would be a clamor for a stockholders' meeting and new officers would be elected, and you'd see Keel right in there running the company himself."

"Why not?" a surly voice demanded. "He's a damned good man. If I was a stockholder and there was such a meetin', I'd sure vote for him. Maybe we ought to ask him to build us a railroad from scratch and forget about old Doc Baker. If he would, I'd put every cent I could raise into it."

Heads nodded all around.

Luke got through, then, and moved down the schoolhouse steps, coming into the yard where he could step clear of the crowd. The night was cold, the stars brilliant, and men moved off in all directions as aroused as when they came to the meeting and leaving even more dissatisfied. Keel hadn't pulled off his coup, but he had

143

gained much that night, moving into open hostility against the WW&CR and making himself a highly regarded figure and a rallying point for the opposition. Would he use this to promote his own company as the farmer had suggested? Luke didn't think so. It would be quicker, cheaper and more profitable to use it to force Baker to his terms.

Chapter 10

The storm that had hardly more than played with the Walla Walla country had got down to business when Luke awakened in the day's first light. His impression was of somebody using a sledge hammer on the wall outside his room; then he understood that this was a loose sign banging on the street. The wind's shriller sounds came gustily with a deepening of the cold in the room. He pulled the covers closer about his ears and his first thought was by habit of the train that had to make its round trip if the WW&CR was to keep its tenuous hold on life.

The hold was more dangerously weak than ever, he knew. Bill Green had stayed in town for the night, and Luke had seen and talked with him for a while in the hotel bar. Green had remained at the schoolhouse until the last of the converts to the cause had done their business with John Boyer.

"It was the biggest vote of confidence in

Doc yet," Green reported. "Maybe a hundred men ready to stand up and be counted on his side in spite of Keel's insinuations. That much would have done Doc's heart good, if he'd been there to see it."

"But the money?" Luke asked.

"Scarcely a third of what Doc needs." Green shook his head. "They just weren't people with much money to spare and when John got it footed up, it come to a little under twenty-five thousand. Frank went to tell Doc, but I don't know how even Dorsey Baker can stretch it to what he's got to have. If the country divides up the way the meeting did, we'll have more friends than before. But the ones against us'll be more set than before."

"And ready dupes," Luke said, "for anything Keel wants from them. It looks like he's only got to sit tight, John, to have the whole thing fall in his lap."

Luke got out of bed with that thought still in his mind and made a speedy business of getting dressed in the cold room. Sherry had saved him from having to speak out against Keel at the meeting, but the prospect was already back to haunt him.

He went down to the lobby to see a virtual ground blizzard blowing beyond the big panes of glass. The night man was still on duty and gave him a sour grin. "If your train makes it up today, it'll have to put runners on."

"You telling me?" Luke said.

There had been trouble aplenty keeping the track clear to that point, although the snowfall hadn't been heavy enough at any one time to prevent the train from getting through. He wished he was down on the Wallula end of the line or that Frank was there to make the decision whether the train should go out at all. If only Doc could afford a snowplow — but then there were so many things the railroad needed and managed to get along without. Heavier locomotives that would ride smoother and pull longer trains, iron rail that would stand up to them, sidings and turntables and water tanks and a telegraph line. Some of those things might have been managed if the stock had been fully subscribed. The amount raised would hardly complete a wooden track, with revenue marginal already and a heavy guard force eating up that.

He had breakfast in the dining room with the early risers, then made his way along the street, whipped and driven snow blinding him. When he reached Pasco's hotel, he found the driver up and as worried as he was over the grim turn in the weather. Even if no one showed up foolhardy enough to want to go down to railhead to catch the train, there might be passengers on the train, provided it got through, who would have to be brought in to town. So Pasco would have to make the run, and the prospect wasn't attractive.

"I'll tell you a worse one," Luke said at the driver's grumping. "That's for a train of ours to stall some passengers in a killing blizzard miles from nowhere. I wish I knew what the weather's like on the Wallula end. With Frank, Truax and me up here, it'll be up to Sam Dunbow to decide whether to take the train out, and if the stage leaves from down there, Sam will feel obliged to compete."

Luke made his way on to the freight office where he found the two guards inside hugging the stove. He didn't reprimand them for their laxness, for deviltry in that kind of weather was the least of his worries. He sent them out and built up the fire so the office would be good and warm by the time Sherry arrived for work, if she made it in. He had barely finished this when Frank Baker arrived, as worried as he was about the train.

"There's nothing we can do about it but trust to Sam's good sense," Luke told him.

"I know," Frank said. He went over to Sherry's desk and sat down. He didn't look like he had got much sleep. "I saw you at the meeting. What did you think of it?"

"It didn't go as good as I hoped," Luke said cautiously. "But better than I feared. How did your dad take the outcome?"

"I don't know." Frank shook his head. "He just listened to what I told him and never said a thing."

"What a pity he won't borrow money. Most men in his position do it all the time."

"You know he'll never do that."

"I don't see why the bank can't buy enough stock, then, to do everything Keel offered to do last night. It's a private bank. His money and Boyer's started it."

"Everyone's tried him on that. John, Bill and even me." Frank threw up his hands. "If the depositors won't put money into the railroad voluntarily, he's not going to do it for them that way."

"It's a pity," Luke reflected, "that some of those principles of his weren't remembered and appreciated last night."

"They were. By about one out of three who were there. That's gain. The ones who swung over to us run heavy to business people, here and out in the other towns. It's the farm crowd that's gone over to Keel in a block."

"I know it," Luke agreed. "Keel's had a fine chance to work on 'em at his store and flour mill."

"If we get more freight business from the merchants, it'll help."

But not enough, Luke was afraid, to enable the company to make up the deficit out of revenue. Meanwhile the OSN would be more encouraged than otherwise to start up the Columbia with their full-fledged line.

Sherry and Tripp arrived in a bobsled at their usual time. Sherry looked blown and rosy-cheeked and a little uncertain about what the others thought of her outburst at the meeting. Frank reassured her. "Sherry, you were marvelous," he told her at once. "I could have kissed you for what you said. I still could, by George."

"Why don't you?" Sherry said with a relieved smile.

They were both teasing, at least Frank was because he had an understanding with one of the teachers at the town school. But Luke was surprised at the wrench it gave him to see Frank laughingly grab and hug

Sherry and kiss her heartily. She was a mighty attractive girl, and it seemed to Luke that she let it take longer than necessary. Then she let her eyes rest on Luke for an instant and took the chair at her desk and fell to work in a very businesslike manner. Luke turned to his own piled-up office work, while Frank went out to the barn where Tripp was taking morning care of the stage and freight horses.

It was hardly an hour later when a man arrived with word that Dorsey Baker wanted to see his son and Luke at the bank. The wind had died down somewhat but by then had mottled the landscape with patches of bare, frozen ground and huge drifts. Going in with Frank, Luke began to ease up on his worry about a prolonged storm. Frank announced his intention of leaving for Wallula as soon as his father was through with him, even if he had to ride a horse clear through. Luke decided to go along.

The bank hadn't yet opened for the day's business, but John Boyer let them in. Luke saw that Truax and Green were already there with Baker, seated around the doctor's desk. It would have been another directors' meeting except for Luke's presence, and he wondered why they

151

wanted him there. The doctor didn't look any more tired and discouraged and no more rested and enheartened than he had at the schoolhouse the night before. There were papers all over his desk, and he got down to business at once.

"I've just been going over the estimates with Newall," he explained to the newcomers, "trying to see where we can cut costs. We can by postponing a good deal that's already been postponed too long."

"So you're going ahead," Frank said.

"I'm considering whether it would be stark madness to go ahead," his father told him. "The money subscribed last night is woefully short of the already meager sum I asked for. Yet if we accept it, we'll be equally bound to my commitment to have the line finished and operating before the next harvest season. The men on John's list have a right to expect what I promised in return for their faith in me."

"If we can be ready by summer," Frank said fervently, "and if they'll give us a fair share of the crop to haul, we'll be over the hump. Everything we've done so far's been makeshift. We can keep on a while longer."

"I said we could cut costs by continuing that way," Baker said reprovingly. "Even so, we'll have to increase revenue just to complete the track to town. That's the vital accomplishment, to have a finished track and trains running from terminal to terminal. It would eliminate much of the handling, and we could cut out our stage and wagon expense, which would help a lot. Can we increase revenue, though, when it was mostly the farmers that went over to Lawson Keel last night? It doesn't look very promising, although the merchants who finally came our way will probably use our services more. Which brings me to the question I wanted to ask you, Luke. Can we cut operating expenses?"

"I don't see how," Luke said truthfully.

"How about dispensing with the guard? There are a lot of men on that payroll, and if we have to keep meeting it, I'd sooner have them building track."

"Golly, Doc —" Luke pushed his hat to the back of his head. "If money wasn't such a pressing matter, I'd say no, not for a minute. Too many people will be itching to see you driven to take Keel's offer. There's the freighters and grazers still hoping to see the whole railroad proposition fall through so things'll go on like they used to. Clint Morgan was an example of that breed. There's plenty like him still around. Taking off the guard would hand 'em an invitation thirty-two miles long. But if it's a case of running the risk or throwing in the sponge, the answer's yes. We can put the guards back to cutting timbers and building track, and I'll try to find another way to protect our weakest points."

"Good." Baker's chary smile broke on his face and vanished. "We're going ahead, gentlemen. Our target's through service to Walla Walla City by June 1st. If we achieve it, I have a little plan in mind to help us tie up the next wheat haul." Everyone waited, but he didn't mean to reveal that yet. He turned to the papers on his desk, dismissing them.

Luke went down to the street with Truax, Green and Frank. They were all heartened, but mainly from having again been in contact with a spirit that nothing could daunt. The date the doctor had set was a little less than five months away and looked fairly easy, a bit over a mile of track to be built each month. But there was no telling what the weather would be doing for at least half that time. There were half-built trestles to be finished and all the grading to be done, the ballast and tie and stringer work, the strapiron surfacing. Materials alone would eat a big hole in the new money. Labor would double that. The transportation business was in its dullest season, with only five months of revenue to balance the budget. And that took only normal problems into consideration.

Luke and Frank left immediately, taking saddle horses since there was no knowing if the train would make it to Whitman Station. Within the hour they doubted the wisdom of having started out themselves, for while the wind had nearly died, the sky turned black and formed a solid overcast. At the end of another hour a steady snowfall pelted them, and drifts from the night's blow held them to a snailing pace. The railroad track, off to their left, was as badly obstructed as the stage and wagon road. There still was no sign of the train when they reached Touchet Station, which it usually would have passed long since.

It was well after dark when finally they rode into Wallula Landing on horses nearly played out. Ever since Divide Station they had known there was never any need to fear for the train and its passengers. On the desert and along the Columbia the wind had blown at gale force, drifting the track solidly for mile-long stretches. At Wallula they learned that Sam Dunbow hadn't even been able to bring the train down from the Slabtown yard. And it was going to be a while, Luke knew, before Sam would be able to do so, for the snow by then fell quietly but in heavy density, and the temperature was falling fast.

Frank took the choked road on to Slabtown, while Luke rode to the town livery barn to put up his horse before going to the hotel. Elvie Elvek was on duty at the barn and seemed more than usually glad to see him. The hostler took the tired animal, but lingered. Luke realized that, there being no connections with Walla Walla City that day, nobody at Wallula knew how the long-discussed stock issue had come out.

"Pshaw, now," Elvek said, when Luke told him about it. "That makes it rough havin' to hear what I figured I ought to tell you. I think Clint Morgan's back in this country, if he ever really cleared out."

Luke said sharply, "What makes you think so?" Elvek had stood him in good stead on several occasions. He listened now with respect. "You seen him?"

"No, but a few days ago, right here in the barn, I heard a couple of fellers mention him like they just seen him. I got to thinking on it. Wondered if people around here've been helpin' him dodge the law without him having to hit it for yonder."

"Could be," Luke said reluctantly. "Who'd you hear talking?"

"That's what made it stick with me. The Holladay boys."

Luke placed them, brothers who traded in horses and furnished Kirk Browder with some of his draft stock. "They'd rented horses here?" he asked.

"No, they put theirs up here when it's bad weather and they aim to make a night of it in town. What I heard Chuck Holladay say to Blackie was, 'Don't forget to get the tobacco Clint wants before they lock up the stores.' There could be more than one Clint, but I never heard of another around here. They used to hang around with Morgan, and it could be they're helpin' him hole up. All I got's a hunch, though, and all I'm givin' you's a tip for what it's worth."

"It could be worth plenty, Elvie," Luke said. "Thanks."

It was the last thing he wanted to hear, however, when he had just agreed to discontinue the expensive guard on the railroad property, and it worried him while he got a room and ate his supper at the hotel. There were too many uncertainties for him to pass on to the law what the stablehand had said. If Morgan was in the country, again or still, and the Holladays were helping him, there was no reason to suppose they were keeping him at their ranch. The marshal's poking around there would only warn them and make the fugitive as difficult as ever to catch, for other sympathizers would lend Morgan their help.

On the other hand, Morgan's hatred of the railroad had become personal as well as general. If he saw a chance to strike yet again, he would do it at whatever risk to himself.

The snow fell all through the night and by morning was piled a foot deep in spots previously swept clean and up to six times that deep in the drifts. The cold wasn't yet of killing intensity, but it was deep enough to guarantee a slow recovery and a lot of problems before that came about. Luke put Morgan out of his mind for the time being. The man was no real danger to a railroad that couldn't be seen except where there was a station shed or a trestle over a stream.

There was no use even going outdoors, and in his room after breakfast Luke sat by the window, smoking and watching the persistent fall of snow. The room was chilly, its only heat being that which drifted upstairs from the lobby and through his open door, and he kept on his coat. It was no comfort to know that everyone else connected with the railroad was as helpless and as restless as he was. That would be especially true of Truax, who had hoped to get his construction camp moved to the site of the new work to be ready to go as soon as the weather broke and grading could be started.

Out on the cattle ranges, which Luke thought of with sudden nostalgia, Bill Green's concern would be doubled. He had not only the railroad but the Baker herds to think about. If the thermometer kept falling and there was a die-off as bad as some had been in past years, that alone could be a crippling financial blow to the doctor.

Chapter 11

Low as his spirits were the first morning he was snowbound in Wallula, Luke wouldn't have predicted that the whole country would be at a frozen standstill on through January and February and well into March. Freeze-ups of that nature weren't new in the region, yet they were rare, and no one ever really expected one to come along again. So day by day, through the first week, everyone anticipated that another day would see the mercury rise again and got out of bed on another morning to find it where it had been before, or lower still.

Since no one could come in to trade, and no travelers braved the elements to come up the river on the steamboats, and finally the steamers themselves stopped coming, the people of Wallula Landing had the town to themselves. The stores became social clubs for those who wearied of spending the livelong day in the saloons or the poolhall. Since the food and fuel were in reassuring supply, it wasn't exactly hardship, yet it wore on the nerves, especially Luke's since he was cooped up with people, who in main part were his enemies.

It grew too cold for him to stay in the hotel room except to sleep, and he took to spending a lot of time at the livery stable, talking with Elvek or George Tedro, who owned the barn. And then, largely to counteract his heavy boredom, he took to dropping in now and then for a drink at Nan's. Thus it was that he discovered Kirk Browder's conviction that he was the man in Nan's past life. Luke didn't know why Browder was so sure there had been such a man, for Nan seemed to have told him little about herself before she came to Wallula and opened her place.

That she had had a lover had somehow been betrayed to Browder, even so, and a jealous husband would not be blind to her inner turmoil each time a certain man entered her presence. The railroad fight having been frozen with everything else, Browder seemed to brood on this fly in the ointment of his life with Nan. And once when Luke dropped in fairly early in the day and found only a few people on hand, with Nan not yet come down from upstairs, Browder came over to the bar where

Luke stood alone with a drink.

Browder said with a superciliousness that betrayed his self-doubt, "Look, Preston. There's other places to put in your time. And there's nobody here you need to see or wants to see you."

"I never come here out of need, Browder," Luke said evenly, "nor because I like the place."

"Then why?"

"It helps kill time."

"That ain't all," Browder said, his temper slipping. "This ain't Colorado, Preston. It's Washington Territory."

"What do you know about Colorado?" Luke asked.

"Some."

It wasn't enough to straighten him out on Nan's affiliations back there, so it probably didn't include anything about Wade Foster and his one-time partnership with Lawson Keel. Luke grinned at him and said nothing. After a moment Browder turned away and went back to the solitaire game he had been playing. Luke realized while he finished his drink that part of his coming here stemmed from the very thing Browder believed. He was trying to keep old feelings stirred up in Nan, not the romantic sentiments that Browder imagined, but the hidden, unresting guilt in her that, if he kept her from putting it to rest, might torment her into making amends.

There were lulls in the part of the storm that locked up the country so tight, clear days of aching cold in which men of sufficient fortitude and will could break trail to such nearby points as concerned them. During one of these Luke bucked his horse through the drifts and reached Slabtown to find it as congealed in inertia as Wallula, and Frank Baker pacing the office floor.

"What're we going to do?" Frank demanded, knowing full well Luke couldn't answer him. "When's it going to stop? Then how long'll it take to thaw out so we can at least run the train?"

"That's what I come up about," Luke said. "You've got a good millwright and a good blacksmith here doing nothing. Why can't they build a snowplow? Not a fancy one like we'd have bought, but something we might be able to clear the track with as soon as the weather lets up enough."

Some of the gloom went out of Frank's face, for he preferred doing almost anything to nothing at all. But he said cautiously, "Snowplow? How?"

"Rigged on the front of a flat car," Luke explained. "Something like an overgrown plowshare. With both locomotives behind it, maybe it would throw the stuff off the track."

"If we don't wind up with a silver thaw."

"That's the danger, and there's a good chance we'll get one."

"Just the same," Frank said, as if afraid he had sounded too forbidding, "we could have it ready to try in case we get a chance. If we rigged a horizontal A-frame ahead of the car, winged it back and out on each side, kind of like a big dart, and faced it with sheet metal — there's plenty of timbers already cut in the yard, and we can make tie-rods in the blacksmith shop — there's an old boiler down by the pond we can get the metal from —"

Excited now, he got paper and pencils, and they worked on it together, drawing a crude plan for the mechanics to follow. The idea was to achieve the cutting surface of a plowshare, raked so as to slice through the snow and peel it up and over the side of the track far enough to clear passage for the trains. If the rails could be exposed sufficiently to engage the car wheels, the area abounded in sand that could be used for traction, if needed.

The more they worked on it, the more possibilities they saw and the more problems. The exciting part was the prospect of getting train service restored well ahead of the freight wagons. Inbound freight was piling up down the river, and the steamboats would be the first back in service, for they had only to wait for the ice that had formed along the shores to break up. Store shelves in all the towns from Wallula to Central Idaho were being cleaned off by the traffic shutdown, and merchants would be hollering for replacements.

It was a chance for the railroad to demonstrate its superiority and also pick up a tidy revenue to offset the present total lack. Nothing would clear the stage and wagon road but a general thaw, and even after a thaw the road would be a quagmire of mud and flood waters. This tied in with facts that began to make it seem to Luke and Frank that their adversity might be turned into an advantage. The wheat haul wouldn't begin until fall, when harvest was over, and would run into early winter. The reason the doctor had set his sights on taking the track on into Walla Walla by the first of June was that the inland merchants always used the summers to build up a stock of goods sufficient to carry them through the long winter months when the roads might be closed tight at any time.

Baker wanted this revenue, too, and he might get it if he could show the merchants that he could give them all-weather service under the most extreme conditions. Such a service would let them carry lower inventories and cut down overhead.

But on the discouraging side was the fact that the railroad itself had to resort to wagons and stages for the last six miles to Walla Walla City. Moreover their plow might work well enough on the stretches where the snowpack was of uniform depth, and much of the track was that way. Yet there were countless drifts, some so immense the makeshift plow might be wholly ineffective against them.

"We'll never know," Luke reflected, "unless we build the thing and see."

They were thoroughly sold by then on the idea that the gamble was worth the small cost, and it was much better than enforced idleness. Besides, Luke preferred to make Slabtown his own headquarters until the country opened up again, and the project gave him an excuse. So with the help of the mill's regular blacksmith and millwright they put in a week cutting out and bolting together their crude model. The weather stayed moody and below zero, but with their undertaking the constant frigidity suited them. The danger would come when the temperature climbed enough to thaw a little by day and freeze again by night, crusting the snow and turning slushy areas to sheets of ice. If, after that, a deep cold socked in again, the results would be disastrous and their plan ruined.

As it was, they ran into many problems. The passenger and long-idled work train stood in the open on the yard tracks, the fireboxes of the little locomotives now so cold they would freeze a hand left to rest on their metal too long. The problem, though, was that snow had drifted around and sometimes over the cars and had to be cleared away at great labor, even to run one of the flats into the machine shop for fitting. But the mechanics had helped to build every freight car owned by the company in that same shop, and the contraption they had put together for a plow went on like a glove. It promised to stay there dependably, whether or not it worked, and they were ready to try it out.

Frank was optimistic and said, the night before the trial, "I'd give a pretty if we could take it all the way down to Wallula. It would give Kirk Browder and his freighter friends the turn of their lives."

Luke grinned but suggested that they wait to crow until they saw whether they had anything to crow about.

The locomotives had been drained to keep them from freezing, and their boilers had to be filled. This had been done the day before, and by daylight the engineers had fired up and built a head of steam, and they pronounced both engines ready to do or die. Every man in Slabtown was on hand to help clear track by hand until they had the improvised plow and its twin drivers on an open length of yard track. The spur was so representative of conditions everywhere that they knew if they made it out to the main line, they could go through to Wallula and maybe to Walla Walla City.

A shout went up when the plow reached the first real snow after the cleared and tramped-up stretch of track. It didn't even spin the drivewheels of the locomotives when the point lifted the snow ahead of it and curled it neatly back and aside along the curve of the moldboard. When the depth increased, the sand hoppers rigged ahead of the drivers gritted the bared rails, and the rig kept crawling forward. It went a third of the way into the first real drift and then, instead of stalling as expected, it tried to climb over the top.

More ballast was needed, which was simple in a region that was mainly basalt. Excited men made short work of gathering and piling a few tons of rock on the flatcar, which the engineers had pulled back in the clear. Then with sanders open and the snorting locomotives digging in, the rig moved forward again. The increased weight held it down until, deep in the drift, it came to a wheel-spinning stop, the snow too deep for the moldboard to throw it clear. They were only a few feet from the reverse slope of the drift, however, which shallowed rapidly. The engines backed off and rammed forward, and momentum did what a steady push could not. Only a little of this bulling was needed, and then the plow turned the snow off to the sides again and came out on a long stretch there was no doubt it could clear.

They could have dug their way on to Wallula, but there was no thought of that now. They had hold of something, but it needed improving, and the plow went back to the car shop. They started over and spent another week on a modified design, which had a longer point and a more gradual lift and flare. Of greater effect was an auxiliary boom, a V at its end and operated by a hand crab, that could be lowered ahead of the point to sweep back drift tops and help the plow clear itself. The new design was even more cumbersome and ugly than its predecessor, but when they took it down the track to the next drift, it went through. There would be worse drifts on the desert and in the open valley of the Walla Walla, but if they weren't too numerous and too bad, hand-shoveling could help to conquer them.

There might have been a celebration in Slabtown after the second tryout had not a warming trend that promised to continue made itself evident during that week. The winds stopped, the sky cleared, and the thermometer climbed. This only stabilized the situation without relieving it, and roads and railroad were still impassable, while ice on the river still kept the steamboats tied up at downstream ports. February was half gone, June 1st was that much nearer, and Newall Truax and his construction outfit hadn't been able to do a lick of work on the new track.

The worry over the rising temperature came from the fact that it wasn't climbing out of the danger zone, but into it. Ahead inescapably was a point where thawing and refreezing would be so delicately balanced that the time and money invested in clearing the track, provided they succeeded in doing it, could be brought to naught overnight. On the other hand was the hope of being ready to handle the freight off the first steamer to come up. It was unprecedented but an operating problem. With Dorsey Baker nailed down on the far end of the line, Luke knew the responsibility for making the gamble was his alone.

"Let's go on it," he told Frank, the night after the second tryout, "and hope we beat the ice to the end of track. If we can't we've thrown away a lot of money, but if we can, we're set."

"Good," Frank said. "That's what I hoped you'd say."

"I sure hope your dad feels the same way."

"If he were here, I think he would."

The work began. They didn't discount the difficulty of what they were undertaking, but they didn't come close to guessing what they were really in for. Two miles a day was the best they could do, while a rotary plow could have fanned through to end of track in a day's time. And then much of the time was spent buried in some drift, often so deep it took the combined efforts of a shovel crew and the plow to get past.

The track behind the outfit had to be sanded and resanded, for the heat of the slow-moving locomotives left slush that froze into ice between the rails, and even on them at times. Fuel and water had to be carried along in a flatcar behind the straining engines. Men who worked up a sweat when their work was needed nearly froze solid when it wasn't. And instead of being taken aback by the threat of restored train service, Wallula Landing laughed at the pygmy contraption pitted against the gargantuan snowblock.

Yet day by day a little more of the track was exposed to the cold winter daylight, as far as Five Mile, then Divide, and finally as far as the Touchet. Punishing as the cold was, it was providential that the temperature never climbed higher than twenty above, staving off the threat of icing that would stop everything again. But the Touchet was as far as they had gotten when the warm-up, born of a Chinook wind, swept in overnight.

The snowplow had, as usual, returned to Slabtown for the night, and in the night Luke awakened to hear dripping water and realized that it came from the roof of the shack in which he slept. For the first time in weeks, no cold knifed into him when he sat up in bed, and he called to Frank, who shared the shack, "Hey — you hear that?"

Frank grunted, said, "Raining?" and all at once came fully awake. "It's thawing. That sure came on fast."

His tone was as worried as it was jubilant. They both knew that a warm-air mass had merely pushed back a cold one and that the cold mass could shove back just as hard and fast. Luke thought of the miles of uncleared track, which would be under an ice sheet if the cold air won the struggle. If on the other hand the warm air prevailed, clearing the wagon roads as well as the rest of the track automatically, they would have lost everything they had worked so desperately to gain at considerable expense.

Frank knew that, too, and what they had to do, and they roused all hands. While the locomotives were being fired, food and blankets were loaded into a box car. This was hooked on behind the engines when, in the last hours of a warm darkness, they ran out to where the work that day had stopped.

The urgency that drove them around the clock for the next three days stemmed from a determination to clear as much track as possible, if not all, before the temperature could plummet again. The men were millhands and mechanics who had fought the Slabtown fire to a standstill. Now they drove themselves until hunger or exhaustion stopped them and, in relays, they ate or slept in the box car moving behind the creeping outfit. And then it began to freeze again at night so that a tough crust had to be broken ahead of the plow.

Yet they worked on, and the third dawn showed them, far down the line, the dots and trees of Whitman Station. While Luke didn't join in the cheer that went up, he felt a deep gratification. The weather pattern seemed to have stablized, and at a point where there would be neither a disastrous new freeze nor a dramatic clearing away of the snow. The plow reached Whitman Station in mid-afternoon that day, a deserted, useless-looking place because six miles of fouled wagon road separated it from Walla Walla City. It was road that had to be conquered, too, before the giant job of clearing the track could pay off.

Chapter 12

It was the first time Luke had seen a grin so heartfelt crease the seams of Dorsey Baker's tired, slack-sided face. They were in the sparsely furnished study of his house on Mill Creek because of the late hour. Lacking horses, Luke and Frank had come in on foot from Whitman, skirting drifts and following shallows on a tiring and time-consuming course. It had been nearly midnight when they reached town, and they had had to get the doctor out of bed. No one at all had undertaken the much longer trip between Wallula and the valley town, so no word of the work being done to clear the track had come in.

"Talk about stealing a march," Baker was saying with an exuberance that matched his grin. "With freight back up from Dalles City to Portland, the steamers'll be working double time, themselves."

"We might find one in Wallula when we

get back there," Frank said. "Warm as it's been lately."

The doctor nodded his head. "The roads might not be open for weeks to come, and till they are, there's no question we'll get all the business we can handle. Which is a lot, because if need be, we can put on two trains. You get the freight to Whitman, Luke, and we'll get it the rest of the way somehow. You, Frank, start bringing up track materials if Luke doesn't need both engines. It'll be that much time saved when Truax can get started finishing the track. You two —" The doctor hesitated, then made an impatient motion with his hand. "I won't try to tell you how I feel about this. Except to say things were looking pretty black."

Luke and Frank were dog-tired, with a lot ahead of them to be accomplished, but they talked for a while longer. Freight arrived at Wallula on OSN waybills and beyond that point was picked up by wagon or train, whichever the consignees chose to patronize. Baker would solicit the business as a matter of form, he said, although there was no doubt that until the wagons could run again that the WW&CR would be implored to bring in the badly needed merchandise. Even merchants farther inland would prefer to have their shipments waiting in Walla Walla City for the interior roads to open than in Wallula. Every effort would be made and no expense spared, Baker promised, to open the road to Whitman Station to company wagons. If that couldn't be done as yet, they would resort to pack trains for as long as necessary.

"I'd start with packstrings," Luke suggested, for he had given much thought to it. "And saddle horses if any passengers show up. Tripp and Pasco could scare up enough horses, and they and the wagon drivers could run 'em. I'd stay off the wagon road, and break trail right down the railroad right of way. The soil is sandy. Even after it turns slushy it'd hold up."

"Sure," Frank said with a laugh. "No use clearing the road for the competition."

"On top of that," Baker said with approval, "it would help clear the right of way for Truax to get started."

Luke nodded. "Every little bit counts with June 1st only a whoop and a holler off."

Frank spent the night there, for it was his home, although he hadn't been able to put in much time there for a long while. The doctor asked Luke to stay, but Luke declined and went to his room at the hotel. Nearly ten weeks had passed since he left Walla Walla City expecting to be away only a few days. He knew no work had piled up for him at the freight office since no business had been done. The engines had taken the snowplow back to Slabtown and would be at Whitman the next afternoon with the first train in weeks. So he would stay on this end of the line only long enough to complete arrangements for the hoped-for business boom, then go back down with the train.

He could have slept around the clock but was at the freight yard the next morning shortly after Tripp and Sherry arrived, expecting to put in another idle day. Pasco was out, but Luke had left word at his hotel for him to scare up Barney Lunt and Lafe Wells, who drove the wagons, and bring them out to the yard. Early as he was, he arrived at the yard to find Frank Baker there ahead of him, so the Yales knew about the cleared track.

"You're sure a pair of snow gophers," Tripp said heartily, offering Luke his hand. "If I'd known what you were up to, I'd have got down there somehow to help."

Sherry was equally pleased, but more to the point than her father. "I think it's marvelous, Luke," she said. "If a rattle-trap railroad with make-do equipment can dig out of a mess like that, there's nothing could stop the kind of line the doctor's been begging for. And this country will have to admit it."

Catching their high spirits, Luke laughed and promised to keep them busy enough from then on to collect for the idling they had done so long. Then Pasco and the wagonhands arrived, and they worked out the details of putting pack and saddle horses on the Walla Walla end until wheeled vehicles could run again. Afterward Tripp made a suggestion Luke adopted, which was to take the long cooped-up stage and freight horses in a herd over the right of way, breaking down and packing the snow, so loaded animals wouldn't have that to do.

Just before noon Dorsey Baker came out to the yard to report that he had been authorized by every important merchant in Walla Walla City to pick up any freight coming into Wallula consigned to them. He had required them to put it in writing since there would be arguments about it on the Wallula end, and he gave Luke the authorizations. Then Luke and Frank rode down to Whitman Station, Pasco going along to bring back their horses. And it was one of the rare thrills of Luke's life when, only minutes behind its regular schedule, the train pulled into sight down the valley and then rolled to a stop at the end of track. It carried only the train crew, but they were all excited.

Dunbow had hardly swung to the ground when he said gustily, "The *Chief*'s tied up at Wallula. She was there when we got down last night. The skipper told me freight's piled up till hell wouldn't hold it at Dalles City and The Deschutes. They're puttin' the *Tenino* on the run, too, till they get it thinned out."

"You bring up any freight?" Luke asked.

The conductor shook his head. "We had trouble there. Kirk Browder's breathin' fire all over Wallula. He claims he's got verbal contracts with the people he's been haulin' for, even if it means the stuff's got to set there till the road's open. The other wagoners're makin' the same claim. The man at the wharfboat wouldn't release any freight to us till it's straightened out."

"Doc figured on that," Luke told him. "And was smart enough to get written instructions for us to load about everything that boat brought up."

They turned the horses over to Pasco,

and it was good to be riding in the dinky passenger car again, empty though it was. A bright sun lay glitteringly on the valley, and it was warm enough for a slow but steady thawing to be taking place. At intervals Luke saw range cattle and horses, skinny but still on their feet. Of more immediate satisfaction was the still badly clogged wagon and stage road that for nearly the entire distance ran in sight of the train. He saw no one trying to buck it even on horseback.

The train went directly to Wallula instead of to the Slabtown yard for the night and backed to a stop beside the wharfboats in the early dusk. The *Chief* lay on the far side of the bobbing barge houses but had finished unloading. Luke showed the wharfmaster the authorizations Baker had turned over to him and announced in no uncertain tones that he intended to load every last item consigned to one of the names. The dockman was plainly uneasy, and maybe partial to the wagoners with whom he had dealt for years, but he made no further objection. The train crew began to load freight.

In addition to a bumper cargo, Luke learned, the steamer had brought in a score of passengers presently at the hotel who had no choice but to take the train or wait around Wallula interminably. He wondered why they hadn't taken the train that day, and went to the hotel to find out. A group of them were in the bar, their dress identifying them as sourdoughs who probably had gone downriver for the holidays and were only now able to start back to their mining claims over in Idaho somewhere. Luke knew none of them but gave them an easy grin and asked why they had laid over.

"Well," a man said hesitantly, "there was this talk."

"What talk?"

"The word went around it was worth a man's life to ride your train right now."

"I see. Well, I'll start some more talk. Which is that our trains are running on schedule from here on, and we'll give our passengers every guarantee and protection we can. Anybody that wants to go up with us tomorrow is welcome. Anybody so chicken-livered that he'd let wild talk scare him out is welcome to stay here till he's as sick of the place as I am."

Luke went from there to Nan's saloon, hoping to find Kirk Browder. The man wasn't there, or, according to Nan, even in Wallula. Luke showed her the authority from the Walla Walla merchants and suggested that she tell Browder about it.

"He hasn't got a legal leg to stand on, Nan," he concluded. "I know he's got one that's not so legal, and my advice to you is to keep him from trying to stand on that."

Nan glanced about uneasily to see if anybody was listening, but no one seemed to be. She looked pale and worn, and the spirit that once had been so much a part of her had given way to resignation. "Luke, I don't have a thing to do with it," she said in a low, frayed voice. "I want you to know that. I don't have any influence over Kirk, either, and you might as well know that. But I'll tell him what you said."

"Nan, why do you stick with it?"

She didn't look at him. "What else is there for me, anymore?"

"You could start liking yourself again."

She looked at him with pained eyes and turned away, and he left.

There were nine passengers aboard when the train went up the valley the next day. Their fares added little to revenue, but their decision to trust the WW&CR meant much. The train was the longest ever to go up the track, and while the run went without incident, Luke fretted every foot of the way. The threat of physical danger that had worried the passengers might not have been an empty one, born of disgruntlement. For the first time in weeks Luke thought of Elvek's hunch that Clint Morgan was hiding out somewhere around Wallula.

It had seemed reasonable that after the ill-feeling Morgan had aroused in Walla Walla City, Lawson Keel would want no more to do with him and hangers-on like the Browder crowd. Yet Keel himself had suffered a serious setback at the stock meeting, even though he had emerged as the leader of a powerful element in the valley. Keel knew now that there was no hope of intimidating Baker into yielding to his pressure, that the one chance of gaining control of the line was to drive the doctor to the wall. The Morgan touch was well suited to that, and the shippers' present, self-interested support of the railroad might bring Morgan back into Keel's favor.

The company men at Walla Walla City had done their jobs well, and Pasco was at Whitman Station with a saddle string more than sufficient to accommodate the passengers on the last six miles. Barney Lunt and Lafe Wells were there with pack-strings instead of their usual wagons, and the wooden saddles were loaded to the limit. The rest of the freight brought up was stored in the shed to be picked up on the packers' next trip. They had brought nothing out from town to go down the valley, but with a successful run behind the train, that might be different soon.

And it was different, so much so that until the end of March, when the wagon road came back into service, the railroad seemed so firmly established it was hard to believe it was still in a fight for its life. True to early reports, the *Tenino* doubled in harness with the *Chief*, and even after the *Yakima* was also put in service, the flow of traffic from downriver didn't slack off. For two and a half months there had been no traffic, and now spring was opening the interior and bringing on the usual summer rush.

Within a few days two trains instead of one went up the valley each day, building a mountain of freight at Whitman Station that had to be sheltered in tents borrowed from the construction department and put under guard. Each night a work train went out to end of track with construction materials for Truax, who waited impatiently for the right of way to clear enough to start the grading crews that must precede everything else.

Within a few days it was evident that the clearing was taking place. Gradually the temperature rose until it no longer fell below freezing even in the dark, windy nights. Slush formed underfoot, impeding the packstrings, and ponds of dirty water grew in the hollows. Saddle traffic appeared on the stage road, but it was mostly local, for soon the ponds were lakes. Streams all the way to Wallula came out of their beds and washed out flimsy wagon bridges and submerged long stretches of the road.

The contrast between the two avenues into the interior couldn't have been brought into sharper focus, or the skill with which Truax had located the railroad more fully shown. Everywhere the track followed the high ground or ran on sturdy grades. The trestles over the streams reached well above flood level and were too strongly built to be endangered by flood force. And these were advantages that would weigh heavily in all the winters to come in which men would need to ship and travel.

But the snowpack dwindled, the flooding subsided, and it was with mixed feelings that Luke saw the day when the first wagon outfits rolled out of Wallula for the upper valley. They were nearly empty but back in business and ready to fight for what to them was only a temporary loss of business. Luke knew that the fight had to come. The railroad's first real furtherance had been produced by vagrant conditions, and the settlement had to be reached in open competition.

It was the first of April when Truax, his camp set up between Whitman Station and Walla Walla City, broke ground on the last stretch of track. The right of way was cut into three divisions, with an outcamp at the first and last. Grading crews were based on each to save time between job and camp and bring the entire grade to completion at about the same time. As soon as wagons could use the right of way, materials and carpenters were moved out to the trestles that were started but left unfinished for lack of funds. This drove the company stages and wagons back to the old road, slowing them down, but that couldn't be avoided. Everyone was hopeful that June 1st would yet see the wagons obsoleted by trains running clear into town.

Dorsey Baker was everywhere by then, cracking a whip that nobody working for him resented because they were solidly with him and so much depended on his success. And then he took the boat down to Portland for another talk with John Ainsworth, determined to see that the steamboat people realized the little WW&CR had weathered yet another crisis and intended to stay in business, even against a competing line. The only change he was able to make, he told Luke afterward, was to inculcate a wait-and-see attitude in Ainsworth's mind.

He had done more than see Ainsworth while in Portland, Baker revealed. Not moved by optimism but realizing that the wooden rails wouldn't hold up very long under the increased traffic, he had ordered enough light iron rails to rebuild the track from Wallula to Walla Walla City. The rails had to come from the East, which had forced him to act with no idea where the money would come from to pay for them. Moreover, he had ordered another, heavier locomotive, wheels and fittings for another passenger car, and a number of freight cars. He meant to be ready for success if it came, and he refused to contemplate the consequences of failure.

Chapter 13

In Wallula, only a few evenings after Baker had talked with him, Luke got a report from Elvek on a strange conversation the hostler had had with Nan Browder. Nan kept a saddle horse at the livery barn and liked to take lonely rides of a morning before she opened her place of business. She had resumed the practice, now that the weather had turned mild and fair.

A day or two earlier she had been in to get her horse, finding Elvek alone at the barn. In a half-frightened way, she had asked him right out if he wasn't a pretty good friend of Luke's and a secret rooter for the railroad. It had scared Elvek, too, for a moment, since he had done more than a little spying and eavesdropping. Much of this had been done in Nan's saloon, and if his sympathies were apparent to Nan, his activities could be so to others who hung out there.

Yet something in Nan's manner had put

down his fears, and Elvek had admitted the truth of what she asked, and that seemed to give her the reassurance she needed herself. So she had told him she thought Luke should be warned not to let down his guard simply because there hadn't been trouble from his enemies when he had more reason to expect it. Trouble was planned, but the freighters or whoever was guiding them had realized that the weeks in which the railroad had a monopoly on the hauling wasn't the time for it. The inland merchants had been anxious to get their shipments and restock their shelves. If anything had put the trains out of operation, just then, it would have backfired worse than Morgan's attempt to blow up the Walla Walla City freight yard. It was different now that there was other transportation to turn to if the trains quit running.

Whether or not that was all Nan knew, it was all Elvek had got out of her. She claimed not to know if Morgan was in the country, as Elvek still suspected, and she professed ignorance of what was being planned.

"Thought I'd pass it on," Elvek concluded, minimizing as he always did the importance of what he had divulged.

"She's married to Browder and makes her money off his kind of people. She could only be tryin' to throw a scare into you. Or trick you into takin' on the expense of putting guards along the line again. It didn't strike me, though, that she was."

"Me, either," Luke agreed.

His belief that Nan had acted in good faith didn't solve the problem her warning created. The line simply couldn't afford to resort to a heavy guard force again. The only alternative was to stop the trouble before it started. Elvek was convinced that Clint Morgan was holed up somewhere near Wallula. If so, Morgan's Nevada cronies might still be with him, and since the three were supposed to have left the country, they were the obvious ones to strike again from their secret hideout. Certainly Morgan would have the emotional drive to do so. His hatred of the railroad had turned him from a fairly prosperous stockman into an outlaw.

A night's sleep only strengthened Luke's conviction that, if Morgan was still in the country, he had to be rooted out. Elvek had given him a lead by connecting Morgan with the horse traders, Chuck and Blackie Holladay. But Luke wanted Pasco's help, for the man was perceptive, quick-witted and had courage enough for two people. He took the upbound train and at the end of track had a private talk with Pasco.

"Elvek, he is probably right," Pasco agreed, when Luke had posted him. "I am so sure of thees, I theenk I am going to have the bad back again *muy pronto.*"

"Not a bad back this time," Luke told him. "I'd as soon too many of our own people, even, didn't know what we're up to. Tell Tripp what I want of you, and he'll square it with Baker. I'm going back down with the train, and you come down tomorrow. You and Tripp can give out that you're going down the river on private business."

"Weel do," Pasco agreed. "I see you tomorrow night at the Wallula Hotel."

"Meanwhile, I'll try to get a line on what the Holladay boys are doing."

The run down the valley knocked a hole in the afternoon, so Luke waited until the next morning to take a private look at the Holladay brothers' layout. This he knew to be south of the Walla Walla River on the edge of the Umatilla uplands, and he rode out right after breakfast, crossing the river south of the town. The day promised to be fair, and all that remained of the snow lay in dead, grey patches on shady bottoms and slopes. Along the Walla Walla, which he followed upstream, willows and cottonwoods showed delicate buds, and now and then he heard a chickadee or lark or some other bird of spring.

He rode steadily east until the wagon road crossed to his side of the river, and then he cut deeper in toward the highlands to avoid being seen by some chance passerby. It was timberless country, and he had to use the terrain itself to keep hidden. The Holladay horse spread, he knew, was in a broad canyon that cut deep into the high ground and was followed by a shortcut trail to the Umatilla.

At the end of a two-hour ride he found himself on a butte that brought him in sight of the Holladay headquarters. The distance let him see only a thin stand of leafless trees, a clutter of corrals and some shacky, weather-stained buildings. He wasn't sure it was smoke he saw staining the air above what appeared to be the house. There were loose horses in a fenced pasture up the canyon, which narrowed rapidly, but he could see none in the corrals.

His only purpose for that day was to study the layout and make certain that the

Holladays were there, and he needed a closer look. He rode on into the first slow-rolling hills of the high country, then crossed the canyon and swung back. This brought him to the kind of place he had hoped to find, a brushy, rock-studded elbow much closer to the ramshackle structures. He spotted the viewpoint and moved on to it afoot, showing as little of himself as possible.

There was not only a fire in the dwelling below him but, on the near side of the trees and structures, a corral holding half a dozen saddle horses that he hadn't been able to see from the other side. His view still wasn't good enough for him to make out the brands, but he didn't think they would tell him much anyway. He knew that somebody was home, with nothing to suggest that this wouldn't be the case the following morning as well. Satisfied for the time being, he withdrew and started back to Wallula Landing.

There was nothing more to do until he had Pasco to help him, and he finished the day taking care of his regular work. But he was at the depot when the train got back, and Pasco was on it. Luke feigned surprise at seeing him there, and Pasco explained for those within earshot that he had been called down to Portland by a brother who lived there and had got in some kind of trouble. Pasco had dressed for the part and wore the checked suit, boiled collar and derby hat he donned for dress-up occasions.

Later, when he had gone to Pasco's hotel room down the hall from his own, Luke said with a laugh, "How're you going to help me beat the sagebrush for Morgan in a trotting rig like that?"

"Ees eet not *magnifico?*" Pasco asked. "But I have the old clothes in the war bag. And the gun."

Luke described his stealthy inspection of the Holladay ranch and the indications that at least one of the brothers was home and still would be the next day. He described the elbow that had given him a good look and how to get there without being seen from the house. He had arranged with Elvek to provide Pasco with a good mount, and Pasco would pick it up and leave in the small hours of the morning. It didn't matter from there on if somebody noticed that he didn't take the steamboat for downriver. By the time it left they would have pulled their trick for better or worse. "Now, hit the hay," Luke concluded, "and be up on that elbow by the time I get out there in the morning. I'll make it as soon after daylight as I can."

"If thees go wrong, Pasco is the one in trouble, not hees *hermano*." But Pasco's doleful remark was counteracted by the excitement in his eyes. He hadn't forgotten their other effort to smoke out Morgan and put an end to him. This time he hoped for better luck.

So did Luke, and that night he slept fitfully. A number of the merchants who had turned to the railroad when it was to their own immediate benefit were again giving Browder and the other wagoners some of their business. The railroad had put on an impressive performance, and this had had its effect on the business people. Yet a force Luke hadn't anticipated was also at work. The Walla Walla was mainly farm country, now, and the storekeepers dared not risk alienating the large faction behind Keel and against Baker. They had to work both sides of the street.

Through the book work Sherry and he did, Luke knew what revenue amounted to and how much of it went out again in operating costs. The other books of the company were in John Boyer's custody, and he had no idea how funds for construction were holding up now that Truax was drawing on them heavily. But he didn't need a balance sheet to know what would happen if another rash of costly mischief broke out. And never could he forget that, unless he found another way to spike Keel's guns, he would be forced to expose the man to his own ruin.

In order for his pretended errand to seem plausible, Luke had to wait until after daybreak to leave town. Pasco had been gone from his room, and Luke knew he was carrying out his part of the plan. This time Luke rode the wagon road openly, crossing the river where it did, and staying with it until he turned off along the canyon trail into the highlands. He wasn't wearing his gun, but it and belt were hidden in his saddlepouches.

Following a rutty wagon road in to the Holladay buildings, Luke had an uneasy feeling of being watched from the time he drew in sight. Even so, he hailed the house as required by the rules of the range and then rode boldly in to it. He wasn't surprised to find Blackie Holladay standing on the broken step in front of a partly open door. He was pretty sure he had a gun trained on him by the other brother, hidden beyond the door.

Both Holladays were rawboned men,

dark-skinned and as rough of appearance as they were of manner. Blackie only nodded curtly at Luke's mild, "Howdy, Holladay," and shifted his weight nervously. He was careful, Luke noticed, not to get in front of the crack in the door.

"What you doin' up this way, Preston?" Blackie said finally. His undisguised hostility could spring from his partisan sentiments, but the gun Luke sensed behind the door spoke of something more personal and dangerous. "Never seen you in these parts before."

"Just wondered if we could dicker a little," Luke said. "Maybe you heard the company had to pick up some extra horses a while back when the wagon road was closed. Now that they aren't needed, we got to get rid of 'em. It struck me you boys might like to put in a bid."

"Us?" Blackie looked at Luke with his suspicions deepened considerably. "Buy railroad horses? You gone loco?"

"You're in the horse business, aren't you?"

"Not when it comes to Dorsey Baker," Holladay exploded. "And you never thought so for a minute, Preston. What you pokin' around here for?"

It was the reaction Luke had hoped to

draw out of him, much too violent to spring from anything but guilty fear. It seemed to him that the crack of the door widened a little, but the man there would have to be Chuck Holladay. The renegades Luke was now convinced they were harboring would have started shooting before he got that close to the shack, and Clint Morgan would have welcomed the chance.

"Take it easy," Luke told him. "A horse is a horse, no matter how you feel about the railroad. There's some good stuff in the lot, but you've got a right to buy where you want and sell where you want. Just thought I'd give you a chance."

Blackie didn't believe that, either, but was in no position to say what he did think. "We don't give a damn what you do with your nags," he growled. "We don't want ary part of 'em or you, and don't you come snoopin' around here again."

Luke shrugged, nodded and turned his horse. He had a puckery feeling in his back until he was out of gun range of the shack, although Chuck could have shot him down easily if that had been their desire. But he knew they were watching to make sure he actually returned to the main road and left the area. He did so because what he wanted from them most was yet to come.

He had gone halfway back to Wallula, meeting nobody, before he stopped and took a long look to the rear. He hadn't expected them to follow and saw no sign that they had. Then he turned away from the road and moved off toward the uplands that there pressed much closer to the road. As soon as the first draw swallowed him, he lifted the speed of his horse.

An hour later he had worked his way back to a peak that could be seen for a considerable distance and that gave him a sweeping view of the lower canyon all the way to the Walla Walla. He had used up a couple of hours since leaving the Holladay spread but knew he might have a long wait yet, so he dismounted, loosened the saddle cinch and ground-tied the horse where it could graze. Then, his back to a rock he sat watching the belowground, not able to see the horse ranch from there and not so interested in it anymore.

It was over an hour before he saw a mounted man come out of a depression far below and start up toward him. He knew this was Pasco long before he could see for sure since nobody else would ride so directly at that particular time toward a widely visible but otherwise useless landmark. A little later he stood up and waved his hat over his head, and Pasco responded. But the climb was steep, and more minutes passed before Pasco, looking excited and gratified, swung out of the saddle.

"Looks like it worked," Luke said.

"Like the charm." Pasco's white teeth flashed. "You are hardly gone when the Holladay *hermanos* rope the *caballos* and give me the very bad time to keep track of them."

"Where'd they go?"

"Up the main canyon, then over a ridge to theese little side canyon. And there is the hideout of *Senor* Morgan. I see heem."

Luke grinned, although he had been confident that it would be Morgan if, as he had hoped, the Holladays felt impelled to pass the word to somebody that Luke Preston had been nosing around in the vicinity. "Just Morgan, Pasco?"

"The Nevada coyotes are there, *tambien*."

Pasco explained carefully, for it would be a difficult place to breach. The only approach not discouragingly difficult was up the main canyon, which had enabled the Holladay brothers to serve as lookouts as well as a source of supply. The canyon floor was wooded, fed by springs that apparently had drawn Indians there in the past to camp because the renegades were living in some old lodges. But the canyon was too small to support horses for long, and since the Holladays had taken no extra horses along, their hasty trip had been made only to warn the outlaws to be on guard.

Luke weighed it carefully. "They never guessed I had somebody posted to watch what they did," he concluded to Pasco. "So we might catch 'em still off guard if we move fast. Morgan's bunch have been kept posted, so they know there's warrants for 'em. They'll be watching for a posse and not expecting it to show up just yet."

"I weesh we had one," Pasco said.

"Me, too. But they're wanted men, and we've got a legal authority to make citizens' arrrests."

"If they weel hold steel while we do it," Pasco agreed.

Luke knew that the chances were slim of taking men so desperate without a fight, but he hadn't come there to shoot them from hiding and turn their bodies over to the law. He knew that Pasco entertained no such bloodthirsty ideas himself. He walked to his horse, got out his gun and belt and buckled it on. Then he tightened the cinch and rose to the saddle.

They first had to make sure the Holladays had returned to their ranch, for the two had incriminated themselves to the point where they would pitch into a fight. What he and Pasco did after that depended on the unfolding of events, once they had been put in motion. "I tell you one theeng," Pasco commented while they rode down from the landmark. "It was the very bad winter for Cleent Morgan and his *amigos*. They look like the mean, hungry *lobos*."

Luke could agree that the long-lasting cold spell must have been punishing to men forced to live in old Indian lodges without an Indian's craft and inurement. It aroused no pity in him, only an awareness that it would have made them the more vicious.

Chapter 14

Pasco spoke in a soft whisper. "They are losing no time, *amigo*. They are feeguring to move the camp."

Luke nodded his head. They had worked their way in above the main canyon in time to see Chuck and Blackie Holladay whip by below them, going down to their horse outfit. They were riding too fast to be through with their errand, so he and Pasco had crossed the canyon behind them and moved down to the elbow where they could see what happened next at the ranch. Pasco had made a good guess, for the brothers had roped more horses from the corrals, cinching riding saddles on three of them. Now they were putting pack saddles on two more.

"I guess they went up to see what Morgan wanted to do about me poking around," Luke answered. "Which was to clear out *pronto* from the looks of it. Two pack horses. They must have accumulated quite a camp."

"*Puede ser* it ees the arsenal, and that ees why they have the big eetch to move."

That made sense to Luke, but what to do about it stumped him. It was lucky they had checked, for if they had tried to jump the hideout in their haste, the Holladays would have come boiling in on top of them. Now it looked like they would have to try to dog Morgan and not lose track of him, and there were a lot of uncertainties involved in that.

Yet there was another chance, so daring and dangerous Luke rubbed his jaw while he considered it. All at once he said decisively, "Supposing you and I take that horse string in to Morgan."

"You mean — ?" Pasco's eyes flashed. "*Amigo*, that ees the teecket."

The horses below them were ready to travel, and one of the brothers had gone into the shack. The other Holladay had mounted and, at the distance, appeared to be rolling a cigarette. They didn't seem jumpy about anything at the moment except getting Morgan and his cronies moved out of reach. Luke and Pasco worked back to their own hidden mounts and swung to saddle.

They didn't descend into the canyon until it had pinched in. When they reached the floor, they dismounted, left their horses and worked back to where a jog gave them a chance to hide themselves. Pasco's eyes were glittering, but there was tension in his face, and Luke felt its counterpart in his own. The sun had climbed by then and was on their hind quarter. There was no wind in the canyon, and the deep quiet let them hear the warning fall of hoofs coming on at a less rushing gait than when the brothers went down.

The sound loudened, but neither of the waiting men moved a muscle until the two sullen-looking horse dealers came around the jog into sight, each leading a short string of horses. There was a rifle in Chuck Holladay's saddle boot, while Blackie wore a holstered pistol. They both grabbed for their weapons when they saw the waiting men ahead of them.

"Don't try it," Luke's rapping voice warned.

Their eyes glued to the pistols in his hand and Pasco's, and both straightened and let their arms go slack, the horses stopped.

"I might've known," Blackie said bitterly, while Chuck growled, "Told you I should've drilled the snoop when I had my sights on him."

"Save your breath," Luke suggested, "and get down from those horses."

Truculence and common sense warred in the pair for a breath or two longer. They were too far away from the hideout for shouts to carry, but the sound of shots might do so, if they wanted to risk dying to warn Morgan. They glanced at each other bitterly and then swung to the ground, stepping away from their mounts in obedience to a motion from Luke's gun. Pasco moved in behind Blackie, then, and plucked the pistol from the man's holster. That took the last fight out of the Holladays, but it didn't remove the mean temper from their eyes.

"Tie 'em up," Luke said.

Pasco did a good job of it, using the brothers' catch ropes and binding them like bedrolls, hands behind and ankles cinched together. He gagged them with their dirty bandanas, then Luke helped drag them behind a boulder so some stray traveler using the canyon wouldn't stumble onto them.

Afterward they rode their own horses until they came to the side canyon that Pasco watched for, the other horses led behind them. At the juncture they switched to the Holladay horses and left their own.

They were grim-faced and steady-moving, for from Pasco's earlier description, the springs and abandoned Indian camp were only a little way in. Hesitation or the look of stealth now could be their undoing.

Luke had nothing but Pasco's glance to warn him when they reached the last crook in a by then very narrow canyon. A moment later the stricture widened out, and ahead he saw a stand of budding trees around the springs, and beyond that the broken outlines of several old lodges. No smoke came from them for their users were too experienced to show it in daylight. And then a voice over there bawled without alarm, "They're back, Clint! You set?"

Luke knew that was as far as dupery would carry them and drawing a slow breath, let his hand drop to the grips of his gun. For another moment the trees would obscure without completely hiding them, and then everything would be in the open. He caught a glimpse of the man who had yelled, a figure remembered from a night that now seemed ages past. If the other two were outside the lodges, he didn't locate them, but there was stuff on the ground they were getting ready to pack out. He nodded to Pasco, and they stopped, swung down and ran forward with drawn guns.

The Nevadan, not wholly alerted until he saw armed men right upon him, looked up from a pack he was tying and blurted, "Holy Christ — it ain't them!"

"Hold it!" Luke shouted. "Move and you're dead!"

Pasco shot and, whirling, Luke saw why. The Nevadan's outburst had drawn the other two to a lodge flap, and they boiled out, grabbing for their guns. Morgan was in the rear, a bearded and wild-looking man, and Pasco's shot had hit the other, spun and knocked him down. Morgan, his gun still half-holstered, made a dive for Pasco, and Luke swung back just in time to fire at the first man, who had managed to clear his gun. This one jerked, stumbled backward and landed on his rump, the weapon dropping from loosened fingers. Luke kicked the gun out of his reach and wheeled to see Morgan shove up from a prone Pasco and bolt for the cover of the trees. Luke aimed at a leg and shot, and Morgan pitched forward. Luke swooped in and got his gun.

Pasco shoved up, shook his head groggily, then sprang to his feet. "Son of a beetch!" he panted. "He has the mule hoofs for feets!"

"He's not doing so good now."

It was over, but Luke knew it would have been a bloody thing had they not got somewhat on top of unsuspecting men before it erupted. As it was, none of the three had given up until knocked out of the fight. Pasco's first shot had broken the wrist of the man who had come out of the lodge ahead of Morgan. Luke's slug had torn through the shoulder of the other Nevadan. Clint Morgan lay cursing steadily, a bullet through the thigh.

"You're lucky," Luke rapped, standing over him. "We could have picked you off like pond ducks from that ridge over there. But you're going to Walla Walla for trial, and your horsey friends are going along. First, though, we'll have a look at your precious packs."

Morgan glowered and muttered something unintelligible, but whatever hope he had entertained of rescue by the Holladays was gone. Pasco had herded the other two over, for they still had sound legs, and he kept his gun on them while Luke opened one of the packs. There were four of these, wrapped in canvas and ready to be moved, and from their shape he expected to find firearms enough to arm a large gang.

He opened the packs one by one, and

they all held track tools: crowbars, sledges, chisels and still more crowbars enough to equip a good-sized demolition crew. Which had been the use intended for them, Luke realized, and why Morgan had hoped to take them along. They might have been stolen from Truax's construction camp, but it was more probable that they had been smuggled in from outside.

Luke felt a grim gratitude for the hunch that had caused him to make this surprise move against Morgan, for if he hadn't already been justified, this alone was sufficient. A dozen well-equipped men, riding at night, could tear up literally miles of track impossible to guard. They could wreck a train by the simple means of removing a rail that might not be seen in time by the engineer. They could have plagued the railroad with such tactics until keeping a schedule would have become impossible, with proportionate benefit of the teamsters.

Nan had known about this, at least the essential details, and had been moved to warn him. There was much he held against her, but for that he was grateful. Going back to stand over Morgan, he said, "You better answer me straight. Was Lawson Keel backing you in this?"

"Who's Keel?" Morgan said sullenly.

"All right. Maybe they can get it out of you at your trial."

"Take me in," Morgan taunted. "They can't draw a jury in this entire country that won't turn me loose." That could be true, but before he could be freed, the railroad fight might be over. "Anyway, you busted my leg," Morgan went on. "How you figure to get me to Walla Walla?"

"Your leg isn't broken. And you can ride unless you'd rather be dragged at the end of a rope."

Luke retied the packs which, while not overly large, made a heavy load for the two pack horses. Morgan had decided not to feign helplessness, maybe in hope of a break somewhere down the line. He had trouble getting into the saddle but made it, and the other two mounted. Carrying Chuck Holladay's rifle, Luke rode behind them, Pasco following with the pack horses. They stopped for the horses they had left at the canyon junction, then picked up the brothers on down the main canyon.

By the time they reached the horse ranch, gunshot reaction had hit Morgan, and he was in genuine distress. The other two wounded men were in better shape, but subdued and tractable. It was different with the Holladays, who not only would escape if they could but would free the others. So Luke put down a human desire to stop at the ranch with them while Pasco went on to get help. It wasn't much more of a ride to the railroad, which he figured they could reach before the train came down from the upper valley.

They barely made it in time to flag the train down, and while this gave Luke and Pasco a few anxious moments, it saved them from a long wait with desperate men beside the track. They turned the horses loose, then, and two hours later were in Wallula Landing with their captives.

But Luke had no intention of trying to hold his prisoners in a town as prone as the horse dealers were to try to turn them loose. The wounded were given medical attention, and that night the WW&CR ran its first special train to the end of track. This consisted of a locomotive and the passenger coach that carried the prisoners and heavy guard drawn from the Slabtown sawmill. It was without triumph but with considerable relief that Luke turned the five men over to the federal officer, who had been unable to catch them. But the warrants were still good, and the marshal was conscientious, and as soon as the men were booked, Luke and Pasco washed their hands of them.

On the sidewalk with Pasco afterward, a town around them that hadn't yet awakened to the new day, Luke dropped a hand on the other's shoulder. "You're working yourself out of a job, *amigo*," he said. "If the railroad's finished, there'll be no need for stages. Or a driver."

"Maybe I go inland," Pasco said with a shrug. "There ees always the job for the good wheepman."

"There's always a job for a good man right here," Luke told him. "And you're too damned good a one to lose."

"You make me a conductor?" Pasco said with interest. "That ees, eef there is more than one train?"

"Better than that," Luke said. "I'm getting to need an assistant. If things go right, I'll have to have him. If you're interested, I think Doc would agree to it."

"Me?" Pasco said, astonished. "Who don't know the *frijoles* about much of anytheeng?"

"What you don't know we can get along without," Luke said with a laugh. "You're *mucho hombre*, and that's what this line'll always have to run on."

Pasco had had one partial night's sleep, another night without any, and went off to his hotel to catch up. Although Luke was also behind, he was too wound up to want to go to bed, and by then daybreak wasn't far off. He walked out to the freight yard, let himself into the office and lighted a lamp. He sat down at his desk, thinking to look over the accumulated work, and was there fast asleep when Sherry arrived.

His first awareness of her, however, was of a hand gently stroking his hair. When he opened his eyes, she was standing there above him, a look of tenderness on her face he had never seen in another woman.

"You're all right," she said quietly. "I worried about you."

Tripp and Baker were the only ones Pasco had told of the plan, but he realized Tripp had told her or she had wormed it out of him. He smiled up at her, moved as he couldn't remember being in his life, and then she got hold of herself and stepped away.

"How'd it go?" she asked in a more matter-of-fact voice.

"They're over town in jail."

"Really?"

It had long been there in his heart, and he had just never let it form into a deliberate thought. He loved her. He wanted her. By his side, at his table, in his bed. But all he had a right to was satisfy her superficially by explaining what had happened in the highlands. She listened with interest, and he knew she had a deep pride in him that he had denied her the right to express. Then Tripp came in from the barn and wanted it told all over again, and a very rare moment was gone.

"Think there'll be a blacklash?" he asked Tripp. "We weren't law officers, after all."

"There could be," Tripp admitted. "In Keel's crowd for sure. Them three men were shot up, and you weren't touched, and they'll distort and lie about how you did it. Just the same, you smelled a rat and nipped it in the bud none too soon."

"And there's news for you, too," Sherry put in. "Newall Truax's starting to lay track this morning."

"No fooling?" Luke asked.

"There won't be much laid at a time," Tripp said. "And till the whole thing's finished, Whitman'll stay at the end of track because of the storage problem. But I'm sure hankerin' to hear 'em pounding spikes right outside these windows."

Luke rolled a cigarette, wondering if that day could now come. The June 1st target date was right on top of them. It wasn't the physical work that made it uncertain, for that could be done in the remaining time. The question was the money to pay for it concurrently, as Baker insisted. The construction outfit ate it up in giant gulps, and revenue had made no staggering contributions to the treasury.

Chapter 15

When somebody suggested dedication ceremonies and a celebration and perhaps an excursion train from Wallula Landing carrying dignitaries primed for oratory, Dorsey Baker only emitted a snort. "The line isn't finished by a damned sight and won't be till we've got iron rails and sidings and turntables and better trains. We'll think about fuss and feathers when it is."

So it was just another day, and a warm one in the first week of June. But, since it would see the first train ever to come into Walla Walla City, a good part of the town was at the depot and strung out along the new wooden track that stretched down to Mill Creek, crossed on the new trestle, and then swept west to Whitman Station that as of that day would be demoted to a way point. The occasion had kindled an excitement that got into the blood even of those who had declared so often that the day would never come.

218

And it nearly hadn't come, for everyone knew that the doctor had been forced to dig to the bottom of his depleted personal resources to finish the last two miles of track. Yet it was now finished, and only a week past the date he had set six months before. It was still a question how much life would be pumped into the WW&CR by the achievement of through service. The summer shipping season was on. Merchants of that and the inland town, thinly threatened by the farmers, were throwing their shipping more and more to the teamsters. The smell of monopoly was in the air again, stronger than before.

It was two-seventeen that June afternoon when a town lad who had shinnied up a tree west of the track let out a whoop and holler. "There she is, comin' round the bend — just look at the smoke pourin' outta her."

In spite of Baker's scorn of ceremonies, there were special gratifications to the occasion for those who had contributed so much to bring it about. With track and trestle materials all cut and stored at the end of track for Truax, Baker had put the Slabtown sawmill to producing plain lumber for sale in Walla Walla City. Every spare flatcar had been loaded with lumber, and every boxcar owned by the company had been coupled into the consist, even if there was no freight behind its closed doors. In consequence it was the longest train ever that came curling around the bend south of town behind the puffing little *Wallula* and *Walla Walla City.*

The freight office in town had been enlarged to include a passenger depot, and there, waiting for the train to come in, were Dorsey Baker, John Boyer and Newall Truax. Bill Green and Frank were on the train, for the doctor had set up a directors' meeting for later in the afternoon. Waiting there, too, with Pasco, Tripp and Sherry, Luke was curious about that meeting. In January, after the stock meeting that had failed him so miserably, the doctor had hinted at a plan to help tie up the next wheat haul. Considering the increasing bitterness of the farmers, the plan would have to be near-magic, and Luke had an idea that Baker was about to explain it.

But at the moment he and those with him were drawn by the train that had now come into view far down the track. While they watched, steam jetted up from the two locomotives, broke itself and jetted again; and seconds later the deep, thrilling sound of whistles rolled over the town. Luke turned his head to see that Sherry was looking at him with a smile as deep and wonderful as if the railroad was a baby newborn to them. He grinned back, for that was the way he felt himself.

Moving closer, he said quietly, "I'd give a pretty to know what's going on behind that poker face of Doc's. "

"Nothing sentimental," Sherry said. "He despises that."

"And nothing vengeful. He despises that worse."

She nodded her head.

A moment later she caught her skirts as they were whipped by the wind from the engines and first cars rolling past, now at slack steam and coasting in to a stop. The engineers pulled their bell cords and tried not to look proud of themselves, and trainmen worked hand brakes along the consist. Bill Green stood on the passenger-coach steps and didn't give a hang who saw him looking proud. He dropped down when the train stopped, Frank behind him. There was a rash of handshaking, and the big event had happened. The trainmen broke the consist to switch the flats of lumber onto the line's first siding and pre-pare for the return trip. But most of the reception party drawn from the town hung around. The scene was too novel, no matter what their partisan feelings, to leave as yet.

Baker led the way to the privacy of the freight office for his meeting, telling Luke and the Yales to come along, for they needed to hear what he was going to say. The only formality was that the doctor faced the others, who stood around the office, keyed-up and waiting. For a moment he only stood listening to the chuffing of the locomotives doing their switching, a new sound in Walla Walla City. Luke knew it pleased him, for there was a gleam of satisfaction in his eyes.

Then he let his gaze flick one by one over Boyer and Frank, Green and Truax. "This won't take long," he told them then. "I intend today to announce a reduction in the rate on general freight, effective immediately. And for wheat, once its started moving. As president and general manager, I have the authority to do this, but I'd like your approval first."

"A cut?" John Boyer stared at him. As company treasurer, he was immediately concerned about the added time a reduction in rates would require to fill the coffers to a safe level. "Why on earth should we do that?"

"To end this talk about a monopoly," Green answered. His grin showed he liked the idea.

"The devil with their talk," Baker said impatiently. "As it stands, they're only paying half what they used to pay, thanks to the railroad. And that didn't stop the monopoly talk. This time we'll only come down a dollar a ton — from six to five. I know from our own wagon-freighting costs that the teamsters can't meet that and stay in business."

"Dorsey," Boyer said sharply. "Have you considered the effect on public opinion? Why, it'll seem to prove everything they've said about you. That you'll run the wagons off the road and then hike the rates to the sky."

Baker's cool eyes stared at him. "Since that isn't my intention, John, I don't see why we should pay any attention to their drivel. We simply must have the business we're entitled to after the investment we've made in this basin. For one thing, unless we become a going concern immediately, the steamboat people are more than apt to build the line they're talking about and run us and the wagons both out of business."

"That's right," Truax agreed. He was plainly in sympathy with Baker, and so was

Green and, Luke thought, probably Frank. "Then let 'em find out what a real freight monopoly's like."

"Just the same, it would backfire," Boyer said doggedly. "All this country would see would be us putting the final kibosh on the wagons. The mean-old-big-us and poor-little-them business, with the greedy-old-Doc Baker bugaboo thrown in."

"It isn't us running the wagons out of business," Baker said with tired patience. "It's progress that's doing it. If we get business in volume, we can haul their freight for five dollars a ton and still turn a handsome profit. When we're in a sound financial position and have the line improved and equipped as it must be, we can come down even lower. What right have the wagons to interfere with a public benefit like that?"

"None," Boyer admitted. He looked at Baker sadly, an astute man with a finger more sensitive to the public pulse than the doctor's. He glanced at the others. "Anyhow, it's four to one. I could be wrong, and I hope to hell I am."

"Good." Baker made his thin smile, finally. He glanced at the other directors. "Is he right about you gentlemen?"

They all nodded their heads.

Luke noticed that Sherry was frowning. She sided with Boyer, and he did himself. On the other hand the urgency that influenced the others was real and powerful.

"I'll make it unanimous," Boyer said, "for the sake of solidarity."

Baker gave him a glance that had much in it of the years they had lived and worked together. Then his thin, nervous fingers opened the folder he had placed on the desk by his side. "I have posters here that I had printed and sent up from Portland so it wouldn't leak out prematurely. Tripp, supposing you tack one outside the depot and a few more around town. I'll give the rest to Sam Dunbow for the way stations and Wallula." He rose to his feet. "Thank you, gentlemen. That's all I had to talk to you about."

Five minutes later Luke was seated at his desk, alone in the room with Sherry. She was troubled and preoccupied, and after a long moment she looked at him.

"Mr. Boyer is absolutely right. It'll backfire. Why run the wagons out of business deliberately? Why not let them fall by the wayside?"

"Well, it's the pressure of necessity," Luke said. "There's the steamboat company's talk of their own railroad. The orders Doe's placed for equipment to improve ours. The five or six months of heavy business before the slack season comes around again."

"I know that. And that future rates won't be blood-sucking, but lower yet. Others'll know it, too, but for every one who does, two more won't. They'll listen to people like Lawson Keel. And I do wish the doctor would listen more than he ever has to Mr. Boyer."

"That's his blind spot," Luke reflected. "He can't see the effect of what he does and says — and even what he is — on the common run of people. Green said that once in connection with raising money, and Frank and Truax agreed. I'm surprised they went along whole hog today."

"I suppose their patience with public stupidity's worn out," Sherry said with a sigh. "Anyway I've got no business shooting off my mouth. I'm just a freight clerk."

Luke heard a hammering and knew that one of the announcements was going up to usher in whatever it would. His mind ran back over the troubles he had had to meet, the latest being his and Pasco's capture of the Morgan gang. The five outlaws were still in jail, for while they had been indicted, they had to wait until the next court session for trial. But there were plenty of their kind left among the teamsters who would now find themselves with their backs really shoved to the wall, for it seemed impossible that the shippers would patronize a slower, demonstrably less dependable service and pay a dollar a ton more in the bargain.

Presently, at least, the sounds around the depot and the glimpses Luke caught through the windows bespoke a railroad humming with success. With the lumber cars cut out, the train was unloading general freight. Barney Lunt and Lafe Wells, who were starting a drayage business now that their wagons would no longer run out to Whitman, were loading such freight as was to be distributed in the town. There was a fair load to go down with the train and a respectable number of passengers.

A little after three o'clock the train left for the down run. Its time had been improved in recent months, the light run down taking only a little over five hours. The train would be in Wallula Landing, Luke knew, before nightfall. And with iron track the run would be reduced even more, and then even the fast stages would be left far back in the dust.

Tripp was doubling as freight and passenger agent now that there were no company horses and wagons requiring his care. With the day's train off his hands, he came in to tell Luke how the posters he had put around town had been received.

"People I seen read 'em looked surprised," he said. "If they're gonna take it the way John Boyer believes, they ain't had time to get started yet. But there was some Browder wagons unloading at Keel's store. I went down there to make sure one of the posters was where the farmers'd see it. But the teamsters had already heard about it, and the things they yelled at me would curl a mule's ears."

"Sticks and stones, Tripp," Luke reminded him.

"They'd have got around to them, too, if I hadn't cleared outta there fast."

By the time Luke knocked off for the day and walked the long main street to his hotel, the town had had time to digest the new development and start to form opinions. The excitement and leniency created by the actual arrival of a train in the town had given way to the old sullen suspicion with which those he met on the sidewalk regarded him. Since the farmers had finished their trading and started home, these were mainly townspeople not directly subject to Lawson Keel's influence. If Dorsey Baker, having achieved his through track, had raised the freight rate or left it where it was, they would have regarded it as natural. Now they were looking for the hook in his generosity and convincing themselves they had found it.

Luke had eaten his supper in the hotel dining room and was crossing the lobby toward the street when a man idling at the cigar stand turned to him and said, "Evening, Preston. You in a rush?"

Luke halted to look at him, seeing a portly man in a sack suit and derby hat. His face looked familiar, and then Luke placed him as Dan Clark, a drummer from some wholesale grocery house in Portland who had come up on the train a few days earlier.

"Not to speak of, Clark," Luke admitted. "How are you?"

"Middling. How about me standing you to a drink?"

Luke hesitated, not wanting to get tied up with a convivial soul trying to escape a lonely evening. But the drummer didn't strike him as having that in mind, so he said, "I reckon I could take time for that."

They were seated in the hotel bar, which

was nearly empty, with whiskey before them, and the drummer had lighted one of the cigars he had just bought before he got around to what was on his mind.

"No names," he said finally, "but I was talking to a friend of yours about an hour ago who wouldn't figure it was smart to be seen talking to you right now himself."

"A merchant?" Luke asked.

Clark nodded and took the cigar from his lips. "Not the biggest frog in the pond and not the littlest. I been calling on him so long we're pretty good friends. So I know he bought himself some railroad stock a while back, and he's given you his shipping business so far. But he don't think he can keep it up much longer."

"He don't want to or won't be able to?" Luke pressed.

"They won't let him. What got him talking was that rate-reduction notice that went up this afternoon. It ought to have pleased him. Instead it scared the hell out of him."

"He's not the only businessman who bought stock, and there's many another who leans our way," Luke said irritably. "I understand the pressure they're under from the farmers. But they stood up to be counted at the stock meeting last January.

Now that it's paid off in through service and a lower rate, it seems to me it's high time they stood up again, if for no other reason than to protect the money they put into it."

"It's not that simple," Clark said, and Luke knew he was in dead earnest. "In a day or two there's gonna be an indignation meeting here in town. To protect the country from this growing octopus — that's exactly the way it's being described."

"To organize a boycott, I suppose."

"That's not the way it's being put. The rumor is that merchants and farmers and every other kind of shipper will be asked to support the wagon freighters to keep them from being driven to the wall."

"At our rate or theirs?"

"Theirs. The wagons can't do business at your rate."

"Maybe the farmers'll pungle up a dollar a ton they don't have to," Luke retorted. "Somebody's got 'em eating out of his hand. But I can't see the merchants doing it except for one reason. To escape being boycotted, themselves."

"That's what they're being threatened with. It looks like Baker gave his enemies just what they've been looking for."

Luke nodded. "Well, thanks for the tip."

"Not that I know what you can do with it," Clark said. "There's no way the railroad can crawfish now and undo the effects. I sold Baker and Boyer when they were country storekeepers. I been for their railroad since the first spike. I've talked it not only in this town but in the others in the basin. Usually I get a feeling I been talking to a fence post."

"I wonder why that is."

"Dunno, unless it's easier for a man to fear something new than to put his faith in it."

Luke had never thought of it that way, and the idea interested him. The new was Dorsey Baker's specialty, if that was the reason so many were afraid of him. For a decade only an intrepid few had dared even to run cattle east of the Cascades because of the Indians, and Baker had been the first to do it in the Walla Walla. From that had grown its first home industry. He had given the valley its first store, its first bank, its first medical service. He had pioneered and changed the whole practice of wheat growing, and now it was becoming the main industry.

Chapter 16

The public indignation meeting was held three days after the first train reached the town, and it was fortunate for the indignant that the weather was dry and warm. No building in Walla Walla City would have held those bent on attending, so the city park had been selected, its bandstand to accommodate the speakers, the expanses of grass to serve the audience. When Luke left his hotel that evening farmers' rigs were strung the length of Main and overran into the side streets. The two blocks of the park were jammed. There was no telling how many of those gathered there were truly aroused, how many merely excited and curious and drawn by the occasion, but one thing was certain. The bulk of them would be receptive to rabble-rousing.

After his talk with Clark, Luke had warned Dorsey Baker of the likelihood of a general boycott, with those not enlisting wholeheartedly being intimidated into taking part. The doctor had dismissed it as he might have waved away a bothersome fly. "They can start one, maybe," he said contemptuously, "but they can't keep it going. It's too much against common sense."

"I know," Luke agreed. "But common sense is something this country hasn't been long on from the start."

Baker regarded him patiently. "What do you think I can do about it?"

"It's out of line for me to be telling you," Luke answered. "But it seems to me you ought to go to their meeting and demand a turn on the speakers' stand and work on what sense there is."

Baker shook his head. "I don't propose to dignify their meeting by so much as recognizing it. Nor would I look with favor on you, Boyer or anybody else in the company doing so. We've built them a railroad. We've given them a rate where, for the first time, wheat production can be really profitable to them. We won't humble ourselves with a public defense of our motives when that's all we ever wanted, talked about or did."

Luke could see Baker's point and how deeply his pride was involved. But the doctor had no more inkling than the general public of the chicanery of the man at the bottom of so many of his troubles and behind the present crisis. Only Luke Preston and Nan Browder were aware of that, and her husband was in a fight now just to stay in business. Nan might very well remain silent to protect him.

So for the second time Luke had gone to Keel's store and confronted the man in the balcony office. It was even harder than he expected, for with every breath he realized more poignantly the cost to himself if Keel stood his ground. There was Sherry now and his acknowledged love for her, as well as his involvement with the railroad and his natural desire to remain a free man. If there was any other way, he would take it, but the time had come when no other way was to be found.

He wasted no words on Keel, saying bluntly, "The last time I come here, you called it a shotgun standoff. If one of us pulled a trigger, we were both dead. What you didn't know and still don't is that I'll pull it if I have to. Which I will, unless you can see your way clear to drop this idea of a boycott against the railroad."

Keel leaned back in his desk chair. He had started shaking his head before Luke had finished talking, and he shook it again for emphasis. He was extremely pleased with himself and very confident.

"It's no longer a standoff," he said finally. "You can thank your doctor friend for changing it. Which his declaration of war on the wagon freighters certainly has. I haven't been sure of Nan, that she wouldn't do me in if she got the chance. But would she come to your rescue when helping you would contribute to her own husband's financial ruin?"

Luke shrugged, and Keel smiled.

"That's a trait of Nan's," Keel resumed. "No matter how she comes to feel about the men in her life, it's her instinct to be loyal. That's the least part of it, though. Without hope of clearing yourself, you're the only one in danger. I can refute what you can say against me if I don't have her to contend with." He leaned forward, his face going hard. "And what will the effect on Baker be if, at a crucial time like this, one of his most valued people turns out to be a swindler hiding from the law? Birds of feather flock together, you know. That's what the public will say. Make no mistake about it."

Luke realized that he had already erred in trying to force a showdown at that point. Correctly or otherwise, Keel was momentarily persuaded that Nan's loyalty to Browder had sealed her lips even more tightly than before. With that conviction he might be tempted to play his trump card, whether or not he needed it, because of the undeniable damage it would do to Baker. Certainly he would play it if his own reputation was threatened with victory almost in his grasp.

"Don't count on Nan," Luke returned. "She knows she owes a debt her conscience is crowding her hard to pay. I've more reason to figure she'd move my way if I called on her than you have to think she'd move yours. Helping me would ease her guilt. Helping you or even Browder through letting me really go to prison would add to it more than she could bear."

He knew he had scored, for uncertainty flickered in Keel's eyes. "All right," Keel said, after a moment. "It's still a standoff."

"Except for what I come here to say. I say it again. If there's no other way to stop you, I'll pull the trigger, regardless of consequences."

Luke turned and left.

So on the night of the indignation meeting Luke came onto the street knowing that his secret weapon against Keel was as neutralized for the time being as Keel's weapon against him. When he rounded a corner, he could hear shouting that, while he drew nearer the fringe of the crowd, turned into some leather-lunged orator already delivering himself of his sentiments. The speaker wasn't Keel, but Keel, Luke saw when he moved closer, was on the bandstand. So were a dozen other men from town and country who had openly supported Keel since the stock meeting.

Keel seemed to be letting the others whip up the emotional storm he was after, for the man speaking sat down and another rose and started the same kind of harangue. Luke recognized this one as Otto Schroder, who teamed out of Walla Walla City on the Dayton-Lewiston haul and wasn't even threatened by the rate reduction.

"Like you just heard Amos Buell say," Schroder bawled, "I ain't against progress when it's for everybody. But I sure as hellfire am when its just for the privileged few and is gonna cost the rest of us our bacon and beans. And that's what's gonna happen if we don't stick together now and put a stop to it. They're gonna run the wagons out of the valley, wagons that's done business here all these years. Then they're gonna build 'em a railroad to Lewiston and to Centerville and run the rest of us freighters out. Anybody need to be told what's gonna happen when there's only one way to ship anything and one way to travel in this country?"

A roar from the crowd attested that nobody needed to be told. The rest followed in the same frayed vein, with speaker after speaker working less to build antagonism toward the railroad, of which there was already plenty, than to enlist sympathy for the menaced teamsters. The response grew ever more noisy and impassioned, for it was the kind of stuff the crowd wanted to hear. When Keel finally spoke, he had the great mass of listeners in the palm of his hand.

"My friends —" he began and then had to wait for another outburst to die down. "I'll be brief since I know that many of you have a long way to travel to get back to your homes tonight. Homes, I might add, that will be safer if we stand together in this crisis. Which we must. The railroad proved itself to be a closed corporation when an effort was made to buy a controlling interest for the people. And now we have this added indication of the monopolistic mind, a freight war to drive the competition out of the valley. We must not let that happen —"

"Who says we're gonna?" somebody bawled, bringing on another uproar.

Keel waited for quiet. "We must not let ourselves be caught in a situation where there is only one public carrier in our valley. And that makes this our fight, even more than the wagon freighters'. We've got to support them wholeheartedly and completely, even if it costs us money we might save if we were blind enough, stupid enough, to fall for the railroad's bait. Because the wagoners simply can't operate at less than their present rates and stay in business, as someone I need not name knows very well."

The howl that followed seemed to shake the leaves of the trees in the park. Keel allowed himself a slight smile and held up his hands for silence.

"That's all, my friends, except for this. If you're not fooled by this sudden bigheartedness of the railroad's, prove it with your complete support of your real friends."

"Try proving otherwise," a voice near Luke muttered, "and see what happens."

Luke turned to see Dan Clark standing beside him with a pained expression on his plump face. Before he could answer, the crowd broke into a milling mass of enthusiastic and neatly gulled humanity. Luke and Clark walked away together.

"The people's friend," the drummer said, when it was quiet enough to talk. "That man'd go a long ways in politics."

"He's probably thinking about that," Luke admitted.

"I called on him the other day. I don't like him, but he's become the firm's best customer up here. He's getting rich just from the farm trade he's corraled by using stuff like we just seen, to the discomfort of my stomach. Pretending to be the great champion of their cause. And that's the only reason he does it. Just to corral their dollars, himself."

"There's more to it than that," Luke said, and told him about the stock meeting in January. "He's banking on the boycott forcing Baker to accept his terms so he can take over the railroad himself."

Clark looked at him. "How'd you know that?"

Luke couldn't answer except to say, "Does it make sense?"

"It sure does."

"And it's something you can point out to your merchant friends. That they ought to be looking at both sides of the coin."

"I will."

The drummer had been given a new insight, and Luke hoped he could do some good with it.

They stepped into a bar for a drink, and then Luke took leave of Clark. By then the dispersing crowd had sifted along the street, many of them to claim their rigs and start home. He was used to their suspicion and hostility, but the gloating that had been added was hard to take. Yet he kept his temper in check and tried to remember that they had been told the same thing so many times, in so many ways, it had become unquestioned fact to them.

The lobby of his hotel was still deserted except for a lone figure seated in one of the chairs under lamps arranged for reading. The man had a copy of the *Washington Statesman* opened in front of him, but Luke saw enough to recognize him and wonder how he had got there without creating even more of a hubbub than the town was in.

He had started for the stairs, but he changed direction, saying, "Hello, Captain. You come up for the indignation meeting?"

John Ainsworth looked up at him, then dropped the paper into an adjoining chair and rose with an extended hand. "I was a trifle late for that," he said with a smile. "How are you, Preston?"

"Fit but puzzled," Luke told him. "You never come up on the train."

Ainsworth was a spare man with an open, amiable face that gave little hint of his power on the Columbia and Willamette Rivers and the driving inner forces that had built up the huge Oregon Steam. A boat captain himself, Luke knew, he had come West with the gold rush to California and for a while had plied the waters of the Sacramento and San Joaquin. Those placid rivers had been too tame for him, and he had come north to the white-water country in time to get in on its gold stampedes and make himself a tycoon.

He liked to tease and said with a smile, "The train? No. They told me in Wallula it was taking my life in my hands. So I hired an old-fashioned horse and got in too late, more's the pity, for the meeting."

Looking into the twinkling eyes, Luke knew Ainsworth had deliberately avoided showing himself in town before the meeting, which might have driven the local citizens into the railroad's arms out of fear of his intentions. He often visited Wallula and went on up to Lewiston, but he rarely ventured inland from the river. Luke thought the night's meeting had something to do with this visit. He couldn't forget that for some six months the OSN seemed to have been waiting to see how the little WW&CR made out before it decided whether to build its own line into the interior.

"How was the meeting?" Ainsworth continued. "Did they go after Dorsey Baker's scalp?"

"He hardly got mentioned," Luke said. "They were too busy bleeding for the wagon outfits he's trying to run out of business. You're apt to undo that, when word gets around you're in town. Most of 'em think that beside you Doc Baker looks like a philanthropist."

Ainsworth laughed. It was his pride rather than embarrassment that he had smashed competition ruthlessly until there were no boats on the river but OSN boats and no portages at the rapids but OSN portages. And, with that accomplished, that he had proceeded to make himself and a handful of associates into enormously rich men.

"Sorry I can't help you out that way," he said, "but I'm heading on for Lewiston in the morning."

"Surveying a railroad on the way?" Luke asked.

Ainsworth glanced at him sharply, surprised at the blunt question. "I just haven't made the overland trip in years. I thought I'd enjoy it." They were attracting attention now. Others had come back to the hotel and, recognizing the bigwig from Portland, some of them had tried to edge close enough to eavesdrop. Aware of that, the captain held out his hand. "Riding's hard on a man used to a deck under his boots, and I'm ready for bed. If I don't see Doc before I leave in the morning, give him my best regards."

"Sure will," Luke promised.

He changed his mind about going up to his room and walked across the lobby and into the bar, reflecting on the odd fact that Baker and Ainsworth really were friends. That, however, wouldn't give John Ainsworth a moment's pause if he chose to build a railroad that would, because of the money behind it, seal the doom of Baker's. He would expect Baker to treat him the same way, whether or not the doctor was capable of it.

Yet Ainsworth had been known to do enormous, unsolicited and sometimes sentimental favors, which he might have done

Baker unwittingly just by passing through Walla Walla City at that particular time. He seemed to have vanished up the stairs, for talk broke out in the lobby that, nursing a nightcap, Luke could hear.

"When John Ainsworth gets saddle sores for the fun of it," a man said gustily, "the fish'll start traveling by trail."

"He's checkin' out a railroad route," another answered. "No matter what he said. The talk's always been they'll come clean up from Portland and go plumb on to Lewiston. Where'll we be with them squeezers ownin' both boats and trains?"

Luke was glad he had asked Ainsworth that impertinent question, which the pair in the lobby must have overheard. It had come from his own concern, which he still felt. Yet if Ainsworth had answered truthfully, it could be an accidental boost that the WW&CR needed desperately.

Whatever Ainsworth's real purpose, he did go on early the next morning, leaving behind him a puzzled and uncertain town. Tripp Yale had heard of the visit by the time Luke reached the depot that day and, like Luke, didn't know whether to be pleased or frightened. "It's gonna make a lot of people think twice," he said, "about lettin' themselves be hounded into joining the boycott. On the other hand —" He broke off and shrugged.

Luke knew what he was thinking. Weathering the boycott would do little good if an outfit as powerful and well-heeled as the OSN moved in.

Even Dorsey Baker, who knew the OSN head better than anyone else in town, was puzzled. He, too, had heard that the man had passed mysteriously through the town and that Luke had been seen talking with him, so he came by the depot on his way to the bank.

"Well, he said to give you his best regards," Luke reported. "Asked if they lifted your scalp at the meeting, said he was making the overland ride for the fun of it, and that's it. What do you make of it?"

"I think," Baker said with his fleet smile, "that it's best not to look a gift horse in the mouth."

"You think he was only giving you a boost?"

"It's the kind of thing he'd do, just like he'd cut me down if that suited his purposes." Baker shook his head. "I don't know to this day whether he's actually thinking of an OSN railroad or only told me that he was to scare me and this country into completing our line. After all, the steamboats will profit if wheat started to move out of here in real volume."

"I hope that's it," Luke said fervently.

"So do I. But we'd be fools to count on it."

Chapter 17

Within a fortnight of the indignation meeting, even Lawson Keel knew that Ainsworth's mere passage through the country had taken much of the steam out of the boycott movement. There had been no opportunity to pin down the captain on his return trip, as everyone hoped to do. Ainsworth took the boat at Lewiston and went back to Portland by water. The questions he had raised went unanswered except as answers were supplied by local conjecture. None of the speculations accepted the idea of the steamboat man making a long horseback ride for pleasure, no matter what he had claimed.

And such thinking caused a great many second thoughts.

While the farmers remained in complete support of Keel, their only present use to him was as a weapon to use on the merchants. They themselves would have nothing to ship until after the harvest. The payloads until then were made up of merchandise almost entirely, inbound to storekeepers not only of Walla Walla City but those throughout the basin and on to the Lewiston country, and of a reverse flow of express, mail and miscellaneous freight from the same places.

With this traffic fanning out from the new railhead or concentrating there downbound, the whole region had a vital interest in the showdown on the main stem from Walla Walla City to Wallula Landing. There had already been a wagon service of sufficient size to handle it. Now there was a through railroad also of sufficient carrying capacity, and there simply wasn't business enough for both services to prosper. In consequence the business element, which was still the year-round backbone of the country, belatedly got down to cases about its own situation.

Back when the wagoners had exercised their own monopoly, it could remember, they and the steamboat company had cheerfully enforced rates twice what the WW&CR had brought them down to. This began to dilute the sympathy whipped up for the teamsters, now that they had become the underdogs. Moreover, the projected OSN line, if built, would certainly put the wagoners out of business, anyway. And merchants farther inland, where wheat growing wasn't yet so extensive, didn't need to wince too much at the prospect of a farmers' boycott of their own businesses.

The upshot was that June ended with the WW&CR holding its own in the inland business and still getting a fair share of the local patronage. Revenue was sufficient for Newall Truax to construct turntables at each end of the line and a siding to facilitate loading and unloading at Wallula. He and Luke went over every foot of track, marking places roughed up by settling or wear so they could be smoothed out and the running time speeded up even more. Luke's goal was a three-hour trip each way, although that might have to wait for iron track and heavier locomotives. And he was as anxious as Dorsey Baker to have sidings at all the way stations before the wheat harvest was ready to move. That would permit cars to be spotted for loading directly from the farm wagons, saving time and expense.

And then news came from Portland that made the nip-and-tuck situation intolerable to both sides in the fight. Baker's huge order for T-iron and rolling stock had gone east over the transcontinental from California, and the same carrier had brought the shipment west to San Francisco. Now the first of it had reached Portland by ship from San Francisco, with the rest to follow shortly. The speed surprised everyone, for before the Union and California Pacific systems came into being, only a few years earlier, such a shipment would not have arrived under six months to a year. It showed what a railroad could do.

Dorsey Baker was both pleased and worried. "I've wondered ever since I placed that order," he told Luke, "whether it was a smart move or a ruinous one. We'll get a chance to find out now. If we can be ready to haul the harvest on a sound iron track, we can show the same kind of speed ourselves."

"You don't know how I've waited for the day, Doc." Luke was seeing the Wallula wharfboats swamped with sacked wheat, with more piled for a mile along the river bank. "And the new Porter-Bell engine."

"We'll call her the *Columbia*," Baker said. "She's a six-wheel switcher with small drivers and weight enough to grip the track and walk off with the longest train we'll ever need to pull." Then, as if embarrassed by his rare extravagance, he frowned. "But there are problems."

"Like paying for it?" Luke said, grinning.

Baker smiled ruefully. "That problem's an old friend of ours, isn't it? John Boyer's been putting money aside from revenue to pay for the order, which is due thirty days after delivery. Lumber sales have been good, and we've credited that to the railroad account, too. Probably we can squeeze it out, even though the stuff's arrived sooner than we expected. But laying the new track — well, that'll cost as much again."

"Can't you ask the eastern suppliers for extra time?"

"An unpaid bill's a debt as much as one created by borrowing money." Baker shook his grizzled head, as if against some subversive temptation in his own mind. "No. The order must be paid for, even if the track laying has to wait. There'll be a whopping freight bill, besides."

It was that aspect, specifically the final haul from Portland to Wallula Landing, that interested Walla Walla City, itself. Tripp expressed the general feeling. "It's gonna smoke out John Ainsworth," he told Luke. "If he really wants his own railroad, he won't be in a sweat to get that track and new machinery up to Wallula. He could let it hang up at the portages and go astray all along the river and even put a freight bill on it that'd break Doc's back. It'd be easy for him to tie us up till too late to haul the harvest on iron. And if he stops us from that, he don't intend to let us haul any harvest any year."

Luke agreed. "But what Ainsworth does might not settle whether we can lay the new track. Truax told me the work itself won't take too long. It's only a matter of taking up the old rails and putting down new, starting at Wallula and working east. It won't even hold up the trains enough to count, with every mile of iron track meaning that much faster time. The trouble's what it's always been — the wherewithal."

"I'm gettin' so I hate that word," Tripp said.

"It'll sure get a fraying," Luke said with a grin, "if they ever write the history of the WW&CR. Building a railroad out of revenue's undertaking enough. When you've got a good part of the country trying to cut off the revenue, it's almost too much. But that's what the track changeover'll have to come from. Even if we don't lose more ground, it'll take months."

Travelers coming up the river by boat

and going on by train or stage were the ones who ended the uncertainty Ainsworth had created in the interior. The railroad materials were moving eastward, these people reported, the light T-iron, car wheels and carriages, the new *Columbia*. Ainsworth hadn't stopped it, nor was he hurrying it, and it began flowing over the portages at the Cascades and Dalles City and finally, in mid-July, the *Chief* tied up at Wallula Landing groaning with a cargo of rails.

Rightly or wrongly, this was taken to mean that the OSN was shelving its own railroad. The impact was potent. With no colossus to fear, at least immediately, shippers who had supported the little WW&CR grudgingly and out of self-interest saw no further need to rise above their passions. Those who had lost farmer trade to merchants supporting the teamsters saw a definite need to recover it. This was most pronounced in Walla Walla City, where L. KEEL & COMPANY had about cornered the rural market.

Enheartened by this turn of the tide, teamsters on hauls to inland towns found a way to help their lower-country brothers by refusing to haul anything that hadn't arrived in Walla Walla City by wagon. Luke thought he knew who was behind that move, too, but charges would have done no good even if he had dared to make them. By the end of July the effect on the railroad was painfully evident, and Truax hadn't laid a rail of the new track piling up at the Slabtown yard.

Yet that wasn't the worst of the matter. Paying for the huge order, which Dorsey Baker would insist on punctually thirty days after the last piece was delivered, would leave the company strapped. The day when revenue fell below operating costs would be the day when, by the dictates of his own principles, Baker would either have to sell a controlling interest in the line or throw in the sponge.

With things going Keel's way again, Luke was surprised when one night he answered a rap on his hotel-room door to find Keel standing there in the hallway. The man was in good spirits and full of his old surface geniality. "Evening, Luke," he said with a smile. "This time it's me who's come to see you."

"What about?"

"Hadn't we better discuss that in your room?"

Luke had no choice but to step back and let Keel enter, then shut the door and muster the courtesy to tell him to take the room's one comfortable chair. Keel ignored the chair and stood looking around.

"So this is where you live your private life," he mused. "Not much comfort for a man of your years."

"It suits me."

Keel lifted an eyebrow. "It would be natural for you to be thinking of a home by now. A wife, children — all the joys and satisfactions of a settled man. I imagine you like women. And Sherry Yale's a very attractive one."

"Keep her out of this," Luke said angrily.

Keel laughed. "That's how I thought it was with you, and what would be more natural, all the time you've worked together? Luke, wouldn't you like to marry her?"

"What business is that of yours?"

"Wouldn't you call it my business when I can make it possible for you to have her and stop worrying about the past?"

"The only way you could do that," Luke growled, "would be to incriminate yourself."

"Oh, no." Keel drew something from the inside pocket of his coat. "All it takes for you to forget it is for me to forget it, too.

And burn this letter I've written to a mutual acquaintance back there. He's still sheriff, and he'd still like to get his hands on Wade Foster. All he needs is a tip where to look."

Luke's shoulders were high, and his eyes burned, for he knew this was going to be very bad. "Something seems to have made you confident of Nan Browder. What?"

Keel chuckled. "Let's just say that I'm no longer worried about her."

Some of the fire had gone out of Luke, for Keel was supremely confident. "What do you want of me, Lawson?" he asked.

"The Walla Walla & Columbia Railroad."

Luke snorted. "How can I give it to you?"

Keel sat down finally, his face turning serious at last. "I've told you more than once I can weather any attack you can make on me. But I'd rather avoid the need, if I can. You want to help make the railroad succeed. I know that. But even more than that, you want Sherry Yale. I saw it in your eyes when you flared up at me about her. I don't love women the way you do, Luke, all out and forever. But I understand your way. If you could have but one thing, I know it would be her."

"Damn you." Keel's understanding and skill at manipulating human feelings was still working fine. "Get to the point."

"All right. I'm worried about John Ainsworth. I felt from the start that he made that mysterious trip through here to foul up the boycott. He's a clever devil, and who knows what he's really up to?"

"He plays your game," Luke said. "With an important difference. He's wily and ruthless, but he's an honest man. He wouldn't betray a friend. He wouldn't lead people to trust him, then turn around and fleece them."

Keel's cheeks had paled. When forced to stop being amused and amusing about his vices and weaknesses, they seemed to trouble him. "I'm winning this fight," he said fiercely, "but not fast enough. I want control of that railroad before the wheat haul, and I don't want Ainsworth tangling my string. Just remember that Baker's finished no matter what you do. You'll only be putting him out of his misery a little sooner."

"How?"

"Slack off."

"I see. Let service get so bad that the railroad won't even tempt the shippers. That's still slow, Lawson."

"But faster than now," Keel snapped. "And fast enough when only that extra push is needed to put the line in the red. Don't think I don't understand Baker as well as you do. I've made a study of the man. The railroad hung up unfinished all that time because he refused to go into debt. So what will he do in a choice between giving up control and keeping his books in red ink?" Keel stood up then, again smiling and cynically amused. "And what will you do, Luke, in a choice between hastening the inevitable and going to prison?"

"It's a thin choice."

"The edge of the razor." Keel moved to the door and turned before he opened it, tapping his breast pocket. "I won't be in a hurry to mail this. On the other hand, I haven't much patience. Let me see results, Luke. Soon."

Luke stared at the door for a long moment after it had closed behind the man. There was an alternative that Keel hadn't mentioned and might not have thought of. That was simply to drop out of the picture at once, going far and covering his trail. He was rendering Baker a vital service by keeping the trains running smoothly and improving their time. But after the stages stopped running to Whitman Station, Baker had agreed to let him put Pasco on as his assistant. Pasco was handling the Wallula end of the job at present, but if need be, he could step in, and he had proved his effectiveness. Above all else, Pasco's hands wouldn't be tied.

The disappearance of a man so prominent in the railroad fight would create a mystery, giving rise to rumors that would in good part be malicious, but this would be less damaging to Baker than the arrest for swindle of one of his key men. Yet there would be those to whom such a mystery would be an unrelievable torment — Pasco, Tripp, the Bakers, Green, and above all Sherry. His pride wouldn't let him explain to them although he could trust them to keep his secret. Except maybe Sherry, who deserved to know why there could be nothing between them and to be given the means of curing herself of him. The others would have to supply their own answers — that he had met with foul play or even that he had sold out to the enemy.

The summer night was only then closing in on the town. The street, when Luke came out of the hotel, was lighted by the windows of saloons and stores that stayed open late at that season, the other hotels, the candy store, the saddlery — all the fronts he had come to know so well. The people he saw moving here and there seemed relaxed at day's end from the tensions that daylight engendered. It was basically a good, a friendly town, and one he had come to like much better than he had known. He turned the corner and went down to the livery barn where he kept his horse.

Riding in to the Yale homestead somewhat later, he was reminded of the dawn, now many months past, when he had come here after the fire at Slabtown, battered and bloody from his fight with Morgan. He thought with a regret like anguish of Sherry's concern for him, her gentle nursing, and then the blunt way he had given her to understand that he was in love with Nan Browder. It had stopped her from expecting anything, but it hadn't changed her feelings. He had only to remember the morning in the freight office, after he and Pasco had brought in the Morgan gang, when the feeling had stood so plainly on her face again.

The Yale house was dark, but it didn't mean that Tripp and Sherry had gone to bed, and Luke rode in to find them enjoying the cool of the early night in their yard. They were both liked and used to neighbors' dropping by and weren't surprised until they saw who the visitor was. They didn't know it wasn't out of preference that he had never paid them a social visit.

So Tripp's question was natural. "Well, howdy. Is something wrong again?"

Something surely was, but Luke didn't want to explain it in Tripp's hearing. "That room of mine's hot," he said. "And I got to thinking how cool it is out here."

Tripp gave him a penetrating look and was plainly pleased. He was thinking that at long last Luke Preston was making a courting call on his daughter. Presently he would give an excuse about a man his age needing his sleep and leave them alone together.

Chapter 18

Tripp did what Luke had hoped, exchanging talk a while, then yawning elaborately and stretching his big, blacksmith's arms. "Well, I don't have a soft job like you two," he said. "I roustered freight today and I got more to rouster tomorrow. So if you'll excuse me, Luke —"

"Sure," Luke said.

Sherry didn't look amused, and her father was barely in the house when she said, "Something *is* wrong, Luke. I can feel it."

"Well, yes," he admitted. "Pretty badly wrong, Sherry."

"What now?"

"I reckon you gathered it's private."

"I wondered."

She was intuitive and receptive, yet suddenly it was hard to say what he must. He drew a long breath. "Well, first I want to set you straight on Nan Browder. I wasn't ever in love with her or her with me. She

264

came into my life in a different way entirely."

Sherry looked at him disbelievingly, as if it was something she had believed so long that it was there to stay. "Then why'd you make me think you were?" she asked finally.

"I'm a wanted man."

"What?"

"There's a warrant for me still good in Colorado. I knew Nan there, and I knew Lawson Keel there. Keel and I had a kind of standoff that's worked around in his favor now. He's put the pressure on me. I'm to help him take over the railroad or he'll turn me in. I'm not standing for either. I'm clearing out, but I had to tell you first. Only you. So you'll know why I couldn't let anything grow between us."

"Oh, Luke."

She said nothing more, but he could hear the sound of her breathing. So he told her the whole thing, how he had arrived in Colorado during the mining boom there, hardly of age and without experience in the world, to be suckered into a stock swindle and made the goat.

"If I'd been older," he said, "I'd have known Keel's stripe from the way he treated Nan. She was Nan Alpert then and she sang in a beer hall. She was in love with him. He took advantage of her, and it wasn't till after I cleared out that she learned he had another woman all along. She learned that after she'd sold her soul to help him. But he fooled me the same way till it was too late to save myself. He run a store there, too, though not as big a one as here, and he grubstaked a miner once in a while when he thought it was a good thing. That gave him a share in any finds. That's how I met him. I'd made a strike that looked real good, but by the time I'd found it, I was busted. I went to Keel, and he backed me and then took me as neat as he took Nan."

Prospectors in hard-rock country rarely worked their discoveries, he told her. It was far too costly, and there were too many investors from coast to coast eager to put money into a good proposition.

"That's the second place I could have saved myself," Luke said, "if I'd been older and more experienced. Keel didn't want to go partners with me, the usual arrangement. He said we'd make out better if I filed the claim in my name and he only acted as my broker. I fell for it and trusted him enough that I signed anything he asked me to. That's how he did me in, for he run a swindle. It was going on everywhere, for that matter, with suckers waiting in line to lose their money. Fake assay reports, salted veins, overevaluations — there's all kinds of ways to make any old kind of prospect look like a bonanza. Keel sold a lot of stock, and when the truth about the mine came out, he laid the fakery on me. He claimed he'd been taken in himself and acted in good faith with the public. To cinch it, he had papers I'd signed that seemed to prove everything he claimed. At least they convinced the grand jury that indicted me."

"And Nan knew about this?" Sherry asked.

"Enough to know I was being railroaded to cover up Keel's snake tracks. She didn't testify against me, but she wouldn't speak up for me, either. I got a tip about the indictment and cleared out to avoid arrest."

"But the money you'd have got," Sherry protested. "What happened to that?"

"Keel pocketed every cent. He had receipts to show he'd turned over everything taken in from stock sales except for his commission. And he offered to refund the commission to the buyers he'd stung. I never saw a cent except for what I got for living expenses and to do the work on the mine that the law requires. But taking off made it look like I'd cleared out with the boodle. And that's it, Sherry. If I let them arrest me, I'll go over the road."

She nodded, and the starlight showed him a face very grave and pained. "Even so, you can't run away again."

"He was bluffing."

"I'm not sure." She rose and walked over to his horse and stood stroking its nose, lost in thought. When she didn't come back he went over to her, and she looked up at his eyes. "It's Nan. I know something about a woman in love. I can understand her keeping quiet rather than expose her lover as a swindler and traitor. As long as you didn't mean anything to her, and I'm so glad to know you didn't. I thought different so long."

"It was you," he said gently. "Almost from the day we met. I got no right to say it, but I love you, Sherry."

He hadn't meant for it to go so far, but abruptly she was in his arms, crying and clinging to him and telling him a blind man would know that she loved him, too. Then his lips silenced her, and he knew she was right about not running away from it again, no matter the cost. It was a long while before she moved away.

"I'd do anything for you," she said. "Even what Nan did for Keel. But I still don't see why she didn't try to righten matters after she was betrayed, too. Afraid of Keel? She could go to the law and have him clapped in jail before he could lift a hand against her."

"She helped him conceal his crime," Luke told her. "That's aiding and abetting. I don't know that they'd actually prosecute her for it, yet there's a chance. But he's been scared she'd do it, regardless, and that's kept him from crowding me till now."

"Why isn't he afraid now?"

"He said he's sure of her."

"That makes me wonder if he isn't bluffing. I know she can't feel anything but loathing for Keel after what he did to her. I've built up a powerful dislike of the woman, but I don't think he could buy her off. And he's desperate, Luke. He's almost got what he wants, and he's afraid of Ainsworth. I don't think he's any more sure of Nan than before. He just tried to make you think so."

"It's a mighty serious matter if he's not bluffing," Luke said.

"Take your chances," Sherry said fiercely. "Keep fighting him. If you have to go to prison, I'll follow you. I'll stay as near you as they'll let me and see you as often as I can, and when you get out, I'll be waiting for you." Suddenly she shook her head. "No. It's wrong to tempt you to gamble the best years of your life. I'll go away with you. You can have me either way. Right now if you want. I love you."

He held her for a long while, thinking how easy it would be to let the fight be lost in a way he couldn't be blamed for, to require no sacrifice of Sherry, to live no longer under the sword himself. Gambling his future might make little difference in whether the railroad stayed in business. If he gambled and helped to save the line and lost, himself, the repercussions would still hurt Baker badly. And there was Nan. What if Keel had threatened her life to be sure of her silence? With her disposed of forever, the man could mail his letter with no fear for himself. He could be bluffing at present, but that was a step he could take if the bluff was called.

Luke added it up and his mind knew he could take neither of Sherry's alternatives but was forced for her sake and Nan's and Baker's to do what Keel demanded. Yet his heart knew something else. Sherry's love and devotion, now so freely declared, was the finest, cleanest, strongest thing life would ever offer him. He would not mock it with his own unworthiness. Keel couldn't act until he saw for himself whether he was being obeyed or defied. Somewhere in that brief period of grace, Luke knew, he had to find a better way than was in sight at present.

"I don't know, Sherry," he said, his voice heavy with feelings he couldn't express. "Right now I can't see much of anything except that coming here tonight was the best move of my life."

"I'm so mighty glad you did," she answered. "Do what you must. Whatever it is, I'm with you."

It was another long moment before they stepped apart. Then he swung quickly into the saddle and was gone into the star-blazing night.

He had left a town serenely indolent in a warm night's comfort, and he returned to one astir with excitement. The stores had closed, and women and children had cleared off the sidewalks. But now men drawn out of the saloons stood in knots, talking and gesticulating, most of them seeming pleased about something. There was another group at the livery barn when Luke reached there to return his horse, but they broke off talking and looked at him in an odd way when he rode into the light of the lanterns hanging over the door.

He swung down, looked back at them, and when nobody spoke, he said, "What's the to-do about?"

A man he didn't know but who seemed to identify him let his face tighten in a derisive grin. "Your catch didn't stay caught, Preston, and I say here's luck to 'em."

Luke glanced at the stablehand, who usually was friendly. "What's that supposed to mean, Henry?"

"The Morgan gang," Henry Spatz muttered. "They just busted outta jail."

Luke gaped at him. "How?"

"Looks like somebody slipped 'em a six-shooter."

They were all willing to talk, then, because they were stimulated and full of rumors and conjectures. It had been more of a delivery than a jailbreak, Luke gathered, for there had been more than the smuggled weapon involved. It had happened in daylight with horses waiting. The turnkey had taken the prisoners their supper around six o'clock and had been overcome, tied up and gagged. Not only the Morgan bunch but two other prisoners, seven in all, had got away and might have had all night if the marshal hadn't taken a notion to drop in at the jail before he went to bed. He'd had a time raising a posse in a town mostly rooting for Morgan.

Luke walked on to the hotel with a mind numb with shock but active enough for him to see the specific nature of the passivity Keel wanted from him. And to see why that would be enough, and fast enough, to satisfy the man's driving urgency. The vengeance Morgan would surely try to wreak, if not caught or opposed or guarded against with utmost care, could turn the trick overnight. A wrecked train, a few burned cars of freight — even the cost of a guard force would be enough to push the railroad beyond the breaking point. Keel would have had little trouble engineering the delivery in a town in sympathy not only with Morgan but with him. And by the same token, the marshal would have the devil's own time apprehending the escapees.

There was to be no grace period at all, no time in which to find a decent yet self-protecting solution, and Keel had known that. How he must have gloated in his secret knowledge that forces were already loosened to gain his end, if Luke Preston was kept from once more bringing Morgan to time. And what an easy way out he had offered. Nobody could blame Luke Preston if, this time, Morgan won a round.

He was pulling off his boots, ready for bed, when the immediate urgency of the situation came through. He lowered his foot still clad, knowing he had a lot to do before he slept. He needed a horse, but returning to the livery for his own would call attention to what he was doing, and that he didn't want. He thought of Barney Lunt, who lived on the edge of town and kept a couple of good saddle horses. Lunt had gone into the transfer business with Lafe Wells, but the years when he drove a railroad wagon to Whitman Station had proved his loyalty. A glance at his watch told Luke it was a little after ten o'clock. He put on his hat again, blew out the lamp, and ten minutes later was rapping on Lunt's door.

Lunt had been in the process of going to bed, himself, but he came to the door quickly. Luke knew from his manner that he had heard about the jailbreak, understood its threat, and was ready to help.

"Barney, I need the loan of a horse," Luke told him without preamble, "and on the quiet. There can be only one reason why Morgan got loose or was turned loose, and he's right apt to make his play before word can reach Wallula. I got to get down there before the train leaves in the morning."

"I got a hoss that can get you there," Lunt agreed. "Where's your gun?"

"No place to hide it, and I didn't want to be seen toting it."

"You gotta have one. I'll give you the loan of mine."

Luke knew within minutes after he slipped out through the ragged edge of town that Lunt's boast was justified. The horse he rode was a long-legged grey that hadn't been worked for several days and was full of go. He had left word with Lunt to tell Tripp where he had gone, and he wondered what Lawson Keel would make of his vanishing from the town.

For some distance west of the town the stage road paralleled the new track which, although it was improbable that Morgan could do any damage that close, Luke found himself watching uneasily. And then, after crossing Mill Creek, the road swung away from the railroad, not to come close again until Whitman Station. It would make for slowed going, but Luke decided to swing over and follow the tracks. It made him feel better to keep his eyes on at least a stretch of the railroad's far-flung property.

Beyond the old railhead the two thoroughfares stuck close together as far west as the desert, and Luke returned to the wagon road for better time. He had barely made the change when he slowed the horse, staring into the forward distance. Riders were coming toward him, barely discernible in the far darkness. He shifted the holster of his gun a little farther forward and rode on, doubting that the Morgan gang would show itself so plainly.

It turned out to be part of the posse that had fogged out of Walla Walla City after the jailbreak had been discovered. There were five of them, disgusted men who suspected that they had been sent on a wild-goose chase. Luke knew none of them personally but recognized them as men standing for law and order, whatever their sympathies in the railroad row.

They had only had an hour of daylight, they reported, and the word of a man who claimed to have seen the escapees cut out of town and head north toward the benchlands and the Snake River country. That could have been a baldfaced lie to throw them off, but it hadn't mattered much, for the posse had picked up no sign.

When darkness drowned the chances of finding any, they had split, the marshal taking the other half on a swing to the east while this group swung west on the chance of flushing something on one of the main runways in the broken country. The only thing they had accomplished was to show that not everyone in Walla Walla City was willing to see the law mocked without trying to do something about it.

Thereafter Luke rode in a peaceful night, putting Dry Creek behind and the Touchet, the divide and the desert. Wallula lay in darkness when he raised it far ahead. He stopped at the landing only long enough to roust Pasco from his hotel room and take him along to Slabtown, which sprawled in the same slumbering serenity. The mill and railroad yard and the great store of new materials were so far untouched.

"They don't worry me much," Luke told Pasco, whom he had filled in on the ride up the river. "Train service is where we're wide open now, and that means we've got to protect both the trains and the track. Don't ask me how, without hiring a scadload of guards we couldn't pay. But we've got to do it."

"*Si*," Pasco agreed somberly. "And don't

ask me how *tampoco*." He shifted in the saddle uneasily. "Thees time Morgan weel not take the chances of getting jumped. He will not stay put long enough. He is the hero, the *caballero* who fights for the leetle people. They will hide and feed and give him the warnings from one end of the country to the other."

"He doesn't need to lift a hand against us," Luke added. "The threat's enough to finish us."

Chapter 19

The only thing different about the morning train out of Wallula was that Luke and Pasco were both aboard, the latter riding in the cab with the engineer to help keep an eye on the track ahead. Except to Pasco and Frank Baker, Luke had said nothing about the escape of Morgan and his six desperate accomplices, and no word had arrived otherwise by the time the train pulled out. If this had happened, Luke knew that the fourteen passengers who showed up would have had second thoughts about entrusting their safety to the WW&CR. And many, if not all of them, would have switched to the Concord stage that left at the same hour.

As it was, the twenty-eight-dollar fare they had paid was in company hands. There was also enough freight in the boxcars switched out from the new Wallula siding to keep the line in the black for one more day at least. This gave Luke no hope for the days ahead. The train dared not run at maximum speed when at any moment it might have to brake to a smoking stop because of a man-made snakehead, a loosened or missing rail, or a weakened trestle ahead. That alone wiped out what he and Truax had gained from their careful work in improving the track.

Luke and Sam Dunbow weren't armed, but they both had guns stashed handily in the passenger car. At any station, or even between stations, the powerful outlaw gang might attempt to board and take over the train, terrorizing the passengers and working their deviltry on the cars and freight. Yet all that developed on the long run to Walla Walla City was that the train arrived an hour behind the schedule it had been maintaining in recent weeks.

The town made no to-do about the arrival of the train, although there must have been considerable curiosity about why it was late. And there wasn't a passenger waiting to go down on the return trip. "It's creepy," Tripp told Luke. "They act like the avengin' angels had been turned loose, instead of a bunch of low-down hard cases."

"They've been worked on too much to see straight," Luke said wearily. "Have you seen Doc Baker since the break?"

Tripp nodded. "He was here this mornin' on his way to the bank. He's tryin' not to look worried about it, but I know he is. And why. Even losin' the passenger business would hurt, when every dollar counts, and it looks like that might be gone already."

Sherry was at her desk and showed Luke a face with tangled feelings when he stepped into the freight office. Barney Lunt and Lafe Wells were there, too, and their drays were backed up to the loading platform behind the freight shed. Their presence kept him from yielding to a powerful impulse to kiss Sherry. He had an idea she wanted that and was remembering the night before, herself.

"Well, you made it," she said, and tried to smile.

"This time." Luke looked at Lunt. "Sorry I couldn't bring back your horse, Barney. If I don't get a chance to ride it up, I'll send somebody up with it."

"Forget the horse," Lunt said. "Me and Lafe come in to tell you we don't have business enough for both our wagons. If things get worse, there won't be enough for even one. So one of us wants to go back to work for you."

"Doing what?" Luke asked, surprised.

"Helpin' ride shotgun on the train."

"Thanks." Luke grinned at him. "I'd like to have either one or both of you. But there just isn't money for extra help."

"Who said anything about money?"

"You know how Doc is. He wouldn't accept gratis work."

"I ain't talkin' about that, either," Lunt said. "Me and Lafe'd both like to own more railroad stock. But startin' our own business and all, we don't have the spare cash to pay for it. You suppose Doc would object to one of us workin' it out?"

Luke stared at him in wonder. "Stock in a company that might be busted in a matter of weeks?"

"Stock," Lunt said calmly, "we'd as leave have as hard cash."

Sherry's voice cut in, strong with excitement. "Why can't we all do that?"

Luke turned to look at her. He had drawn his pay regularly but only because Baker was a stickler for meeting the payroll as punctually as he paid his other bills. He had put what he could back into the company and knew the others had, too. It hadn't seemed like much of a contribution until now when, as Tripp had said, every dollar counted like ten would have in the past. Sherry's suggestion began to excite him the way Lunt's had her. It was an act of faith that might satisfy Baker's stern conscience, for the doctor surely believed the stock was still worth par. It would cut down the drain on cash enough to offset the loss of passenger business at the least. Also it would let him add a good man to the train guard.

Sherry didn't wait for agreement but hurried outside and came back presently with Tripp, Sam Dunbow and the engineer and brakeman from the train. She had already told them what she had in mind, and they were more than willing to take their wages in stock for as long as necessary. The question was whether Dorsey Baker would agree to it or look on it as an intolerable act of charity on their part.

"He's at the bank, Luke," Sherry urged. "You go see him."

"Yeah." Lunt and Wells had just flipped a dollar and Lunt grinned. "You're lookin' at your new shotgun messenger, and I sure hanker to go down with you on that train."

Walking upstairs to the Baker-Boyer bank, ten minutes later, Luke wondered what effect the struggle now grown so bitter was having on the bank itself and what the effect would be if the WW&CR did not survive. So far the public seemed to have kept the two enterprises separate in its collective mind. The bank was a sound institution of a kind they knew and was Walla Walla City's first, with likable John Boyer its mainstay as far as its depositors were concerned. It was the railroad, its practicability and then its motives that they had come to distrust and refuse to support. For a moment Luke had a shocked vision of the railroad's failing in this climactic storm of fear and hate, taking the bank with it. And then, inevitably in a vicious chain, Baker's cattle and farming operations.

Baker was glad to see him and wanted to know about the trip up with the train. Luke sat in a chair by the doctor's desk and explained that the lateness was simply due to the need to run slowly.

"That's what I come to see you about," he concluded. "Maybe we're as well off without any passenger business, as long as the Morgan bunch is loose and threatening us. Without passengers to worry about, we can risk more speed."

Baker shook his head. "The train crew's lives are worth as much as the passengers'."

"Sure, but they're more willing to put them on the line. They just proved it to me." Luke explained about the spontaneous offer from the group at the depot. He thought he knew others who would feel the same way. He didn't intend to press it with anybody, but he wanted Baker's permission to offer stock in lieu of wages if he needed more help. He didn't think he was going to get permission, for by the time he was finished, the doctor was scowling at him.

And then a smile flickered on Baker's face, and he said, "I don't think it would have made me feel any better if the entire stock issue had been subscribed last January. It's the widow's mite."

"It's all right?"

"I haven't any choice. We've got to protect ourselves against mischief, with no other way to pay for it. The new track and equipment's paid for, even if it's useless to us at present. But it cleaned us out of cash. From here on we've got to take it in at least as fast as it goes out. If we can't do that, I'll trade my bank stock for the railroad stock that I don't own, myself, and close out the WW&CR."

Luke had known it would be that way, yet it was chilling to hear it. "You still wouldn't listen to the Keel offer?" he asked.

"Not for a minute."

"Would you sell out to the OSN?"

"No. Look what their rates on the steamers used to be."

"Why don't you let it leak out that it's what you'll do, though, if they drive you to it?"

"That's a temptation." Baker sighed. "But I've never done business that way and I'm too old to start."

The trip back to Wallula was also uneventful, and Barney Lunt went down with the train. By then word of Morgan's escape was loose in the town, which seemed as surprised as Walla Walla City had been to see the train come in unmolested. They could see a possible reason why it had not been. With no passengers to keep soothed, the six company men who arrived with the train were openly armed. That was nearly as many men as now made up the Morgan gang, and their faces suggested that they were just as tough.

While the freight was being unloaded for transfer to the steamboats, Luke walked up to the livery barn and, catching Elvie Elvek alone there, asked him how he would like to go to work for the railroad.

Elvek stared at him, astounded. "Don't reckon there's anything I'd like better," he said. "But what good could you get out of a cuss like me?"

"You've been plenty of help already," Luke told him. "But I'd better warn you, you'd have to take your pay in railroad stock for a while."

"That'd suit me to a T. That stock's gonna be worth plenty someday."

"Thanks, and that's the kind of spirit we want. Can you start tomorrow?"

"Right now, if you want. All I got to do is clap on my hat, and she's already clapped on."

"Well, you won't go far. I want to make you our Wallula agent."

"Depot agent?" Elvek's mouth hinged ajar. "Me?"

Luke explained. It was work he had once done and had put Pasco on, but now he wanted Pasco's help elsewhere. It amounted to keeping an eye on the railroad property in Wallula and especially the freight coming over the wharfboats to see that no shenanigans were pulled on consignments billed over the WW&CR. There was the outbound freight to be watched, also, to see that it wasn't trifled with and that it went on the steamers as speedily as freight arriving by wagon. Elvek's shoulders seemed to straighten while he listened, and his jaw set. Luke knew he could be counted on.

Luke turned away with his own face tensing. What he meant to do would prove conclusively to Lawson Keel that he was still doing his utmost to defeat him. He wanted to talk to Nan, and before her place filled with its nightly hangers-on, so he crossed the street and walked down to her door. The only ones he found inside were a yawning barkeep and a pair of town oldsters in a back-comer cribbage game. The bartender closed his mouth and looked at Luke with unfriendly eyes.

"I don't want any of your rotgut," Luke told him. "I want to see Nan Browder." He canted his eyes at the quarters above. "She upstairs?"

The bartender said coldly, "She ain't around, Preston."

"Where is she?"

"She went down the river."

Luke didn't believe him. "Where's Browder?"

"He's got a business to run, you know. If you want to see him, though, he's usually here after supper."

"Nan go to Portland?"

"Reckon so."

"How long's she been gone?"

"Quite a spell."

Luke shrugged and walked out, but outside the door he turned left to the corner of the building. There an outside stairway rose to a landing outside the Browders' living quarters, and he took the treads quietly. When he reached the door at the top, he pulled in a long breath, then rapped lightly, the reassuring drumming of a friendly caller. He had done this several times and was about to give up and leave when his ears responded to a faint sound. He saw the doorknob turn slowly, then the door opened a crack, and he saw Nan's face beyond.

She started to shove the door closed, but his foot stopped that. She made no commotion when he pushed against the wood and finally she stopped resisting. He stepped in, aware of the fear and consternation in her eyes. She was dressed as she usually was in the evenings downstairs, but out of those surroundings she looked younger, prettier and much more vulnerable.

"No, Luke, no," she said in a hoarse whisper. "Go away."

"Not till we've had a little talk."

"Then quietly. Kirk would kill you if he

knew you were up here with me."

"He'd kill me for a few other reasons, too," Luke said dryly, "if he could cut the mustard. I'm not interested in him, Nan. I came to talk about Lawson Keel."

"I don't want to talk about him. I told you once before I can't help you."

"I know that. But you're going to talk again, or I am going to let that barkeep down there know I'm up here."

"All right. What about Lawson?"

"Have you seen him lately? Or been in touch with him any way?"

Her eyes became even more guarded. "Why?"

"Just answer."

"I saw him recently."

"You sell your soul to him again?"

Temper flashed in her eyes. "I never sold myself to Lawson Keel. I was in love with that man. I thought you knew it."

"Then I don't see why you don't hate him like poison now."

She looked away from him. "Maybe I do. But how can I help you without Kirk learning everything? Have you stopped to think of that?"

He hadn't, and the idea surprised him. "You care that much about Kirk Browder?"

"We get along. It's a marriage. All I've got."

"Then hear this. Keel's threatened to turn me in. If he does, it'll all come out, anyway. He'll call on you to help clear him."

"He promised he wouldn't. He doesn't think he needs that, with all there is against you."

"Do you trust him even yet, Nan?"

She looked back to him helplessly. "Have I a choice? I helped you twice. I tipped you off about Lawson. And then about Morgan. Please. Let that be enough."

"Nan, I think you'd help yourself a whale of a lot if you got the whole stinking thing off your conscience."

"No. Stop it."

"All right, Nan. Live with it."

He had shut the door and turned to go down the stairs before he saw, at the bottom of the steps, the angry, belligerent and somehow lewdly aroused face of the bartender. Their voices — they both had got carried away and must have talked louder than they realized. The man stood at the bottom of the stairs a moment while Luke, staring at him steadily, came down. Then he turned and left. When Luke reached the sidewalk, it was empty. He debated going into the saloon to warn the man to keep his mouth shut or going back to tell Nan. It would do no good. Kirk Browder would hear about his wife's visitor, and nothing would be said of the anger that had flared between them.

The next morning Luke started a plan he hoped would keep the trains running with maximum speed and safety, removing the only two valid reasons for a boycott by either shippers or passengers. The new *Columbia* had stood on a spur at Slabtown, tested and ready to go to work but held back until the iron track had gone down. Like the other two locomotives, it was a woodburner, and the millyard held inexhaustible quantities of slab. So there was little extra expense in putting the *Columbia* in service, and Luke made use of its extra power and speed.

The new engine went out ahead of the regular train with a man riding the cowcatcher to make a constant, close inspection of the track ahead. Two more armed men rode the tender. Even rails that looked worn, and capable of loosing a snakehead naturally, were checked. Special care was taken at the trestles, and due to its bursts of speed, this escort kept easily ahead of the main train, where more armed men showed themselves warningly atop the cars. The train, that day, passed station after station on time and rolled into Walla Walla City five minutes earlier than ever before.

"Wait till this gets around," Tripp cried, clapping Luke on the shoulder. "An armed convoy, by God."

But Sherry took a grimmer view of it. "Like Indian country. Isn't it something for this valley to be proud of — that it's necessary?"

Luke agreed with her and hoped there were many others who would see it in the same light. The insanity of bigotry and prejudice had to end sometime, and without it a Lawson Keel could get nowhere.

Chapter 20

It was the middle of August, after two weeks of convoying the trains, before Luke sensed that the tide of public sentiment was beginning to turn. He knew there were good reasons for it. The Morgan gang, whatever its original intentions, had so far failed to muster the courage to challenge the bristling gun crews with the trains or even to molest the track. The marshal had failed completely to pick up their trail. So when the rumor went around that the wild bunch had simply skipped the country, even Luke gave it some credence.

The renegades' threat, itself, had been a potent weapon at the start and it still would be if the railroad had to bear, in a cash outlay, the cost of the armed guard. That might have been Keel's whole design, with Morgan and his cronies all too willing to let their menace benefit Keel while they, themselves, put distance between themselves and the jail that had held them.

Even so, Luke knew he dared not discontinue or weaken the guard. The outlaws could only be waiting for him to relax his vigilance.

Yet the threat was losing its force with the public, and now there were a few passengers each way every day. The volume of freight entrusted to the line held its own, then showed a slight increase, and the WW&CR stayed in the black, although barely. Yet that wasn't enough. There was iron track to lay and sidings to build before the first shipments came out of the ripening miles of wheat. That was only weeks away, and the farmers were as bitterly set against the line as ever.

Riding the trains himself now, Luke had plenty of time to think about it and remember that every inch the railroad gained brought his personal life into greater jeopardy. He had defied Keel and so far had neutralized the effect of the jail delivery. After his discouraging talk with Nan Browder he knew Keel hadn't bluffed about not fearing her. So Keel's letter could have gone to Colorado. Any day could see the local marshal turn his attention to a new case, one certain to rock the country as strongly as the jailbreak had. Strengthened by Sherry's love and loyalty,

Luke bore this with stoic calm, resolved, before it happened, to do as much for the railroad as he could.

Meanwhile there was Kirk Browder to think about as a result of the talk with Nan. That Browder had been tipped off by the spying bartender became certain on the evening following the visit, when Luke had been on the overnight, Wallula end of the run. He had seen Browder on the street, and the glower the man gave him had had much more in it than the old factional antagonism.

Luke had been with Pasco, who noticed it and said, "*Senor* Browder he has waited the long time to see Morgan deliver the wallop. He does not like the way you keep messing eet up."

"It's not that right now, Pasco," Luke said. Browder's eyes had given him a creepy feeling, and he wanted somebody around who would watch when his back was turned to the man. "He thinks I'm interested in his wife."

"Who would not be?" Pasco said approvingly. "She ees the beautiful *mujer.*"

"I used to know her, that's all, and he's got a mistaken idea of how it was."

"Watch heem. He is the sidewinder like Morgan."

Luke thought that in this instance Browder was mainly an intensely jealous husband with a total lack of trust in his wife. But Browder had done nothing since then, and Luke's concern had become mainly for Nan, who must be having a rough time. He had little reason, after her lack of compassion for him, but he was growing sorry for her and her desperate effort to hold onto so miserable a marriage and life.

It was the third week in August when Luke realized that the valley had a sense of shame after all. It made him think of what Sherry had said about the convoy, "Like Indian country . . ." Yet it wasn't contrition on the part of those who had so passionately maligned and resisted the WW&CR. Rather, the new spirit became manifest in those who had little if anything to ship, no money to invest in stock, and who rarely traveled. They were also without organization, except as they were united by a common intelligence and decency.

Their only reason for shame was their inertia in a situation they had believed not to affect them very much personally until they could no longer blink the fact that everyone was affected. The newspaper, which had tried to chart a bland course, came out with a stinging editorial that not only chastised the perpetrators of the boycott but those who had let themselves be intimidated. In two of the churches sermons were preached in the same vein, which encouraged the newspaper editor to lambaste the backcountry teamsters who refused to haul freight handled by the railroad. Astonishing numbers of people expressed gratification that their own sentiments had finally been voiced. A noisy minority had been so dominating that it had made its own feelings seem general, and the record was being set straight on that.

The trouble was, that was about all that was being accomplished, for the businessmen and the farmers were the ones on whom the life of the railroad depended. The farmers remained implacable, the merchants divided in their support. But the latter weren't as evenly divided as before.

"We showed a profit last week," Sherry told Luke one day between the arrival and departure of the train. "Not much, but the biggest since the boycott. You suppose it's caving in?"

Luke didn't know but hoped so. "Anyway, the merchants are Keel's weakest allies. I sure wish there was a way to hammer 'em harder."

The way came to the WW&CR with no effort on his part. Newall Truax's construction gang had been paid off and allowed to scatter. But a number of them were local men who were still on hand and, it turned out, unhappy with the way the railroad they had helped to build was being treated.

Truax had been away on personal business, and he had just returned to Walla Walla City when four of these men dropped in to see him. They didn't happen to be doing anything just then, they mentioned, and they'd as soon keep busy. A couple of them knew Barney Lunt and had heard how Baker was letting him earn a few shares of railroad stock. They'd as leave own a little stock, themselves, and it didn't take too large a crew to replace wooden rails with iron, since the grade and timber work was all done.

They were some of the best men Truax had had working for him, and he conceded that Baker might be agreeable to such an arrangement. By the time he had seen the doctor and obtained official authority, the potential track crew had doubled in size. When the engineer took them down to

Wallula on the following day's train, there were a round dozen of them, as large a crew as he could use.

"When I was talking to Doc about it," Truax told Luke on the way down, "it looked like ten years fell off of him. You know how he hates to grin but can't help himself sometimes. Well, one busted loose that showed every tooth in his mouth. He knows it's not charitableness. Those fellows think railroad stock's as sound as money and that it's a good deal all around."

Luke might not have been any happier than Baker, but he was no less happy to see the T-iron line out at last, rail by rail, toward Walla Walla City. Revenue had grown enough that Truax could set up a small camp to feed and sleep the crew that interrupted its work only twice a day to let the trains go by. As much as a mile of track was replaced each day, and this increased as the job shook down, until it seemed sure there would be an iron track in time for the wheat harvest. Its benefit was amply proved on the completed section. With the smoothness and sure grip of iron on the wheel flanges, the trains doubled their speed with safety.

Luke and his train riders began to notice

something else. Wayfarers on the road had long ignored the passing trains or given them a deriding attention. Now it was more common than not to receive a friendly wave of the hand. To a lesser extent this was true of the farmhouses that stood in sight of the track. The occupants of a number of them were much friendlier when they could act as individuals rather than as part of an organized faction.

The promise of truly fast connections with the river port did its part, but mainly it was this growing spirit in the country that began to break down the merchants' support of Lawson Keel and his cause. They began to find that they could be boycotted by railroad friends as well as railroad enemies, which made it a standoff whether they themselves boycotted the WW&CR. One by one they began to risk the loss of farm trade by coming over to the railroad, and while they did lose farm trade, they made it up elsewhere. But the inland teamsters, still in sympathetic support of their brethren on the main stem, stuck to their refusal to haul anything carried or to be carried by the WW&CR.

It was Baker's nature to be uncommunicative, but he couldn't contain the news he brought to the depot one day while the train was waiting there before starting back for the river landing. He called everyone into the freight office.

"We're sufficiently in the black," he told them, "to put you people back on the payroll. That's true of the track crew, also, although it looks like they'll be finished in another two or three weeks. So, effective —"

"Now, wait a minute, Doc," Tripp Yale cut in. "You mean you're shuttin' us out from buyin' more stock?"

"Why, no." Baker looked at him in surprise. "You all have expenses. I assumed you'd rather have the money."

"Not me," Tripp said, and the others agreed with him. "If there's some spare cash, why don't we build ourselves some station sidings?"

Baker was overwhelmed to a point where he could say nothing for a moment. He looked at them with gleaming eyes. "I'm glad you said 'we', Tripp. It's your railroad, too, and if you want a bigger share of it, you can certainly buy it any way you want. But the sidings — we might not haul a bushel of wheat, you know. We've gotten nowhere with the farmers. And they're the only ones sidings would benefit."

"I vote my stock for sidings," Tripp said,

his eyes twinkling as he looked around. "How about the rest of you?"

Baker regarded their smiling faces and nodding heads and laughed. "Motion carried."

And then the harvest started. It was visible down the valley to the edge of the desert, and what the train riders could see was only a minuscule part. Once when he sighted a crawling reaper, Luke was reminded that out on the bunchgrass Bill Green would be starting his fall beef harvest. He thought of that life and the one he had known prior to it, the hard but exciting life of a prospector, and for a moment regretted that the dull tilling of the soil was so swiftly replacing all that. The feeling passed, but it left him with an unexpected insight into those who so uneasily and so stubbornly resisted change.

The people of the valley had changed locations when they came to settle, but they hadn't expected or wanted to change their way of life. That was being forced on them by circumstances, by the times, by realistic and far-seeing men like John Ainsworth and Dorsey Baker. To resent circumstances was to resent God, in their lights, and to resent the times was to waste anger on something nearly as unfathomable. But it was possible and not necessarily unproductive for them to resent their fellow men.

It was that same evening that Luke found Elvie Elvek waiting excitedly for him at the Wallula station. Luke knew he was spilling over with something, but Elvek didn't want to talk about it until he had drawn Luke out of earshot of the loungers who had also met the train. "Dunno if it's good news or bad, Luke," Elvek said then. "It come up on the steamer today. It was in the Portland paper a couple of days ago. Clint Morgan's been shot and killed."

"Where?" Luke gasped.

"Way over in Montana," Elvek told him. "It was in the *Oregonian*, a feller said. Morgan's bunch tried to stick up a bank at Deer Lodge and must have bungled it plenty. Blackie Holladay was killed, too, and Chuck shot up and caught."

"I'll be blamed," Luke mused. "They cleared out of this country right after they broke jail."

"Sure looks that way. They weren't gettin' much help anywhere if they had to tackle a bank to raise money. The Nevada skunks got away, and the pair that broke jail with 'em, but they sure won't hanker for these parts again." Elvek shook his head. "I don't know if that helps us any. This town's took it hard. All the time they been waitin' for Morgan to make a big play and fix everything up for them. Now they know he ain't goin' to, and there's no tellin' what they'll do themselves."

Luke agreed that it would be foolish to discontinue the hampering train guard as yet, for he could see for himself that the development had put an ugly mood on the town. Muttering lips and scowling faces presented themselves anywhere he went or looked, until the train was unloaded and run up to the Slabtown yard for the night. He was even more worried when the train pulled out the next morning, although he couldn't say just why. No one had tried to make trouble or even voiced threatening talk. And at that hour Wallula's streets were empty except for the train and stage hands and passengers for the upper valley.

The run across the desert went swiftly now, the blow-sand at last conquered and stabilized, and the smooth track permitting high speed. The flag was up at Five Mile Station, and a man and woman got aboard and paid the fare to Walla Walla City. At Divide, the first station in the valley proper, a gang of Truax's men was starting work on a siding. The train didn't stop and ran on, entering the great sea of ripe wheat, at the point cutting across a flat horseshoe bend in the Walla Walla River.

The train had nearly come to the river again when Dunbow, who had been riding the back platform, stepped into the coach and dropped down on the rear seat beside Luke. Nodding rearward, he said quietly, "Something's pilin' up, back there. Sure looks like smoke to me."

Luke rose and went out with him to the platform. What he saw made his shoulder muscles pull tight. A black, roiling cloud lay almost directly behind them, teased by a light, northwest breeze and not as far back as the station they had just passed. By then it was even less a natural cloud than it had looked to Dunbow.

"Grass fire," he said.

"Grass?" Dunbow asked in a tight voice.

"Stop the train. We've got to look into it."

The conductor had to run forward over the car tops to halt the train. Waiting for that, Luke kept his eyes on the sooty mass, which the wind was moving slowly toward him and southeastward into the bend of the river. The train slowed, stopped and began to back up.

Dunbow came back and said breathlessly, "You can see the flames from on top. It's in the wheat."

"You know something else?" Luke asked.

"I sure do. We're gonna get blamed for it. They'll say it was engine sparks, sure as hell."

"They sure will." There were spark arresters on the stacks of both engines, but if this thing proved as bad as it looked, few would believe the safeguards had done their job. In a moment Luke could see the flames himself, a narrow band of fiery lace under the rolling smoke. "It's all south of the track," he judged.

Dunbow nodded. "Wind's carrying it into the horseshoe."

There were two wheat ranches within the loop of the river bend, and south of the river the bare highlands rose abruptly the length of the bend. The river would probably contain the fire in that direction. Possibly its reverse curve would stop it from spreading east into the abruptly widening main valley.

And then it exploded before their eyes, a hurtling hurricane of intense heat. The train had to stop again because of the choking smoke. They could only watch helplessly.

The *Columbia* had stopped and come

back to where the train stood motionless. The ranch houses, which were over against the river, were lost to sight. Luke could only hope that their occupants had seen the warning in time to escape across the river and out of the way. But nothing could save the buildings or the wheat in the pocket, over a mile square of it. The fire front seemed to stretch to the river already, for it had moved faster in that direction. Yet it was edging eastward, also, and only that leg of the river bend stood between it and an entire valley of explosively ripe wheat. Sickened, he watched the backwash of smoke cutting his nostrils and lungs, black embers snowing down on him and the others by then.

It was a long while before he could say with any degree of conviction, "I think the river'll hold it. The breeze isn't strong enough to take it south or right to carry it east."

"*Amigo,*" Pasco said at his elbow, "the *hombre* who set thees is steel around. It went too fast for him to get very far away."

"I know," Luke said, "but he had a horse and probably crossed south ahead of the fire and lost himself in the high ground. We've got nothing to chase him with. What I want to know right now is what happened to those farm families."

It was another hour before he could cross the mile of smoking, foot-scorching stubble to the nearest, still-burning ruins of a house, barn and outbuildings. The owner, his wife and two children had got across the river in time, and the same was true of the bachelor on the next ranch. But they were furious people. Nothing would ever convince them that the fire hadn't been started carelessly, if not maliciously, by the train.

"Baker'll pay for my crop!" the bachelor bawled. "And if there's any way I can bring criminal charges, I'll bring 'em!"

The man nodded his agreement.

Chapter 21

It was the train, ironically, that brought the first word to Walla Walla City of the damage it was supposed to have done, although it was the passengers who spread it quickly through the town. Dorsey Baker, drawn to the depot by the lateness of the train, heard it from Luke and said wearily, "It's purpose was to create another public outrage. No doubt it's succeeded amply."

"That's my opinion, too," Luke agreed. "They picked a spot where it wasn't apt to do much damage, yet enough to turn the trick."

"It'd be the ruin of them, instead of us, if we could prove that."

"We can't." Luke shook his head. The arsonist must have come in the way he left, for the men working on the Divide siding had noticed nothing out of the way until smoke attracted their attention, too far off for them to get there before the fire was out of hand. The char left afterward, which

310

Luke had seen for himself, showed the fire had been set in a patch of dried, wild grass on the right of way, a strong hint that a spark or ember from one of the engines had been the origin. The breeze had carried it on, mounting swiftly, into the wheat. Its happening immediately after the train and two locomotives had passed was damning evidence. "It was just mad talk about criminal charges, Doc, but they've got a good chance to stick you for damages."

Baker nodded. "And that's only part of it. What chance do we have to haul the harvest now? Every farmer in the valley will be as mad as the ones in the pocket."

Luke agreed. "I even heard a man talking about an injunction to stop the trains running and endangering the wheat."

But the doctor was already thinking of corrective measures. "We'll hold the train here for twenty-four hours, Luke," he said. "I'll invite the public — by George, I'll insist that they look our engines over themselves and see how impossible it is that they could have started a fire. I'd like to remind this country that we operated through other wheat harvests. And that it's strange we didn't cause our first fire till

311

right now, when things are turning against the teamsters."

Luke thought that the inspection was a good idea and welcomed the layover for private reasons. It seemed forever that he had been able to see Sherry only at the depot during the turnaround and then never alone. She was pleased when he went into the freight office to tell her about it and invited him to her house for supper. He had, she reminded him, taken exactly one meal there, the morning he arrived in a mauled state after his fight with Morgan. She hadn't cooked it for him, even then, but for her father.

Tripp volunteered to spread Baker's inspection invitation and went up one side of Main Street and down the other, going into stores, saloons and everywhere else that people gathered. He was respected in the town, regardless of his working for the railroad, and he didn't make light of their aroused feelings.

"It could've been a terrible thing," he agreed time and again. "If that fire'd got into the big valley, the crop loss would have been frightful and only a miracle could've kept lives from going with it. If our engines can do a thing like that, we're the first to say they should be stopped from running. We're certain they can't, but you people have got a right to make sure for yourselves. Come and look 'em over."

At first it seemed that nobody was going to respond. It was the newspaper editor, trying to make up his mind if a new facet of the railroad's operation had been disclosed that was really a public menace, who gathered an impromptu committee from among the businessmen and came to the depot. The engineers showed them firsthand how the fine-screened arresters made it impossible for an ember to escape that was hot enough to ignite the grass by the track. They ran the locomotives out past the edge of town and back, pouring the steam to make them chuff and not a spark flew upward with the smoke or dropped from the fireboxes. By that time a large crowd had gathered to watch.

It was hard to tell what impression had been made on the crowd, but the committee was convinced and curious. "Then how did it start?" the editor asked Baker. "Right there beside the track and right after the train went by."

"And right now," Baker added, "I hope you'll raise that question in an editorial."

Sherry's supper was first-rate and would have been so, even if it hadn't been Luke's first home-cooked meal in ages, and even if the cooking hadn't been done by the woman he loved. Afterward they sat in the cool yard, where Tripp said, "Well, we ain't much worse off with the farmers than before. If we can hold our own with the others we ought to weather it."

"I think Doc made a smart move," Luke answered. "The bulk of the people have more sense than I used to think. But it's my feeling we're a lot worse off with the farmers. Something's finally happened they can really belly-ache about, and they're gonna make the most of it."

"Let 'em, then."

Luke shook his head. "We've got to have the farm business, Tripp. We've got to do more than make ends meet. How about the several hundred thousand dollars, most of it Baker's, that has been invested in the railroad? It's not only wrong that it should be continually in danger, but there ought to be a return on the investment and a good one, considering what a risky investment it's been."

"You're right," Tripp admitted. "Somehow the farmers've got to be won around."

"I've come to think there's no winning 'em over, Tripp. They'll have to be brought around. I don't know how, but they're not going to see the light till they're driven to it."

It was hardly dark when Tripp again pleaded the weariness of his age and went off to bed. And then for the first time in far too long, Luke was holding Sherry in his arms again, feeling her hungry lips on his. For a long while that was all they wanted. But there was something on her mind that she voiced at last.

"What do you think Keel's done about Colorado? I know I encouraged you to think he was bluffing. But I wake up every morning, now, wondering if it'll be the day I find out how wrong I was. I know it's worse for you."

"There've been enough butterflies hatched in my stomach," Luke admitted, "to stock a good-sized orchard. I've come to think he was partly bluffing and partly wasn't. I went to see Nan. She's scared to death of her husband finding out Keel was once her lover. Keel knows that. On the other hand, you can't be around her and not know, if you ever knew her at all, that her conscience is giving her hell. If Keel can find another way to win, he'll use it. If he can't, he'll take a chance on her."

"Do you think he was behind the wheat fire?"

"He's sure not unhappy about it. But it's my hunch somebody from Wallula set it. Somebody in Browder's own crowd."

"It's dreadful." Sherry crept back into his arms. "You're a fine man, Luke. You've fought him with everything you've got, and I wanted you to and for us to win. Yet if we do, it's pretty apt to be a bad thing for us personally."

It was true, and Luke couldn't help wondering what right he had had to involve her in it.

Business began to fall off again, and the blackened bay in the river bend remained to remind twice a day when the trains passed why that was. And elsewhere in the valley the harvest got into full swing, with reapers and horse-operated threshers to be seen even from the windows of the trains. And then the first sacked wheat began to move, and it went by wagon to Wallula Landing. All along the road wheels ground up dust, and teamsters returned to jeering at the passing trains. The wheat began to pile up at Wallula and for some reason it stayed there.

"Wonder what's holding it up," Luke said to Elvek.

"Dunno," Elvek answered. "I tried to pump a purser. All he'd say was there's something from the head office they got to wait for."

Wheat piled up for several days without any of it being taken aboard the steamboats. And then Luke came down with the train, one afternoon, to find a town once more stunned by shock and chagrin.

A gleeful Elvek awaited his arrival, but all the man would say was, "Come and see for yourself. It's better readin' than hearin' about."

Luke walked over to the nearest wharfboat with him, seeing as they crossed the gangplank a new placard tacked to the wall.

"Take a look at that," Elvek said.

Luke read it with disbelieving eyes:

NOTICE TO SHIPPERS

Effective immediately: In accordance with special contract with the Walla Walla & Columbia River Railroad Company and because of recently increased demands on shipping facilities, the Oregon Steam Navigation Company will give priority to preferred freight. Only such freight as is consigned to the above

railroad for shipment to the Wallula Landing is classified as preferred freight.
(Signed) J. C. Ainsworth, Pres.
Oregon Steam Navigation Company

"And there," Elvek said, waving a lanky arm at the long stacks of wheat, "is an example of what's gonna happen to freight that ain't preferred."

"The foxy son of a gun," Luke said with a chuckle. "His rival line never was anything but a way to help Doc out." And the wheat that had been allowed to pile up deliberately was a pointed reminder. There were alternate ways for it to be shipped down to the river, but there was only one way to ship it down the river to market.

"What's this special contract business?" Elvek wondered.

"You've got me. If Doc Baker knew this was coming I'll eat your boots. I gotta hunch it's Ainsworth's way of getting it across that he means business."

Elvek started to turn, then hesitated and said quietly, "We got company."

Swinging around, Luke saw at the shore end of the gangplank Pete Lastrade and a dozen other Browder cronies, drivers and wagon-yard hands. Behind them half the town was coming along the road to see what was going to happen. The train men had grown aware of the gathering, and Pasco and Barney Lunt were moving along the siding.

Elvek following, Luke walked back to the shore end of the gangplank, and he wasn't surprised when Lastrade shifted over to block him. Luke looked at them with flat eyes, seeing men no longer arrogant and derisive but reeling from a smashing blow to their way of life.

"I wouldn't start crowin' yet, Preston," Lastrade said bitterly. "You ain't hauled any wheat this fall, and this won't bring you any."

"Before you give off too much head," Luke cut in, "let me ask you all a question. Did you people get graveled when the inland teamsters refused to haul a thing we handled? With you charging a dollar a ton more?" Lastrade blustered, but Luke motioned him quiet. "Let me finish. Ainsworth's not refusing to handle what you haul. He just says he's giving priority to what we haul, faster and for less money. So who's running this profit-gouging monopoly we keep hearing about, us or you?"

"Don't think the farmers won't see through this," Lastrade fumed. "They'll back us all the harder."

"They haven't been heard from yet," Luke retorted. "Now stand aside. I aim to step ashore."

Lastrade wanted to make a fight of it. His eyes flicked from side to side but failed to find whatever it was he needed. He edged over and let Luke and Elvek pass. It was, somehow, symbolic and final.

Fast as the train trip had become, word of Ainsworth's announcement beat the train to Walla Walla City. Luke arrived the next day to learn that Browder, and nearly everyone else owning a wagon outfit, had come up in the night by horse to see Lawson Keel and take steps to rally the farmers. Baker had heard it but met Luke at the train, wanting confirmation.

"It's so," Luke told him. "And it says by special contract with the WW&CR. Did you know anything about it?"

"Not an inkling. He has his little amusements. It could have pleased him to make a public thing of offering me his hand."

"You think Keel can hold the farmers?" Luke asked.

"This won't cure them of their prejudice. But it'll cost them more than the extra dollar a ton now to keep on gratifying it. They won't get paid for their wheat till it reaches Portland. They're not going to see it lay on the wharfboats and river bank for days and maybe weeks, especially when prices could drop overnight." Baker shook his head. "Yet they might stick to their guns. Stubbornness has driven men to suicide before now."

It had nearly driven Baker that far, Luke reflected, although the doctor's had been a laudable cause. "There's one help we're going to get," he said. "I think we can put an end to the pesky job of guarding the trains. With Ainsworth backing us openly, they won't try more monkey business. He's got a powerful weapon he's still holding back."

"Yes, he could refuse to haul their wheat at all. I think it would be wise to discontinue the guard, even if some hothead might still make mischief. The less hostile we look ourselves, now, the better the effect will be."

Luke remembered having told Tripp that the farmers would never be won over and would have to be brought around. It looked like the way to do that had been found. The next day the trains went back to normal service, now needing only three hours running time each way. Work on the sidings was rushed to completion, yet no wheat arrived for the cars. The increase in business that the railroad felt at once came again from the business people. Their own freight was subject to Ainsworth's new ruling. Unless billed via the railroad, merchandise coming up the river was slow in reaching Wallula and the last to be unloaded there. Merchants with thinning shelves saw trade going to more sensible competitors with well-stocked shelves. Pressures mounted until finally the inland teamsters caved in and called off their strike.

Luke had no idea what Lawson Keel was doing, for Keel called no new public meeting. Yet he still seemed to have the farmers in the palm of his hand. The first sign that this wasn't entirely true came when the wheat going down to Wallula by wagon began to slack off, still with none of it coming to the railroad. The farmers were simply refraining from shipping, Luke realized, for the stacks at the landing grew much faster than they were being reduced by the boats.

Luke had a shrewd idea who planted the report, that appeared a few days later in the numerous copies of the Portland *Oregonian* that came regularly into the valley. The item was to the effect that the clippers coming into that seaport were having difficulty making up cargoes due to the Walla Walla farmers holding their wheat off the market. The trading captains were said to be paying premium prices. It didn't even have to be true, for it was credible and its effect on the valley was electric. The piled-up wheat at Wallula wasn't about to go to market, but anything going by train could be in Portland speedily.

"Let one farmer fold," Tripp told Luke, "and there'll be a stampede."

Luke and Sherry were alone in the freight office that same afternoon when Amos Buell walked in. He was from Pebble Creek, where he had one of the largest wheat ranches in the valley, and he had been one of the fire-breathing speakers at Keel's indignation meeting. Instead of that chronic indignation, his weather-stained face now wore a look of crowding excitement.

"Look, Preston," Buell said without preamble. "How many spare cars have you people got?"

"What kind of cars?" Luke repressed a grin and from the corner of his eye saw Sherry's look of astonishment.

"Box, flat — any damn' thing that'll haul my wheat," Buell said. "I want 'em on the

Whitman siding as soon as you can get 'em there. And I'm speakin' for every damned car you can scrape up."

"Why, Mr. Buell," Luke said reprovingly. "You wouldn't be trying to shut your neighbors out so you can make a killing in that fat Portland market, surely."

Buell's neck seemed to turn a little redder, but he had a lot of pride to swallow if he was to get what he now wanted. "It's first come first served, ain't it?" he demanded.

"It sure is," Luke agreed. "And there's no question you're first."

"When can you have the first cars at Whitman?" Buell said impatiently.

"Tomorrow morning."

"Good. And don't you forget I spoke for everything you've got free or get free. I got a big crop."

"That's kind of monopolizing, Mr. Buell —"

But Buell went stomping out.

Luke thought Sherry was choking, but in a moment she got her breath. "The old hypocrite!" she said delightedly. "Just look at what happened to his high dudgeon when he got *his* chance."

Chapter 22

For many weeks Lawson Keel had believed his inability to play his trump card to be a weakness born of his secret fears. Now he realized that holding it back, however involuntarily, had been one of the luckiest things he could have done. After Amos Buell's miserable betrayal, it gave him his one chance to righten matters and restore a most promising situation that Buell's defection had shattered.

Riding through the night, Keel uneasily watched the bare hills that there at the divide pinched in upon him, for confined places always set up in him a choking feeling of oppression. He had left Walla Walla City shortly after midnight, slipping away, and now rode stealthily but swiftly, for he had to reach his destination before it got light. The wagon road at that point was fairly on top of the railroad, at which he looked not with hostility but with a hunger sprung in his jaws like acid and with, also, a boundless anger.

In the two weeks since Buell crossed over to the enemy and began so cynically to flood the Portland market with his wheat, the whole rural valley had clamored for railroad cars so they could get in on the killing themselves. Wagon transportation had come to a standstill. The swiftness of the transformation had shaken Keel. Every straw-chewing, cowhide-booted one of them seemed only to have been waiting for someone else to make the break. Now the wagoners, instead of the railroad, were the targets of their abuse. Not only were the teamsters blamed for trying to extort an extra dollar a ton and getting a vast amount of wheat bogged down at Wallula. They were now accused — and Keel thought correctly — of starting the wheat fire whose char he had a short while ago ridden past. Keel's only feeling for the teamsters was his undying hope to run them out of business himself soon. But he needed them and their cause to champion, until that time came about.

He was relieved when the benighted hills and their forbidding shadows began to stand farther apart, and he rode swiftly on to cross the river with the wagon road. In another twenty minutes he turned left, leaving the road and beginning to follow the paired ruts running south toward the canyon-bound and now deserted ranch of the Holladay brothers. He had seen no one since leaving Walla Walla City and was confident that he hadn't been seen. That was of utmost importance, for while he was sure she would meet him, he was far from certain what he would be required to do.

There wasn't much of the night left when finally Keel rode in among the ramshackle buildings of the abandoned horse ranch. He swung down, looked around carefully and saw no sign of some range bum having moved in. So he put his horse in the barn, went over to the shacky house and stepped in.

He had started to strike a match when he remembered that a burning lamp would be taking an unnecessary chance, even though few people traveled through that particular region. But if he hurried, he could have a fire to boil coffee while there was still enough darkness to hide the smoke. He had been there before and knew the layout, and there was enough filtered moonlight for him to be able to get around. He fumbled in the woodbox by the stove for kindling and chunks of split wood and got a fire started. He hurried out to the well for water and presently had a pot of coffee cooking.

The place was far from pleasant, for it was a boars' nest that had been left in a hurry and shut up for months. He could smell spoiled food and vintage human and rodent odors, and he lighted a cigar to offset them, standing by the window where he could see the ground he had crossed coming in. It would be a while before she got there, for she would want it to look only as if she had left Wallula on one of her morning rides. If she had got his note — but there was no doubt of that. Fortunately he had known that Nan picked up the mail, Browder rarely being in Wallula during the day.

Coffee, fire and cigar smells began to mask the stench in the room. The black granite pot was boiling, so Keel pushed it over with a stick of wood and used the rest of the water in the bucket to douse the fire and put an end to the smoke from the chimney. He found a chipped cup that seemed reasonably sanitary and filled it with scalding coffee. His cigar had burned down to where it generated a savory taste that went well with the coffee. He was a man of strong sensual appetites and pleasures and he relished it.

He began to savor even his thoughts of the woman he was forcing to meet him in this lonely emptiness. She was still a beauty, although a not too happy maturity had replaced the fresh youngness in which he had once found delight. It hadn't been as easy as she thought to give that up, or to leave her alone after he learned that she, too, had come to this new frontier. But the Walla Walla wasn't mining country where little attention was paid to light alliances. He had had an awareness of his power over people and a desire for it to carry him to high places. So he had denied himself some of his former pleasures except as he could enjoy them in secret during his frequent visits to Portland. Keel shook his head to clear it of such lulling thoughts. What he had to exact from Nan now was something else.

Daylight took away the pleasant feeling of snugness he had managed to engender, and he looked around the room with distaste. He didn't know if it was his own fastidiousness or a memory of Nan's that made him gather the clutter of used dishes and utensils and dump them behind the shack and straighten the smelly blankets on the bunks. Afterward he left the door open for fresh air.

Nan arrived so much earlier than he expected that she was halfway across the flat before, striding restlessly past the window, he chanced to glance out and see her. He was outdoors when she rode in, a stunning figure in a divided skirt that let her fork the animal the way he liked to see a woman ride.

Keel had a smile on his face and said genially, "Hello, Nan. Good of you to come."

"Let's keep it straight, Lawson," she said in a cool voice. "It wasn't good of me. We both know I came because I'm scared. What do you want now?"

"Come indoors," Keel said. "It's going to take a while."

"No," Nan said sharply.

"Afraid of me, Nan?" he said and laughed. "Or of yourself?"

She dismounted angrily and followed him into the shack. He stifled an impulse to shut the door, for there was nobody within miles and the place still needed fresh air. He suggested that she sit down but she shook her head, a lovely woman he again regretted having had to give up. He lighted a fresh cigar, fumbling with his thoughts.

"You left earlier than I expected," he

commented. "Where's Kirk this morning?"

"I don't know."

"I warned you that this has to be a secret, Nan. Is it?"

"As far as I know."

He hadn't had a chance since Blackhawk to be really alone with her, to talk and cajole and try to get through to her. It bothered him that she could be so insulated when once she had had only quickness and vitality and a woman's willing surrender to him. He drew on his cigar. "Well, Nan. We seem to have lost the railroad fight."

"I didn't. I haven't much cared."

"Come off it, Nan." Keel stared at her. "You're married to a teamster, aren't you? And they're all but out of business, aren't they?"

"Not necessarily." Nan tossed her head. "There'll always be wagon runs. The railroads can't go everywhere. They're none of them ruined if they'll stop being bullheaded and go where they're still needed."

That was true, and he should have known Nan was astute enough to see it. But he had to keep them bullheaded and irate and ready to fight to the last man. Pretending surprise, Keel said, "Are you proposing to let your husband leave the

country like a whipped dog with a drag-
ging tail?"

"It's not like that. Even if it was, I can't
stop it."

"I can," Keel snapped. "But I need your
help."

"What can you do now?"

"I can make John Ainsworth regret his
alliance with Baker. Sufficiently to break it
off fast. Ainsworth's a pirate, but he's got
principles. He cares for things like personal
integrity, trustworthiness and all that."

Nan moved a hand impatiently. "Let's
get to the point, Lawson. You think that if
you expose Luke Preston as an indicted
swindler hiding from the law, you can tar
Baker with the same brush and make
honest John Ainsworth withdraw his support. That finally does the doctor in, puts
you in control of the railroad, and *then* the
farmers and teamsters find out just how
much their champion you've been. Am I
right, Lawson?"

His glibness had deserted him momentarily. He could only watch her silently.

"You insult my intelligence," she resumed, "with your silly appeal to my concern for Kirk. I'm not the trusting young
innocent you used to know. But I'm still a
coward, as you learned the last time you

sounded me out on this. How come you're still afraid of me?"

"You're showing why," Keel said angrily. "You're not like you used to be. I can't figure you anymore, and I've got to be sure what you'll do before I start something I can't stop."

"There's one thing you can be sure of," Nan returned. "The only thing you can scare me with is my husband finding out about us. That I was a wife to you in everything but name for three long years. How can I help in another of your rotten frameups without all that coming out?"

"Let it come out," Keel said recklessly. "You can't care about that roughneck. And I'll make it up to you."

"With money? Or with another ration of your phony love?"

"Nan, I'm going places. You must know that, and there's no reason why we can't get together again."

"There isn't?"

"You never understood this. It wasn't easy to give you up. Before you came here, I was remembering what we had." He was surprised at how much he really meant it. She was and remained the most attractive woman he had ever met. "Help me, Nan. And give me another chance."

Her eyes filled with contempt. "Listen. Kirk Browder's a roughneck. He'll play dirty in a fight that means everything to him. But compared to you, he's a man. If I have to pay the price of his learning the truth about me, I'll do it to save *him* from your greed and to help Luke Preston."

It was the comparison with Browder as much as his acceptance that nothing could reach or change her mind that pushed him into his final resort. "That's too bad, Nan," he said. "It makes it much harder for you."

"Lawson — what are you going to do?"

He was moving toward her, and he was between her and the door. "Only what you're making me do. I'm going to kill you."

Her eyes shut, the lids barely touching, and then they sprang open filled with a steely defiance. She whispered. "It doesn't surprise me," and when on the edge of his sight he saw her hand slide toward the slash of her riding skirt, he knew she had brought the pocket gun he himself had once given her for protection against mining-camp hoodlums. He sprang forward, sliding his arms under hers to keep her hand out of that pocket. He clamped his mouth to hers hard enough to crush her lips, his fingers laced together behind the small of her back, and he pulled in with all his strength.

"I'm going to break it," he panted against her bleeding mouth. "And then I'm going to watch you die."

The voice was low, male and behind him.

"Let go of her."

Keel was hardly aware of Nan slipping from his arms to the dirty floor, for his consciousness was wholly centered on his exposed back. It took all his effort to turn toward the open door that framed the crouching figure of Kirk Browder. The pistol in the teamster's fist didn't fire, and a wild hope sprang up in Keel that the deadly embrace had been misunderstood. Better to confront an outraged husband than be caught in the act of murder.

"So it was you," Browder said in a flat voice, "all the time."

"Kirk." Nan wasn't badly hurt, Keel saw. She was getting up. "You don't understand."

"I reckon I do. I listened a while. So he's the one. All the time I thought it was Preston."

"Put down the gun, Kirk," Keel said with a nervous laugh. "She isn't worth it. There've been a lot of men. Me. Preston.

Who knows who else?"

"That's a lie," Nan said.

Browder glanced at his wife and nodded his head. "I know it is, and if I hadn't followed you, you'd be dead. A little bird told me about Preston being up in our rooms with you. I never said anything to you. I just been keeping tabs, figuring to catch you with him and kill you both."

"Luke came to ask help that I should have given him a long while ago," Nan said. Her voice was dull now, resigned. She looked at Keel. "And this man was trying to kill me because he's afraid I will. I helped him in a frame-up. I guess you heard enough to know why. I was in love with him. I was living with him."

Again Browder nodded his head. His eyes were pained, baffled, and it struck Keel that the fellow really cared for her, a capacity as surprising to him as Nan's desire to preserve her marriage.

"What sort of frame-up?" Browder asked.

"He wants control of the railroad. He's used you and the farmers and was trying to use me to get it. Don't think he'd have let you stay in business if he'd succeeded. He's money-mad and power-mad and woman-mad. I couldn't warn you. I was

336

too afraid of you finding out about me."

"Why were you afraid of that?" Browder said softly.

Nan looked at him with level eyes. "I want to keep on being your wife."

Something in Browder's eyes warned Keel that he was in the deepest trouble yet. He felt dizzy, weak, and said desperately, "Don't listen to her, Kirk. She's trying to pull the wool over your eyes —"

"Shut your dirty mouth," Browder snapped. "All right, Nan. What's he got on Preston?"

Keel had to stand there and listen to her explain everything, knowing that afterward there would be no chance of his ever leading the country again. Unless — his one chance was this unsuspected feeling of Browder's for Nan.

"Now, listen to me," he said insistently, when Nan was finished. "You're not going to shoot me, Kirk, unless you want to have to testify that you caught me here with your wife. You can't even repeat what she told you without it coming out how she happened to know. So you'd damned well better keep her quiet if she gets the idea she's free now to help Preston clear himself. Unless you want the whole country to know how long I slept with your wife."

"I told you to shut your mouth!"

Keel smiled at him. The man was very vulnerable there. Then Browder motioned for Nan to leave the room, and she did so, going out to her waiting horse. The teamster's eyes held a killing gleam when they raked Keel.

"You're right," he said harshly. "I'd like to gut-shoot you, but I don't dare. And I don't feel kindly enough toward Luke Preston to let her crawl through the dirt to help him."

"Good," Keel said.

"Hear me out," Browder rapped, "before you say that. I'll find a way to take care of you, Keel, without hurting her. Don't ever think I won't."

A chill crept into Keel while he watched Browder back out and pull the door shut behind him. He heard their low voices and then a silence and waited there numb and motionless until he saw the two of them riding off across the flat. Browder had meant every word he said, and Keel knew that from there on he would have to live with the threat of it hanging over his head. Nan's voice rang in his ears as if she were still in the room: "Kirk Browder's a roughneck. He'll play dirty in a fight that means everything to him. But compared to you, he's a man." Keel shuddered and went out to the barn to get his horse.

It was odd that his only desire now was to be left alone, to stir up no more hornets' nests himself, and to hope that, in return, his enemies would leave him in peace.

Chapter 23

Luke was experiencing his own feeling of novelty, but it was more pleasant than Lawson Keel's. Once the farmers had swung over to the railroad, they had berated the teamsters the loudest of anyone. Now they were damning Keel for the counsel and leadership that had failed so miserably, and the boycott he had started had been turned on him. Only the hand-to-mouth grade of farmers continued to take wheat to his flour mill, taking out the proceeds in trade in his store. Since he had gambled everything on his control of the farmers, Keel was mortally hurt and seemed to know it. The fight, the old flashing dominance was gone.

Luke's problem was no longer how to keep the trains running in the face of every obstacle but how to scrape up enough empty freight cars to meet the demand. New ones were being built as fast as possible in the Slabtown shop, but they weren't enough to make up the shortage.

Wheat poured in on the WW&CR in a golden flood, and farmers who had cursed the railroad and sworn to boycott it forever begged for its services and talked of doubling their planting for the coming year.

"Amos Buell never made his killing in Portland," Sherry said with dry amusement. "Wheat just wasn't that scarce and high. But that greedy hypocrite started something he and nobody else can ever stop."

Few wanted to stop it any longer, not even Kirk Browder. Luke was astonished when one evening Browder came to his room in the Wallula Hotel. The teamster wasn't used to the change yet and was stiff and formal almost to the point of belligerence. But he was straightforward.

"This don't come easy, Preston," he said, "but I got to say it. For a long while I laid something at your door that didn't belong there. And I'm glad I found it out."

Luke looked at him searchingly, gathering the weighty import of what he had heard. "You find the right door?" he asked.

"And then some. He nearly killed her a while back. If I hadn't been tryin' to catch her with *you*, she'd be dead."

"So now you know about Blackhawk." Luke eyed him warily, for Browder had plenty of other reasons to hate him.

"The whole stinkin' story. And it's the only reason Keel ain't dead himself."

"He's about dead, anyway, as far as this country's concerned," Luke said.

"Does that satisfy you?" Browder asked.

"No, it doesn't."

"Nor me. It ain't his using us people that sticks in my craw. He's payin' for that already. It's what he tried to do to Nan after what he'd done already." Then Luke sat listening to Browder's account of what had happened at the deserted horse ranch. "But he slipped up," Browder said. "Them brainy ones do, in time. He wrote her that note, takin' it for granted a married woman'd burn up such a thing after she'd read it. Nan didn't, though. She had a feelin' he might harm her and left it where I'd find it and know what happened."

"That's a strong piece of evidence," Luke said. "And an attempted murder's a worse charge than the one I'd like to see him stand trial for."

"Yeah," Browder agreed, "but there's still Nan's good name and what they might do to her for withholding evidence she might have given to the grand jury, back there."

"There's still my good name, too," Luke

said impatiently. "I understand her instinct to protect herself, and yours to protect her. But listen, Browder. Circumstances put her where she could have established the truth of that Blackhawk swindle. It put a responsibility on her she had no right to shrug off. I've got a right to a clean bill of health. I love a woman, too. I want to marry her and raise a family and get up of a morning not scared for them or for myself."

"She wants to make it right," Browder said. "It was me she didn't want to know about her and Keel, and now I know anyhow. And it's me tryin' to spare her more, not her. I'm movin' my business to Umatilla Landing. Its backcountry's growing and there's some good hauls outta there. When Nan's sold her business, she'll follow and just keep house and raise a family. I ain't gonna have her messed up anymore."

"What am I supposed to do?" Luke exploded. "Be happy to know Keel's got himself in a fix where he's not apt to make me trouble?"

"No." Browder leaned forward. "If he was to confess to the Blackhawk business, it wouldn't be necessary for Nan to take part. And he might rather confess to that than to stand trial for tryin' to kill a woman, here in a country that's come to hate him like poison. That's my hunch, but it's a gamble. If he balked, we'd have to crawfish, or it'd all have to come out about Nan. And about you, too, when you could let it go and be safe. I just figured to talk it over with you."

"I see," Luke said, looking wonderingly at the man. There was no doubt of his loving Nan, or that she was anything worse than a woman with weaknesses she couldn't help. He understood Browder's temptation to let things ride. He felt it himself. There was nothing about Wade Foster that he cared to reclaim, not even the name, and it had been his lack of family attachments that had encouraged him to move west to Colorado. Luke Preston was here, sound, healthy, at liberty and in love. Everything he wanted was here — Sherry, his job on the railroad, the valley he had served well, and people like Baker, Green, Pasco and all the rest. He knew that Sherry was only waiting for him to mention wedding bells. After a moment, he added, "It's pretty decent of you, Browder. You didn't have to tell me a thing. After the fight you lost, I wouldn't blame you if you hadn't."

Discomfited, Browder said gruffly, "What do you think?"

"Give me a little time."

Browder nodded, rose to his feet and left.

Riding up the valley on the train the next morning, Luke tried to look at the situation in the light of his interests and Sherry's alone. No doubt about it, it wasn't enough to get out from under the sword that had hung over him so long. He wanted and had a right to a clear record, while the Browders had no right to expect consideration from him. The temptation was strong to return to Colorado and take his chances, forcing Nan and now Browder, under the power of subpoena, to come there and tell the truth. That would give him his best chance with the least risk to himself.

That night, sitting in the Yale yard, Luke told Sherry about Keel's attempt on Nan's life. And then he explained Browder's idea of using it in a gamble to drive Keel into confessing the swindle and frame-up in Blackhawk.

"It's a powerful weapon," he told her. "Keel would have to go before a jury drawn from a country that's soured on him plenty. And for violence against a woman, which no jury anywhere looks on kindly. There's a good chance he'd choose the lesser of two evils."

"But if he didn't?" Sherry asked.

"I'd have thrown away a big advantage I could have had by going to Colorado and hiring a good lawyer to dig out the truth. And let him use legal means to compel Nan to tell the truth, regardless of the effect on her."

"You men," Sherry said, "and your worry about a woman's good name. I can understand Browder's. She's his wife. But why you?"

"I guess because she suffered as much from Keel as I did. I don't like the idea of piling more onto her just to set my own record straight."

"She piled it onto you to keep herself in the clear."

"Not exactly. She was in love with Keel. And she cares something for Browder, because later it was his finding out that she was scared of. And Browder's right. If it worked, Keel's confession would spare her and clear me overnight."

"Then try it, Luke. I don't think you could be happy clearing yourself at Nan's expense. Or with just letting things ride as they are."

He smiled at her, not knowing until then that she had said what he had hoped to hear. "If it works, will you marry me right away?"

"You know I'll marry you either way. Now or ten years from now. Exonerated or convicted."

He held her in his arms, then rode back to town. By the time he had gone to bed he knew that he had to act alone, using what Browder had told him but without Browder's participation. Keel knew too well how Browder felt about Nan. If his nerve was as good as it once was, he would try to turn that weakness in Browder to his own advantage.

It was after ten o'clock the next morning when Luke went to Keel's store. The man was there in his balcony office, still pretending to be one of the town's leading merchandisers, although his three clerks were idle and there wasn't a customer in the store. Only the bookkeeper was missing, and Luke knew why that was. There was no longer bookwork enough even to keep Keel occupied, for he sat idling, smoking a cigar.

Luke climbed the stairs knowing he was being watched both from below and above. He strode across the deserted boot and shoe department and through the railing gate. Keel kept watching him, jumpy and worn and looking much older than the last time Luke saw him.

Luke sat down by the desk without invitation and said, "Well, Lawson, you mailed your letter."

Keel's head jerked up. "No, I didn't."

"I don't mean the one you threatened to send to Colorado. I'm talking about the one you sent to Nan Browder."

Keel's cheeks went white. "What do you know about that?" he gasped.

"Want me to say where those loafing clerks can listen?"

Keel flung a frightened glance toward the lower floor. "No."

"Then we better go somewhere private. There's plenty I've got to say about it."

Keel nodded, putting down his cigar. He rose, and Luke followed him across the boot department into a wareroom in back. There Keel shut the door.

"All right," he said. "What about that letter?"

"You thought Nan'd destroy it. A guilty wife would, if it was only an invitation from an old lover to meet him in secret. But Nan got to know you between Blackhawk and here. She might even have suspected you'd try to break her back and watch her die."

"How could you know that?" Keel blurted. It was inconceivable to him that Browder, who had so long hated the railroad, would have divulged it to Luke. Or that Nan would have done so unless she intended to prosecute him and righten the old wrong. "Who told you?"

"Did anybody have to tell me?" Luke grinned at him. "Maybe her husband wasn't the only one who got curious about that rendezvous at the Holladays' shack. That'd make two witnesses to your attempt to murder her after you lured her there, wouldn't it?"

"You?" Keel gasped. "You followed me?"

"I'll explain my part," Luke said calmly, "when you stand trial for it. I'll also explain why you did it. And that'll go a long way toward backing up what I'll say about Blackhawk won't it?"

"No," Keel protested. "Damn it, I lost my head, but I didn't hurt her. Leave me alone. You're safe. I won't give you any trouble or cause her any." When he saw he was making no headway, his voice turned pleading. "Look — I've lost my business. I'm going broke. I'm up to my neck in bills I can't pay, and the jobbers will close me out. I'm worse off than when we met in Colorado. Isn't that enough to satisfy you?"

"Not by a long shot. You might get five years for swindle. It'd be twenty for trying to kill a woman who got dangerous to you. You'd have to stand trial for that here, where you might be tied to that dynamite job of Morgan's that nearly blew up the town. And the jail delivery. Even the wheat fire that could've been a major disaster."

Keel eyed him wonderingly. "Are you offering an alternative?"

"If you care to listen. I'm offering a chance not to have to stand trial at all. You could avoid it, and try for five years instead of twenty, with a confession about what happened in Blackhawk."

"You're wrong," Keel said bitterly. "I don't have to do either one." His hand slid into the side pocket of his coat. It could have been his finger that shaped itself threateningly under the cloth, but Luke dared not take a chance. Keel's eyes glittered with their old cunning. "I didn't know who it would be. But I knew that sooner or later somebody in this cursed country would give me trouble. Don't make me shoot you. I'm going out of here. If you try to stop me or start a chase after me before I get clear, I'll shoot myself. Then where would you be with your hopes of coming clear?"

Luke glanced again at the tubular bulge in the cloth of the man's coat, weighing his chances. Keel seemed too sure of himself to be bluffing. Luke said nothing and watched him reach behind to open the door, then back through and pull the door shut. For a while he had thought he had won his gamble, but that had been dead wrong.

The realization that it could be worse than that came to him like a freezing wind. Keel was cunning enough to improve his chances of escape by taking a hostage. And what more effective hostage could he choose than Sherry, alone and unsuspecting in the freight office? Luke jerked open the door and moved through, and something came down on his head that blinded and staggered him. He thought, *Tricked!* And then blackness swept in, and he forgot everything.

His first renewed sensations were of spluttering, blowing, and a cold, soggy wetness. Somebody's voice said urgently, "Hey, what's goin' on? Preston — come out of it —" and he managed to open his eyes. Two or three faces swam above him, blurred and revolving, and when he moved his head, it roared with pain. "Give him the rest of the pail, Milt," a voice said,

351

"Keel really bore down on him with that stool."

Water hit Luke in the face, cold and needling. He sucked in a heavy breath and pushed up to a sitting position. When he opened his eyes, his vision was sufficiently clear to show him the three store clerks hovering above him. He knew where he was and why and dropped his gaze to see, lying by the door, the heavy stool Keel had used to lay him out.

A clerk said, "What kind of hell did you raise here, Preston?"

"Where's Keel?" Luke's voice was ragged and hoarse.

"All I know is we heard a thunk and grunt up here. Then he opened the safe and cleaned out the tills downstairs and went out of here fast. We come up and here you were, cold as a whore's heart. What kind of a twist did you put in his tail, anyhow?"

"How long ago'd he leave?" Luke asked, trying to stand.

"Five minutes, maybe."

"He take a gun?"

"Far as I know he never kept one here. What's up? He clearin' out? How about our wages? We ain't been paid in three weeks."

Luke had got to his feet, groggy and

dizzy, and he headed for the stairs. The clamorous clerks followed, and he turned at the street to say, "You might as well lock up the place. He's walked off and left it. If he wasn't running."

He went out to the street, his head still pounding but again able to think of Sherry and the danger of Keel's using her to shield himself. The man hadn't been armed or he wouldn't have resorted to that stool to gain time to get what money was in the store. He could have taken a new gun from stock, but it would have cost him time to test and load it, and he apparently had even been afraid of his unpaid clerks. The livery barn where Keel kept his riding horse was up the block on the far side of Main, and Luke went there on the run.

His arrival, hatless and water-soaked, created the first excitement at the barn. Keel had been there and picked up his horse, the stablehand said, and apparently had done it quietly so as not to attract attention. The hostler didn't know which way he had headed after riding out to the main street. Luke helped him saddle another horse, countering his questions with demands for speed. He estimated that he had fallen behind Keel ten or fifteen minutes by the time he reached Main, himself.

He had barely come to the main thoroughfare when he saw Barney Lunt approaching from the left in his dray. Spurring over to him, Luke said urgently, "Barney, you seen Lawson Keel the last few minutes?"

"Just did. Why?"

"Which way'd he go?"

"I met him up the street a few blocks, and that's all I know. What's the ruckus?"

"Tell you later, if I see you later," Luke called and rode on at a gallop, indifferent to the commotion it caused along the street. To have met Lunt, Keel had to be riding east. That meant he had been afraid to go to the depot unarmed and had struck off toward Dixie and Waitsburgh and the wide-open spaces of Idaho.

Proof that he was on the right track came at Spring Creek where a farmhouse stood near the road. A tired-looking woman was pulling feed carrots in a patch across from the road and appeared to have been there some time. She was weather-stained, thin and hard-eyed.

"Keel?" she said at Luke's clipped question. "Yeah, I seen the son of a bitch. Just a while ago."

"Riding fast?"

"Not very. What's he done now?"

354

Keel was no longer a heroic figure even to the hardscrabble rural gentry, and he seemed to be saving his horse for a long ride. He didn't expect to be pursued, perhaps because of his bluff about killing himself, maybe because he hadn't expected his clerks to revive his victim so soon. Luke rode on at his own headlong speed.

He had reached Dry Creek Canyon, with a straight road for some distance ahead, before he sighted his man, then only a small, receding figure in the distance. Dixie wasn't far beyond and, wanting to nail him before there, Luke demanded the last speed in his horse. It was several minutes before the rider ahead grew aware of him. When instantly he spurted forward, Luke knew it had to be Keel.

But the contest was between a horse somewhat spared and a horse used hard. If anything the gap widened, and then the hillsides came closer together, and Keel vanished around a turn in the road.

What Luke did while he rounded the bend himself was born of a hard-gained acquaintance with the wiliness of which Keel was capable under stress. The road beyond disclosed no more open stretches and hugged the hill on the left. Luke slowed and reined his horse over to that shoulder, watching with straining eyes for the sign that would tell him Keel had pulled off to let him pass ahead before doubling back. He found it where a small, brushy draw cut a notch in the hill, scuffed horse tracks showing a fast-moving horse had turned in there. But Luke rode on, giving it only a cursory look from the corner of his eye, until another bend cut him from sight. Then he stopped, dismounted and trailed reins.

He had no gun, and there was a chance he was wrong about Keel being unarmed, but without hesitating he started back, leaving the road and angling up the slope, well covered by rock and brush. His heart hammered, less from the exertion than from his fear that Keel, in his haste, would ride out of the draw too soon and get away. And then he came close enough to see the man, still standing at the head of his horse, intently watching the road to the east. Luke had to nail him before he could mount, and he went in fast.

Keel wheeled at the sound of crashing brush, his eyelids jarring apart, and then he whirled and tried to get a foot in the stirrup. It was too late, for Luke let out a yell and slapped the horse on the rump, sending it bolting out to the road. Keel, thrown off balance, stumbled backward but managed to stay on his feet.

"You devil!" he screamed and came surging forward with driving fists.

It took a single blow from Luke, started low and whipping upward, to stop him. Keel's teeth clicked, his head snapping back. He hit softly in the leaf mold underfoot, but even so, his eyes rolled up in his head.

Luke was hunkered beside him, relaxed and smoking a cigarette, when Keel looked up at him with clearing eyes.

"End of the road, Lawson," Luke said.

Keel nodded. There was no fight left in him, no wiliness, no self-serving will. "I'll go back to Colorado," he whimpered, "if it's all I'll have to answer for."

"It'll be all if you go back in custody, Lawson. After a full confession to the marshal here of what happened back there. On paper and over your signature."

Keel worked his mouth and swallowed. "All right, damn you. All right."

From the window of the transcontinental train the bewintered desert reminded Luke of the long fight against the blizzard now nearly a year behind. Snow swept away over the bare Nevada mountains, but the steam cars were warm, and ahead, beyond the Sierras, California waited, the golden land that the sun was said never to forsake. That would be the beginning of their honeymoon, although Sherry had been with him through the weeks it had taken for the state of Colorado to drop the charges against him and give him the right to sit here unafraid and smiling at the world's most beautiful girl.

She occupied the seat opposite him and seemed to be sharing his thoughts, for she was smiling, too. "I wonder what they're doing back home," she mused.

"I can tell you what Doc Baker's doing," Luke said with a chuckle. "Planning more railroad. He was talking about going on up the Walla Walla even before we left."

"He'll build it. And you'll be running it. But you're going to have to get you a new freight clerk." Sherry looked down at her hands. "Unless you don't mind a cradle in the office."

"Already?" Luke nearly shouted.

"What do you mean, already? We've been married nearly two months."

About the Author

Chad Merriman was the pseudonym Giff Cheshire used for his first novel, *Blood on the Sun*, published by Fawcett Gold Medal in 1952. He was born in 1905 on a homestead in Cheshire, Oregon. The county was named for his grandfather who had crossed the plains in 1852 by wagon from Tennessee and the homestead was the same one his grandfather had claimed upon his arrival. Cheshire's early life was colored by the atmosphere of the Old West which in the first decade of the century had not yet been modified by the automobile. He attended public schools in Junction City and, following high school, enlisted in the U.S. Marine Corps and saw duty in Central America. In 1929 he came to the Portland area in Oregon and from 1929 to 1943 worked for the U.S. Corps of Engineers. By 1944, after moving to Beaverton, Oregon, he found he could make a living writing Western and North-Western short fiction for the magazine market and presently stories under the by-line Giff Cheshire began appearing in *Lariat Story Magazine*, *Dime Western*, and *North-West Romances*. His short story *Strangers in the Evening* won the Zane Grey Award in 1949. Cheshire's Western fiction was characterized from the beginning by a wider historical panorama of the frontier than just cattle ranching and frequently the settings for his later novels are in his native Oregon. *Thunder on the Mountain* (1960) focuses on Chief Joseph and the Nez Perce war, while *Wenatchee Bend* (1966) and *A Mighty Big River* (1967) are among his best-known titles. However, his Chad Merriman novels for Fawcett Gold Medal remain among his most popular works, notable for their complex characters, expert pacing, and authentic backgrounds.

RBR